MUSES and CONSUMMATIONS

Douglas Wicken

To Mark:

Great seeing
you again.

Doug.

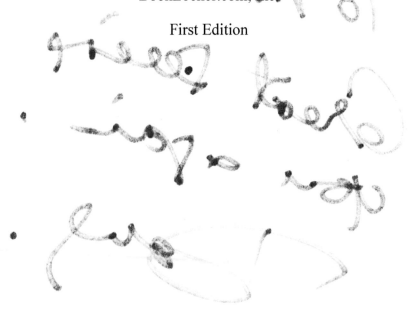

DEDICATED TO MOM

Beatrice Mae (Hickox) Wicken

She bears no resemblance to any of the mothers in this novel.

IN APPRECIATION

Thanks to the following people who assisted me in so many ways by reading early drafts and offering comments, assisting with research, formatting and design, holding hands when needed, being a friend at critical times, tolerating my endless rants and relentless philosophical meanderings, and by being family.

Patti Gower
Scott Whalen
Gudrun Heiss
Bill White
Natalie McMullen
Frank O'Connor
Gord Horne
Daniel Williams
Joe Callahan
Peter Snell
Sher Kariz
Bernie Carroll
Scott Wicken, Shelley Young and Rowan
Craig and Nena Wicken, Luka and Gabrijela
Karin Heiss, Daryl Ralph, Oliver and Ella
Kyle Gell, Kathy Karakasidis and Olivia
Kimberley Gell and Silas

01

"Getting old is Hell," Damon shouts from the teak bench surrounded by ancient pines; magnificent creatures, broad at the base and surging straight as a prairie highway to the sky. His voice ricochets from trunk to trunk as if the trees themselves were voicing their agreement. Miraculously, these few majestic, towering evergreens have survived the gluttonous demands of human settlement for centuries only because a few people who cared enough about them adopted, and subsequently protected them; worshipped them even.

"Of course," he acknowledges, staring upward at the trees, "I'm not telling you guys anything about aging, am I? You still have a few years on me." He swigs directly from a half-emptied bottle of Canadian Club. "The stories you could tell. My God, what stories they would be." Damon pauses in hopes that one of them would accept his challenge and relate its family history to him, but there's only the silence as one would experience in the woods, accepting the wind and occasional rustles of twigs and pine needles as a kind of base fog that is always present and no longer constitutes a sound, but an existence.

Damon stands with the pines as evidence of human longevity; one of the lucky few who, like them, has managed against the odds, to outlive the threats of illness, war, famine and insanity, to savour the memories of those who have failed to be so fortunate. He can only assume that these magnificent survivors must also carry, within them, visions of their poor relatives and neighbours who have succumbed to the axes and chainsaws and blights and flames, leaving them alone to stand in sole representation of their entire race.

At his side, on the bench, sits an urn, not terribly fancy; adequate, functional, and with extreme taste, that's the way she would have wanted it. Ever since Lavinia died, more than nine years ago, Damon has kept the urn on the ledge of the Steinway grand piano in the parlour.

"I just couldn't let her go," he sobs to the trees. "There were too many years to make up for, too many questions that still needed answers. That's why I've waited until now to spread her ashes onto her final resting place. This is where she wanted to be, with all of you. She viewed this as her most sacred place on earth, as if your surging trunks and branches were her spiritual pipeline to the great beyond."

It's a place that was dear to Lavinia, and to Damon even still, throughout their many years of appreciating this beautiful corner of Muskoka where the family cottage, winterized and established as a year-round residence decades ago, sits watching as a sentry over the lake. Lavinia had located the bench strategically for a view of not only the lake, but of the cottage as well, especially to provide a vantage point through the parlour window to the piano. Equally important was that the teak bench could be viewed with similar ease from inside the parlour windows, especially when the outer porch lights fanned their diffused luminance across the grass to the pines. On many occasions, Damon performed his magical improvisational sketches on the piano while Lavinia sat on this very bench, reading, or just soaking up the music.

"Yeah. Getting old is Hell. If it isn't one thing it's another; you can't escape it. There are the aches and pains of ankles, knees, hips and lower back, not to mention the implementation of various medicines, from eye drops for glaucoma at the top end to Prep H for hemorrhoids at the bottom, always something to squirt, insert, or rub into every orifice in our deteriorating bodies. What I really hate most though, are those condescending assholes in restaurants, medical clinics, hotels and hospitals, just about everywhere, who assume that, because I've survived long enough to attain the status of senior citizenry, I've returned to my infancy and am no longer capable of understanding adult conversation. Are *we* having a good time, Mr. Farrell? Isn't it time *we* took our medicine, Mr. Farrell? My, my, Mr. Farrell, aren't *we* looking dapper today? Shall *we* have a little bit of lunch? Give me a fucking break."

The pines respond their agreement with his ranting by waving slowly with the breeze that blows in from across the lake, sometimes viciously, but tonight merely a quiver. Damon can sympathize with their creaking limbs that snap just like his own bursitis-ridden shoulders.

"I knew you'd agree," he tells them. "You know what my answer to those bastards is? I'll tell you." He points his forefinger toward the closest pine. "My usual answer is to inform them, in no respectful manner, that *we* aren't doing anything together. Unfortunately, they don't get it. They just assume that I'm another old fart who's become grumpy in my old age. The truth is I just can't tolerate stupidity; I never could. I'm probably one of the most tolerant people on this earth, except when it comes down to laziness and stupidity. That's where I draw the line."

He stops ranting to the trees and becomes much quieter, pondering the task he has chosen to undertake this special clear starry night, to allow his memories of Lavinia and the cottage to pass through him once again. Like her, he has learned to find solace among the great ancient pines. Damon shivers and closes his eyes; teardrops dampen his lashes and creep down over his cheeks. He can do nothing to stop them. In his solitude he wishes to return to nine years before, when he met Naomi, and his lonely pathetic life began to turn around.

02

Staring into the open bowels of the piano, Damon Farrell's fingers plunge heartily into a free-spirited introduction to the last tune of the night. His left hand suggests a Latin motif but, for the moment, it lacks any framework of time. The long fingers of his right hand stretch open arpeggios over the upper range of the keyboard, harmonically locking into a two-chord vamp. He's alone for the time being, his mind and body synchronizing and focusing on the job at hand. Once settled into a pulse, the elements of rhythm and harmony coincide as a precursor to Kenny Dorham's 'Blue Bossa,' which the younger members of the band attach to as a unitary force. The hard two-beat samba tempo encourages long, burning solos from the horns before the bassist, Tiny Prescott, breaks tempo to begin constructing the tune all over again, starting with deep throaty notes that pin down a tonal centre; he eventually embellishes them with a flurry of thumb-positioned chromatics, before returning to a pre-theme vamp. The horns take the tune out with multiple turnarounds, while the audience expresses their satisfaction.

"Good night folks. You've been listening to The Damon Farrell Quintet," Damon announces before listing the individual players and waving his hand toward them, all young musicians from the local college where Damon has been teaching improvisation for more than 25 years, except for Tiny, who Damon met while in high school. Each musician bows or nods his head in acknowledgment of the applause when introduced.

Damon turns to the audience. "Thanks for being here and experiencing this music with us. Good night all."

Horns are swabbed and packed meticulously into their felt lined cases, Tiny wipes down the bass strings with a rag and loosens his bow, and the drummer detunes his snare and toms, and covers his tubs with a bed sheet. Damon remains at the piano. "Good gig guys. See you all tomorrow."

Lydia shuts the lights down before calling it a night, leaving the club in darkness but for the mandatory red 'EXIT' signs over the front and back doors and one dim red mood lamp above the stage that casts its glow over the piano.

"I'll see you tomorrow, Damon," she calls before locking the front door.

"Yeah, tomorrow, Lydia. See you tomorrow." There's always tomorrow, he mutters to himself in a low gravelly voice. His hands wander the vintage Steinway's keyboard as if searching for the best keys to press, but he knows there are no best keys; there are no right or wrong ones either.

Damon has spent most of his 60 years searching the keyboard. Since he was five, when his Aunt Lavinia talked his mother into buying a piano for the house and starting him on lessons with old Mrs. Howarth, who taught young children to play the piano, with the assistance of 'Melodies for Ten Little Fingers,' Damon has never looked back. His life is music: performing it, composing it, and instructing others at the college how to do the same. He faithfully remembers the conversation that occurred when Aunt Lavinia approached his mother more than 55 years before.

* * *

With the rapping of our doorknocker, I run to answer. Aunt Lavinia enters and gives me a huge hug and a smacking lipsticky kiss on the lips, even before the door is closed behind her. Lavender permeates the vestibule. Her two-toned Studebaker sits at a slant in front of the house, one front wheel parked on top of the curb. She always says how much she hates driving in Hamilton, the big city.

"So, you finally came to visit, did you?" Mother states as her typical welcome. "When was the last time? Was it as far back as Christmas? You didn't call to let us know you were coming. I didn't prepare a bed for you."

"Oh, I'm not staying, Helen. Don't you worry. I've just come to give a gift to young Damon," Aunt Lavinia offers with a friendly but

stern determined tightness to her face. "A gift that will last him his entire life."

"What are you getting at Lavinia?" mother responds. "You're not meddling in Damon's life again, are you? You know how Charles feels about that, don't you?" She pauses, realizing that her sister doesn't hear any of what she's saying. "Don't turn me off Lavinia. You always ignore me when I'm stating the obvious, as if you're accusing me of not knowing what I'm talking about, but I know you better than that. You're just waiting to deliver the Coup de Grace. There's something else yet to come, I can feel it. But first, let me tell you that I know how to bring Damon up and to take care of his needs. We don't need any more meddling from you. Besides, what can you possibly offer Damon that we don't already give him? Isn't it enough that he visits you every summer? We are capable of giving him a good life. Charles earns a respectable income and we've already started a savings plan for his education, just so you know. Hopefully it's an education in business or medicine, a profession with some status attached to it instead of doodling around in the arts."

Mother emphasizes her final words by tapping her right forefinger onto the surface of the kitchen table.

"Oh cool off, Helen. This isn't anything you can't afford. It's just something that you would never think of doing for him." Lavinia pauses, licking her upper lip with her tongue while she ponders her next statement. "Well, you might, but Charles would never even consider it, not in a million years, and it's something critical to Damon's future sanity."

Mother sighs deeply. "OK Lavinia. Let it out. What is it that Damon needs for his sanity that we won't provide for?"

"Piano lessons," Aunt Lavinia blurts before mother can add anything more to her sentence. "He needs some artistic exposure; something that isn't about killing." She refers to Charles' love of hunting and fishing. "His father would never address the creative needs of young Damon, you know that, don't you? He's all about sports and the kind of outdoor stuff that centers on killing... while

6

getting drunk in the process. Is that the kind of son you want Damon to be?"

Mother becomes more agitated the longer Aunt Lavinia rattles on.

"Lavinia," mother finally addresses with stern tightened lips. "Charles is a good father. He means well. Yes, he does like his sports and his outdoor stuff. That's what he knows. Besides, there's nothing wrong with a boy learning about the wild. Charles was talking about putting Damon into the Cubs, so he'll learn to appreciate the outdoors."

Aunt Lavinia jumps in. "I suppose you want him to wear the uniform and pledge himself to God, the King and country. Haven't we lost enough young men… no, I stand corrected… young boys already. We would do well to teach all young children to play more piano, paint more pictures, write more stories, and dance more ballet. That would be a vast improvement in how…"

"Ballet?" Mother stares directly at Aunt Lavinia; her mouth hangs open in disbelief. "You want us to send Damon to ballet lessons now? Hah! That'll be the day. We're not raising some kind of a pansy. Forget it!"

"Oh, for Christ's sake Helen. I didn't suggest you send him to dance lessons. I told you that I'm offering him piano lessons, that's all."

"You won't gain any ground by abusing the Lord's name in this house, Lavinia. Besides, we don't even have a piano. He wouldn't have anything to practice on, would he?"

Aunt Lavinia stands straight as the ancient pines at the cottage, with a smug seriousness about her face, an appearance that I know too well. Mother feels the Coup de Grace coming.

"Do you remember old Mrs. Howarth? She's been teaching young children to play the piano since I was a little girl. Surely you remember her: thin, tall, with wiry fingers, wears her hair up in a tight bun?"

Mother feigns ignorance.

Aunt Lavinia continues. "Well at any rate, I've commissioned her to provide Damon with his first year of piano lessons. It won't cost you or Charles a penny."

"What about the cost of a piano? We can't afford that."

"That too, is being looked after. Within a couple of days, Johnson's Piano Emporium will deliver a used, but well-cared-for, Heintzman upright piano, and they'll tune it immediately. Damon's first lesson is on Thursday next at Mrs. Howarth's." She turns to me. "I'll call you on Friday to see how your first lesson went Damon."

"Charles isn't going to like this at all Lavinia, but I'll see what I can do. I can't make any promises, but I'll try to swing him over. Charles will object to receiving the money; you know how he is about charity and welfare."

Aunt Lavinia finally loses her cool. "Damn it Helen. You're half of that marriage. If you're going to raise Damon, then be his mother and stand up to that asshole you call a husband. I'm not giving you charity or welfare; I'm giving Damon a gift, and that's my right."

At that, Aunt Lavinia leaves the room, pausing at the front door. "Yoo-hoo, Damon," she calls. Say goodbye to your crazy Aunt Lavinia. Give me a big hug. You're going to love playing the piano, aren't you?"

I kiss her on the cheek and wrap my arms around her neck. "Thank you Aunt Lavinia. I love you."

"That's my boy." She lands another lipsticky kiss on my lips. "Remember, I'll call you on Friday."

I watch her Studebaker meander down the road until it disappears.

* * *

'Good old Aunt Lavinia.' Damon lets his fingers wander across the keys until they find something to work with. Most of his reflective playing happens late at night, after the gigs are over and Lydia has closed the club. Reflective practicing is different from his experimental practicing, which he normally does for two hours each afternoon at the college. He would like to practice more than that but his tight teaching and playing schedules get in the way. His late night reflective time is more of a response to how the gig went that particular night and how the guys played. He places far more importance on the cohesiveness and energy of the band's collective sound, than on whatever virtuosity exists within each player, including his own output. He learned that kind of respect from the examples that Miles Davis set for his groups. Like Miles, Damon never tells the musicians how or what to play; he rarely talks to them about the music they're playing but he can gab for hours about the philosophy of music and creative activity, or about energy and pulse. He prefers to let each player express himself from within the group, using the other musicians as catalysts for one's creative energy. The whole is bigger than the sum of its individual parts. Some nights the pulse is right on and he can feel the energy inside; on other nights it doesn't happen. That's just the way it is.

His reflective practicing is dark and somber; it didn't happen tonight.

'There's always tomorrow,' he reflects as he turns down the lid on the keyboard and lowers the top. 'There's always tomorrow.'

He climbs the steep narrow stairs leading to his second floor apartment, conveniently located above the club. He's lived here for more than a decade after securing a deal with Lydia that would guarantee him a venue for his jazz as long as she owns the club. He has access to the piano anytime, and can hire any sidemen he wishes for the gigs. The only condition is that he must guarantee the consistency and quality of the music. Lydia knows and trusts his judgment. Besides, with her husband, bassist Tiny Prescott, playing with him every weekend, Lydia always knows where he is.

It's a small two-bedroom apartment; in one bedroom he sleeps, the other he uses as a composing and thinking room. There's a Yamaha electronic midi piano in the corner, and a Macintosh computer on the desk. Against the far wall, a CD player and a turntable sit at the ready.

Damon relieves himself, brushes his teeth and stares into the mirror. A wrinkle-browed, grey-haired old man with several days of salt and pepper stubble stares back.

"Who the hell are you anyway?" he demands aloud from the reflection and imagines hearing an answer.

'I'm the old fart you've evolved into. Take a good look. You're a lonely old bastard with nothing to look forward to but playing the piano. You can't make love to a piano; it's just a thing. You need a life, man.'

Damon dims the lights and retires for the night; the digital clock tells him it's 2:10 a.m.

His bedroom overlooks Queen Street West in the Parkdale/Roncesvalles area of Toronto, a neighbourhood in transition. Light from the street filters through vinyl venetian blinds that clatter against the frame of the open window; the combined essence of no less than five culturally diverse restaurants enter through the same blinds. Headlights and taillights from passing cars flash red and white across the ceiling in both directions. At seemingly regular intervals sirens from police and ambulance vehicles carve through the usual din of traffic and pedestrian movement; occasionally small packs of inebriants offer their audible contributions by smashing beer bottles against the brick building facades and by voicing, like carrion crows, their nightly chorus of "Fuck you and fuck you too," to each other in passing. Tonight, a pair of pigeons squats on the window ledge cooing their love songs and dropping deposits on the sill in Pollock-like patterns.

Damon points his remote at the CD player and John Coltrane's 'Ballads' joins the outer chorus in hopes of encouraging sleep, but it doesn't come easily. He refuses to succumb to the night until Nancy With The Laughing Face begins, eight tracks in. His sleeping mind wanders, drawing him deeper into the all-too-familiar dark caverns of his persistent nightmare.

* * *

Powerful waves retaliate against our approach. The beach is still some distance away and the essence of seasickness puke blends with

10

sea and salt smells: dead fish, kelp, and fuel oil from the landing craft. None of us can anticipate what lies ahead. The gate of the landing craft scrapes open with the full force of fingernails against slate, smashing into waist deep water. Like penguins we plunge into the dark sea toward our doom. Once in the water, the cacophony of war befalls us. One young lad trips and is immediately submerged under the landing craft, sent to his finish before even touching ground.

An enemy shell lands on the beach. We, the safe ones, endure screams from our unlucky comrades. Tanks struggle to move, their tracks digging their own hopeless graves in the rocks. Another comrade falls, his legs peppered away from beneath him. He utters not a sound but his blood broadcasts from his stumps staining the uniforms of others close by. Seawater-drenched trousers become heavier. A boy to the right of me belly flops onto the stones to avoid crossfire that cuts down several on my left. The redhead from Stoney Creek, the boy we affectionately call Gingertop, is gone, almost to the last piece of him. His helmet, insulated by remnants of red hair, is all that remains, inside up.

There's no place to hide, nothing, just the beach ahead of me. I struggle up from the shore on my belly, suddenly blocked by a pile of bloodied corpses and charred war machinery that won't stop churning their infernal engines. Like spent, rumbling volcanoes erupting nothing but smoke and thunder, they resist surrender. My head echoes from the steady volleys of enemy fire, by the screams of pain from poor legless and armless bastards who don't even know why they're here, by the repetitive banter of cross-laden padres and priests who, hovering like turkey vultures eager to pluck out souls from the hearts still pumping, promise eternal salvation to the masses of dying who can do nothing but damn the very gods they're being asked to submit to.

The odours of salt and sea are now overpowered by the stench of urine, excrement, blood, fuel oil and death, so stinging that it eats away the mucous membrane from my nostrils.

Unable to climb the corpses, I hunker down behind them. The surf rolls up to my waist, eroding the soil beneath me. It draws at me to return. With one last effort, I lift my exhausted and waterlogged carcass in a final attempt to advance with the last yell of bravado remaining.

A pinprick of bright light appears in the distance like Venus on a clear moonless country night. Soaring toward me, it gains in speed and magnitude until saturating my entire field of vision. It strikes me, consumes me, ignites me with patterns, red and orange and yellow, squiggling, dancing, interacting, an orgy of untamed shapes accompanied by the repetitive paradiddling of machine gun fire peppering from all directions and a choir of the dying screaming in agony, praying for and damning its gods. There is nowhere to escape.

An oncoming bullet cuts across my left temple, separating my brain from my optical nerve. It forces me backwards, blinded into the rolling surf. I try fighting against the waves, but they drag me under the surface. The salt stings my eyes. I see nothing. I only sense, with my mind's eye, my own blood escaping from the gaping hole in my skull. The undertow sucks at my body.

Water rises up over my thighs and across my chest. I can no longer breathe, drowning in my own blood. Open-eyed corpses float beneath the surface, brushing against me, staring into my eyes. Am I one of them?

Suddenly it's quiet. The surf ebbs and flows without sound, the dancing spoils of oil, gas, urine and blood pirouetting above me on the surface, backlit by the overcast sky like gossamer webs on a dewy morning. The choir and the paradiddles stop. As I submit to the drifting undertow, a tunnel of brightness appears in the distance. A large fishlike creature approaches, the brightness encircling it like an aura. It ventures forward without fear, its dorsal fin swaying slowly but determinedly left to right. It circles my pathetic remains, possibly considering me as a meal. After several circles, it veers to leave me. I have been reduced to less value than a tasty meal for a scavenger. As the creature wends further away it turns to look once more in my direction. The beast transforms into a beautiful sensuous woman —

Aphrodite has come for me. She treads water before returning, drawing closer and closer until she becomes accessible to my touch, but my arms don't obey. Her eyes remain fixed on mine; wondrous eyes that beckon me to join her. Her body, naked and desirable, dances for me alone in an aquatic ballet. I yearn for her and reach out to touch her with the last energy remaining but she turns away and disappears into the vanishing light. I'm left in darkness, abandoned with my excitement unrequited, the only form of life remaining in this pathetic remnant of societal madness.

* * *

Damon struggles to liberate himself from the nightmare; his perspiration-soaked body bolts upright from the pillow. Darkness permeates the room but for the Queen Street ambiance. He rises from the bed without fully wakening and limps across the floor toward the open window. On the street below, a crack whore stands dazed, clutching a lamppost for balance and hoping for traffic that doesn't come. The clock registers 4:05. Damon slams the window shut and returns to bed.

* * *

I arrive in Muskoka by train for my annual birthday celebration with Aunt Lavinia at the cottage. She meets me at the station in her Studebaker, a two-toned green and beige model with a wraparound back window and a nose that looks like a rocket. Inside, it smells of lavender, like when Aunt Lavinia hugs me.

We arrive at the cottage and I climb the stairs to my bedroom; a sign above the door designates it as 'Damon's Private Room.' No one else ever sleeps in that bedroom.

Aunt Lavinia remains in the kitchen. I know she's baking my double chocolate cake, but I'm not allowed to see her bake it; it's one of our rituals. There are 13 blue candles and one special white one for good luck but we have to wait until dark before lighting them; that too is one of the rituals.

Aunt Lavinia does everything with a sense of drama. She loves the theatre. Every year she plays one role or another in the local

Little Theatre presentation. One year she played Stella, in another she was Jane Eyre. It doesn't matter to her which role they assign her, she puts everything she has into it. Somewhere in the cottage, there's a box containing all the newspaper reviews of her performances.

Once darkness arrives, we proceed outside to the porch and light the candles. Crickets sing from the lawn and from under the pines, adding musical accompaniment to the festive occasion. Aunt Lavinia sings along with the crickets as she lights the candles. "We'll meet again, don't know where, don't know when, but I know we'll meet again, some..." Her voice breaks as she lights the special white 'good luck' candle, but the crickets keep singing. She wipes a small tear from her eye with the back of her hand before cutting the cake and then starts singing.

"Happy Birthday to you, Happy Birthday to you, Happy Birthday dear Damon, Happy Bir..."

* * *

His dream is interrupted abruptly by the piercing 'Wah-Wah-Wah' of a police cruiser in pursuit as it screams past his window. Happy Birthday still sings in his mind. There is an ominous quality to a single unaccompanied voice singing Happy Birthday, as if there exists only one friend in the entire universe who cares. The clock reads 7:40, much too early for a jazz musician to start the day, but he has a 9:00 a.m. appointment to see Doctor Hilary Kinderman, his therapist up in Yorkville. He must also conduct a late-afternoon improvisation workshop at the college following his personal two-hour rehearsal in the theatre.

03

Naomi Parsons hoists her bicycle up the steep front stairs of the renovated three-story house in the Annex; she pushes her personal code into the security system before ascending the stairs to her own second floor apartment on the north side of the building. Setting the bike against the wall she removes her helmet and proceeds directly into the living room.

Today's rehearsal was satisfactory but she's becoming increasingly bored with the banality of the repertoire that the company chooses to perform.

"It's too safe and predictable," she mutters aloud to Terpsie, her tortoiseshell cat whose full name is Terpsichore, after the Greek muse of dance. "I want more challenging material. The choreography is much too tightly organized, with no room to stretch out, no space for personal expression. I want freedom; I need it, dammit."

Terpsie meows and rolls over several times on the floor; Naomi rubs her feline muse's belly.

Penderecki's Flute Concerto fills the apartment with sound. In the kitchen she removes a cup of Greek yogurt from the frig and stands for a moment against her Ikea table for two, staring thoughtlessly out the window into the unkempt but fenced back yard. A pile of catalogues occupies one of her kitchen chairs, a chartreuse bulky-knit wool sweater drapes over the back of the other.

"How can I change my life around? How can I turn my dance into something worthwhile doing?" Terpsie meows something in response.

Before entering the shower, Naomi undresses and stares at her nakedness in the hall mirror. 'Look at me. I'm 28 years old, I've lived alone since I left my mother's home for university, and I'm working in a schlocky dance company that's more than satisfied with its mediocrity. If I don't do something soon, I'll be 30, and then what?

I'll go crazy, that's what. There are only so many years left before I won't be able to dance anymore; what will I do then?'

She examines her body carefully, twisting it, bending it, stretching it, and performing a brief breast examination as a matter of course. Her physical perfection reflects back at her, a body that demonstrates the hard work she applies to it; the warm ups, the exercising, the endurance and the stamina, not to mention the hours of dance routines she subjects her muscles to each day. There is no question that she can still handle more adventurous work, but for how much longer?

After scanning her body in the mirror, she focuses on her face, projecting a series of facial isometrics until succumbing to laughter at the reflected results.

'What about the rest of me?' she asks. 'I'm intelligent, but I have no one to talk to, no one to interact with. Certainly the bimbos and losers in the company are no challenge; all they ever talk about is whose getting laid and the calories they're burning up. I have no time for that crap. They don't even talk about dancing, for Christ's sake.'

Naomi runs her fingers through her ebony black, closely cropped hair, with a style more random than arranged and chosen for convenience over style.

'Maybe I should let my hair grow. I used to have long hair; long, wavy and soft.'

With these thoughts, Naomi turns from the mirror and enters her shower, followed by her evening meditation seated in a lotus position before slipping into her Ikea queen sized bed with snow white duvet and four matching eiderdown pillows.

Her bedroom window sits two floors above a relatively quiet side street but the continuing din of evening traffic is heard from the main thoroughfare a block away. Unbleached muslin drapes hang loosely over her window filtering some of the light and sound from her private domain. What does pass through creates a cinematic interplay of light patterns that frolic across her ceiling until she succumbs to sleep.

* * *

From the top of my bed I stare upwards into the shimmering patterns of light that form images only discernible to my sleeping mind. I see dancers in the patterns, two to be exact, a man and a woman, both quite young and attractive. They soar above me with such ease and grace, unaffected by the gravity that holds me to my bed; I want so much to join them. My child's body tingles with a desire to dance, my legs and arms attempt to form the movements I see above me but the couple ignores my existence. I close my eyes and make a wish, just like when I blow out the candles on my birthday cake. Mother always told me to make a wish and it will come true, but I should never reveal what I wish to anyone. 'I wish I could be a dancer and be free.'

The ceiling rises higher and higher until it's no longer visible, leaving in its wake an intense azure sky with billowing white clouds. The male dancer hovers above my bed; he appears muscular and strong. His left arm extends around my miniscule waist and I'm hoisted into the sky where we dance together as partners. Within his arms I age rapidly into the mature body of a young woman. We remain in contact for an extended time and I tingle at his touch, firm and in control. Gradually, he allows me more space until only our fingers touch. I yearn to be free, but at the last moment, he pulls me back to him.

The female dancer, until now watching from a distance, suddenly pries me from the male and replaces me as his partner. I sense a triangle emerging that pits she and I against each other in competition for the man, a battle I want no part in so I recede from the conflict. In my retreat, the male follows me, clutching my arm with more pressure than the first time. His demeanor is more forceful and demanding. The more I resist, the more insistent he becomes; his hands grope at my right leg until I'm able to propel myself from him with pressure from my left. I am finally free.

In my escape, the female dances to my side; her arms touch mine softly. We dance as a couple, at times gentle and graceful, at others wild and free. Our arms and legs intertwine as a tangled garden, and then free themselves so only the tips of our fingers remain in contact. Gradually she draws me closer to her until our bodies connect in a sensuous embrace; my entire being is electrified when she places her lips against mine. I want to share my desire with her.

Suddenly, an image cuts through the dream; my mother's face screams at me but I hear nothing, as if she's screaming from a great distance or from a television with the sound muted. Her face fills my entire field of vision but gradually zooms outward to include more of her surroundings. She's in a room on the fifth floor of a large building; there are bars on the window she screams from. The light against her face flashes in a variety of warm hues, from yellow to bright red. As the image continues to zoom wider I see flames at the base of the building; they rise slowly until threatening the fifth floor from where my mother screams. Her window zooms closer and I watch as her hands present an object to me through the bars. Upon closer examination I see a small child, a baby, cradled in her trembling hands. The flames rise higher until they touch my mother's hands. She drops the child into the flames and I follow in pursuit, descending ever so rapidly toward the source of the flames but it seems endless as if no bottom exists. I am tumbling into the flames of Hell with no way to escape and I am no closer to saving the child.

Suddenly, an image of a hand-carved wooden cross stops my descent. It dangles back and forth before my eyes from a silver chain with hypnotic consistency. An unbearable pain overtakes my body.

* * *

Naomi awakens suddenly from her nightmare; it is still dark and she's soaked with perspiration. She flips on the reading light from her night table and scans the room before stepping out of bed. On her way to the washroom she passes the mirror in the hallway, stopping to catch her reflection. Her mother's maddened face screams mutedly back at her. After splashing cold water over her face, Naomi passes the mirror again and faces her own image. She studies her naked self again wondering how she deserves this Hell and why it happens so often. Knowing she will resist any attempt to return to sleep, she opens the closet door and retrieves her gown.

18

"I have to get a life, to get out more," she tells the mirror. "This shit is going to kill me. I need something else in my life." Terpsie rubs against her legs.

After breakfast she places a call to Doctor Hilary M. Kinderman, a psychotherapist specializing in the delusions and illusions of the creative artist and arranges a consultation for the following Thursday morning. In the meantime she re-experiences the nightmare, but it appears only in short images that flash through her mind at random intervals, day or night: the image of the cross dangling from a silver chain, the face of her screaming mother, the baby falling into the flames of Hell. More and more, she fears going to bed at night and, as a result, suffers from severe sleep deprivation.

Later the same day, to avoid the boredom of hanging around her apartment staring at the carpet, she decides to go out, to experience Toronto's night life, an action she has avoided doing for many months. One of the choreographers in the company told her about a small informal jazz club on Queen Street West where the music is happening, and where she can sit with a glass of wine without being hassled by the waiter every 10 minutes. She arranges a taxi and heads out into the night.

It's Friday night. The Concept is jammed with regulars: university students and professors, yuppies in suits, musicians, some hookers, and a small gathering of doctors and lawyers. There are gyrators and finger-poppers, lovers and thinkers. Some women's husbands sit with other men's wives in dark corner booths. The heartbeat is hard bop. It slices through the crowd, careens off dusty, picture-dotted walls, and penetrates the bodies and souls of everyone. The residue from past smokers still hangs in the rafters and hides in the plaster.

Jesse Townsend's tenor sax blazes through Trane's Giant Steps with all the naïve energy reflective of his mere 22 years, as if he's already hard-wired to the master. The deeper he delves inside the rotating structure of the tune, the further he edges outward, expanding the distance between him and the solid foundation of the rhythm section. The tune burns on as if driven by a unifying spirit. After eight burning choruses, Jesse relinquishes his solo to the equally young trumpeter, Zach Harris, who opens with a series of long tones riding over the pulse, gradually constructing his contribution into a frenzied bevy of double and triple tongued arpeggios that cut through the changes as if they don't exist.

From the keyboard of the club's vintage Steinway, Damon Farrell feeds the young horn players the structure they need to get their job done. At times, that's as simple as some well-placed intervals of thirds and sevenths; at others it's a fat-voiced complement of flat nines and sharp elevens laid down hard over a double diminished scale like a dense blanket of sound that refuses to resolve. Tiny Prescott, the bassist and husband of Lydia, the club's owner, sticks to his job of laying down the fundamentals for the entire band; his opportunity for a personal statement will come later.

Damon's time arrives; his left hand releases spacious intervals in support of his right hand lines that thread through Trane's changes, weaving a tapestry of tonal chromatics and textures. During longer phrases he withholds his breath in anticipation, not absolutely sure of what the outcome will be, only to suck in new oxygen for the phrase yet to come. Choruses pass by like oncoming traffic on a throughway, each one more complex than its predecessor until Damon nods to the horns from under the piano lid; they return with the head, the familiar theme that brings the classic to a close.

Naomi's arrival at The Concept is in mid-set and there's already a full house. She locates a small two-seater wooden table with mismatched chairs in a dark corner beside the bandstand, just behind the pianist. Not much can be seen from her table but she views that as an advantage, allowing her some protection from social interaction, a desirable feature for her first night out in months. A waiter brings her a glass of Chardonnay as requested.

Despite Naomi's longstanding involvement with jazz dance, her exposure to the music that gave it its name has been limited. Her personal CD library includes several vocalists like Diana Krall, and a few soft jazz recommendations from the attendant at the record store:

Kenny G, George Benson and Chris Botti, while much of her listening leans toward more stylized repetitive-beat dance, pop and hip-hop music, for obvious reasons. The 20th century classical examples that fill out her CD collection are there to satisfy her intellectual hunger. Nothing however, has prepared her for what The Damon Farrell Quintet is feeding her this night at The Concept.

It's the energy that excites her most, the driving pulse from the rhythm section that provides an apparent freedom for the horns to weave their emotional cries into a trance, before struggling, in a cacophony of shrieks and squawks, to free themselves further, only to pass the mantle to the next soloist. The pulse, balanced tenuously between the bass player and the drummer, always seems on edge, not quite steadily maintained, but more intuitive; again an apparent freedom that appeals to Naomi's current desires in dance. At the end of each performer's solo, there is applause from the audience, which the performer acknowledges with a slight nod of the head or an occasional smile. Odd scraps of paper adorn the music stands that Naomi assumes is their music, but no one seems to keep their eyes open long enough to read any of it. She observes that there must be some internal group dynamic that keeps everyone connected, but otherwise they each appear to be stretching out from their own centre only to return to the core, like ambitious teenagers leaving home to seek excitement but being drawn back to the family for security. The alpha of this family appears to be the pianist, as the other musicians look toward him for direction. Damon and the bassist are the elders, well beyond 50, Naomi surmises, while she estimates the others to be of college student age, younger than herself.

At the completion of Giant Steps, a tune that Naomi can't identify but thoroughly enjoys, Damon Farrell stands to announce a 20-minute break and to introduce the members of the band. He then settles at a table not far from where Naomi is seated, and is soon joined by the tenor saxophonist, Jesse Townsend. They sit without verbally communicating for several minutes until Jesse speaks to Damon.

"Hey man, have you thought any more about doing the festival thing this year? I talked to the committee and they need a decision by Monday so they can get the promo stuff ready. The gig is ours if we want it. What do you think?"

"Why don't you put something together, Jesse? You know how I feel about jazz festivals. I'm not comfortable with them."

"I just thought we could get some exposure from it; maybe pick up a couple more festival gigs around the province, you know."

"Look at this place, man. You can't stuff another body in here without breaking the law, not that I care about the law, but my point is, do we need any more exposure?"

"I just thought that…"

"Let me ask you," Damon poses to the young tenor player, "Who's the headliner this year? Is it Sonny Rollins? Or is it Wayne Shorter, or Charles Lloyd? How about some younger cats that can really burn, like Christian McBride, or that trumpet player, Ambrose Akinmusire? No man, the headliner is Dixie Witherspoon and the D-Cups, or whatever they call themselves: country singers from Nashville with fringed, low-buttoned cowboy shirts that jiggle while they sing, and high-riding cowhide skirts. How are you dressing for the festival this year, Jesse?"

"That's not really fair, man."

Damon snickers. "I know, Jesse, but try to see my point. I've been at this game for more than 50 years, and the only gig I'll ever get at the Jazz Festival in my own town is on a Wednesday afternoon at two o'clock at an outside stage in Cabbagetown, while four bimbos with only three chords between them will clean out the coffers for more than 20 big ones, probably much more than that, for an hour of work. I'm so far removed from that scene, I don't even know how much they get paid anymore."

Damon stops for breath, but feels compelled to add, "And not only that, they'll sleep in a four-suite layout at the best five star hotel in town and eat like swine."

Jesse starts to laugh out load. "Shit man, sometimes you're funnier than Hell. You know that jazz has never made any money.

Never, in your most colourful hallucinations, are you ever going to make that kind of bread at a jazz festival."

"There you go. You hit the chord square on the tonic. You just called it a *jazz* festival. I have no problem taking the small loaf of bread, even if I only get a few slices here and there, as long as everyone's playing *jazz*. Why call it a jazz festival when the performers are playing country music? Don't get me wrong, Jesse, I've listened to country music. Don't tell anybody else, but I actually enjoyed some of it."

Jesse laughs at the thought of Damon listening to country music, but Damon continues, "You don't believe me do you? Once I actually went to a country music festival up north from the city, and guess what? They were playing *country* music. Imagine that."

"I get your point, man. I just thought we could reach more people and maybe show them how jazz is done."

"Listen up, Jesse. How many times have I said this, and how many times have I said that I'm only going to say this once? I don't do this, this thing we call jazz, for other people. This is a thing I do for me. This is internal, it's personal, it's something that comes from inside and goes right back there. If other people get something from it, that's great, but that's not *why* I do it. In the same way of thinking, I'll do it as well as I can at the time, and if somebody pays me a lot of bread for it, that's good, but that's still not why I do it. Dig?"

Jesse nods.

"Good. That's good. The way I see it is, as long as I can do it for me, the music will retain its honesty. The more honest the music is, the better I feel. Here, at The Concept, I have some control over how honest our music is going to be. This is as honest as music ever gets. That's why I love it here, and why I don't go looking for other places to play. I'd have to sacrifice something to please more people. Why would I want to do that?"

Naomi soaks in the conversation between Damon and Jesse like a sponge. She agrees with most of what Damon is saying because she faces similar attitudes in the company she dances with. If she were more outgoing she would probably join their conversation, but her preference is to remain at her table in the dark corner absorbing the ambiance.

Damon and Jesse return to the stage for their final set of the night, opening with a Chick Corea ballad, Crystal Silence. Jesse picks up his flute and plays the entire tune in rubato as a duet, with only Damon's piano accompaniment for support; the other players remain seated at a table further back in the darkness from Naomi's. The audience is quieted by the tenderness and subtlety of the performance as if they were attending a chamber music concert, only to burst into hearty applause when the flute and piano fade into their own silence. The night proves to be a turning point for Naomi, who senses an emotional tear rolling across her cheek, a personal acknowledgment that she's not alone; that there are others who share her commitment and passion.

04

At the completion of Damon's session with Doctor Kinderman, he exits to the nearest café, orders a dark roast from the barista and settles at an umbrella-shaded table adjacent to a row of shrubbery that separates the patio from an upscale hair salon next door. It's mid-morning and the café boasts a substantial gathering of patrons. The tall, two-seater table with a white marble top and black wrought iron base, is one of only two tables available. From his tall perch he observes a client, obviously late for her hair appointment, leap from a double-parked taxi and hustle toward the salon. She carries a fashionable black bag with an exclusive logo, and seems more able than most to maneuver the cobblestone walkway on her stilettos. Hyperactive traffic, vehicular and pedestrian, assault his vision, his hearing energized instead by a Paul Bley-Kenny Wheeler Duet recording centering in his brain from his Walkman through a pair of high end Sennheiser headphones. He uses the opportunity to correct some music manuscripts in preparation for a session later in the afternoon.

The morning begins for Naomi Parsons. She stretches leg and torso muscles that have rested during the night while she slept; but she didn't sleep soundly. She rarely sleeps well anymore since her nightmares have increased. They have always haunted her, the visual snippets of her disturbing past that appear to her in brief stroboscopic flashes of light, but recently they have been repeating more regularly, and in enhanced detail. A rigorous training in dance has taught her to look beyond the interruptive influences that would affect her concentration by mentally removing herself from where she is physically, a meditative process that allows her to imagine her own body dancing before her as if someone else is moving. Lately, however, the trance has been relinquishing its power to the nightmarish visions that she can't erase.

On this May morning, Naomi leaves the safe haven of her apartment for her first session with Dr. Kinderman. She locks the door and strolls from her red brick second-floor apartment into a promising spring day. The magnolia bush in the front lawn has reached full blossom and a robin cheeps a mid-morning greeting from its freshly woven nest. The walk to the therapist's office takes her past upscale loft apartments, over-priced art and furniture galleries, and refurbished offices, a neighborhood that years before Naomi's time, housed Yorkville's lively nightlife scene.

For Naomi, the Village's history means nothing. She leaves the comfortable seclusion of her renovated suite with enough time to spend over a latte at a nearby café before revealing her disturbing past to Doctor Kinderman. With latte in hand she locates the only patio table remaining.

The café is busy as usual on this gorgeous spring day as the mid-morning coffee-breakers assume their normal places throughout the patio. From his table, Damon uses his well-spaced sips of dark roast as a break from editing manuscripts and to scan the clientele around him. A pair of fresh faces has occupied the table to his left, and a strikingly attractive young woman walks toward the only remaining empty table to his rear. She is tall and presents herself with incredible posture, not the silliness one associates with models, but with the kind of healthy erectness more likely to belong to someone who works out, possibly a gymnast, or a dancer, perhaps. Once accepting that nothing else has changed, Damon returns to his manuscripts.

Naomi scans the patio, noticing that most tables accommodate pairs of people: men with women, men with men, and women with women. At only one table besides her own is someone sitting alone; an older man with long greyish hair and sporting a black beret is facing the outer perimeters of the patio with his back facing Naomi; expensive headphones straddle the beret and cover the man's ears.

She wonders how many of the twosomes aren't really couples at all, but just acquaintances. How many are lovers? What about the two women from the hair salon with the quasi-trendy fashions; are they lovers or just work mates? And what about the two women, who

26

arrive separately and meet here, hugging and kissing each other on the cheek? Do they love each other, are they truly friends, or is the act purely a façade between people who share the same man, possibly one being his wife and completely unaware of the other's participation?

Naomi, who has chosen to live alone but often questions her motive, ponders the body language that couples assume to display their friendships. A man touches his partner's cheek softly with the back of his hand; she smiles and blushes, her eyelids turn downward. Two men overlap their hands on the table and peer directly into each other's eyes, again smiling. Two business partners conduct a sales conference over cappuccinos, while two women prefer to self-indulge in their orange sorbets over any communication between them whatsoever, their eyes scanning blankly across the patio without focusing.

Naomi returns her attention to the older man and is able to identify him as the pianist in the band at The Concept from the previous Friday. Her reclusive demeanor forces her to resist any attempt to approach the man; she settles instead to observe him from a distance. His head bobs and vibrates in obvious response to the music in his brain, the same characteristic that revealed his identity to her from watching him perform at the club. From his actions, Naomi senses the tempo and intensity of the selection he's hearing, the internal muscles in her body adopting a sympathetic rhythm.

One glance at her watch tells her to sip the last of her latte and move on to her appointment. In passing Damon's table she inadvertently brushes against his elbow dumping the remains of his dark roast over the white marble.

"Oh my. I'm so-o-o sorry," Naomi apologizes. She reaches for a napkin.

"No problem, my dear. I can clean this up."

"It was my fault, I'm so-o-o sorry. I hope it didn't spill on your clothes."

"Not to worry." Damon looks at her. "It did spill on you however." He gestures toward a damp stain on her beige jacket.

"Oh shoot," she complains. "I'm such a klutz." After wiping the spot with a damp napkin, she offers, "Please let me buy you another coffee. I feel so-o-o bad about this."

"Heavens no, my dear. I've let it go cold and it was almost empty anyway. I'll get another one. Can I get something for you while I'm at it?"

"Thank you, but I'm due in a meeting right now." She looks blankly at her watch knowing all along that she's late for her appointment.

Damon nods and returns to the barista for his refill.

Later at The Concept, Damon and his sidemen gather at a table before the first set begins. Tiny relates a humorous tale about how he got his first gig at the age of 15, after only two lessons on the double bass.

"The cat told me that as long as I knew where G and D was, I could start gigging. I only had two lessons, one on the G-string and the other on the D-string. He said that nobody was going to hear me anyway, so it didn't matter whether I knew anything about the other two strings. That's how I got my first gig."

"Isn't it about time you learned about the other two strings?" Damon jibes.

The rest of the band laughs. Jesse adds an amusing anecdote about why drummers can't get dates, and the drummer reciprocates with a joke that paints sax players as possessing low libidos. As with any discussions between musicians, the subject always resolves into a sharing of musical ideas.

Zach, the trumpet player, asks Damon, "How do you manage to stretch out so far beyond the changes and still sound like you're connected to the tune, man?"

Damon pauses for the most appropriate response before starting. "I'm sure you remember my lecture when I talked about the relationship between chords and scales; that was more than a year ago, Zach."

"Yeah man, I remember, but it's one thing to learn something, and quite another to do something with it."

Damon answers. "Look at it this way. When you started to learn music, you all did the major scale thing, you know: do, re, mi, fah, sol, etc. I think we do a disservice to young musicians when we start them out with that thing, because it's too limiting. Their heads are too screwed into that do, re, mi sound. Everything that's happened in music since Bach has been to break away from that, to find new sounds. We should all start by learning the chromatic scale first; it has all 12 tones to work with, and all of our western-based music uses that scale."

"I dig that man, but what does it have to do with freedom?"

"The main problem with how young jazz musicians learn their craft, is that they focus in on chords, which granted, is part of the process, but the other, more important part is the scales. You play a horn, man, a melodic instrument, and you have all 12 notes of the chromatic scale to choose from. One way or another, all 12 notes relate to each and every chord. Granted, some of those notes sound more harmonically pleasing than others, but your job as an improvising musician, is to create more interesting music. One way to do that is to utilize the entire chromatic scale. Our job isn't to make the music as pleasing as possible, or 'hummingly accessible;' that's the job of the commercial musician. Jazz is an art form, with the same legitimacy as symphonic music, or opera. We do art a disservice when our only goal is to satisfy the consumer. Then, music is no longer an art form, but a commodity, competing with Corn Flakes, Javex, Playtex and Hummers."

From the table behind the musicians, Naomi chokes on her Chardonnay in a fit of laughter. The musicians turn to her only to witness the wine dripping from her chin.

Damon connects, "Hey, aren't you the same woman who spilled my coffee yesterday? Now you're spitting wine at us. What's up?"

Naomi is suddenly struck with extreme embarrassment, unable to speak or move. She senses her face heating up and wants to leave the scene but her legs refuse to obey. Damon rises from the musicians' table and joins her.

"I suppose I owe you an apology for my rudeness," he offers.

Naomi regains her composure, assumes the onus for the incident, and apologizes to Damon. "I'm so-o-o sorry for interrupting you guys, but I found your conversation so-o-o funny, especially when you compared art to Corn Flakes. That was good. I thought only Andy Warhol could get away with that."

Damon counters, "Only another artist would find that funny. What do you play?"

"Oh, I don't play any instrument." She pauses between each sentence. "I'm not a musician. I'm a dancer. But I understand what you're saying. It's the same thing in dance. We have the same concerns, and many dancers are afraid to embrace the entire gamut of possibilities. What I'm trying to say is, they're afraid to search for freedom in their dance."

Damon nods to the waiter before leaving Naomi's table. We have to play some music right now, but don't go away. We can talk some more after this set. By the way, I'm Damon; Damon Farrell, and you are…?"

"Naomi, Naomi Parsons." She offers her hand and they shake. "I won't be going anywhere. I came to hear the music."

After the band steps up to the small stage, the waiter arrives at Naomi's table with a glass of Chardonnay. "It's on the house, courtesy of Mr. Farrell."

Damon announces the first tune before sitting at the piano. "Our first tune of the night is for Naomi, an appropriately titled tune by Eddie Harris, "Freedom Jazz Dance."

Naomi blushes in the darkness at the attention given her while the rhythm section cuts through the introduction and the horns follow with the jagged-edged fourth-based melody.

Damon joins Naomi at her table following the end of the first set. "So, Naomi, what brings a dancer into a jazz club? Is it the rhythm, the ambiance, or maybe it's the young cats in the band?"

"Well, I'm not here for the young 'cats' as you call them. I was here last week, mainly because I just wanted to get out of the house, but I really enjoyed the music, so I came back. Mainly, I like the attitude of the music and the conversations you have with the other musicians, which, I admit, I've been eavesdropping on. Your music has a freedom that I've been trying to find in my dancing. Incidentally, thank you for the song you played for me. That was great."

"You call them songs, I call them tunes. I guess if there was a singer up there, they would be songs, wouldn't they?"

"So, how much freedom was there in that 'tune,' Freedom Jazz Dance?" When the two horns played together it sounded like it was arranged, but then all hell broke loose. Was that freedom?"

Damon ponders his answer carefully. "Hmmm. Freedom, freedom, freedom. What a concept. Let's say there is more freedom in that tune than in many others, mainly because it has only one chord to worry about. That gives the players a huge sandbox to play in." He thinks further. "Do you understand music? Like, if I talk about chords and scales, do you know what I'm talking about?"

"Can you explain it in less technical terms? Like, if I want to be free while I'm dancing, I just try to ignore the choreography, although the choreographer may take offence. Or, I could concentrate on some concept or emotion in my head, and interpret it with my body, like in contemporary dance. That could be a form of freedom, I suppose."

"For many years, there's been a 'free jazz' movement, at least as far back as Ornette Coleman, or Jimmy Giuffre, in the early '60s. These players often pursued the free concept by just starting to play, sometimes totally ignoring the integral structure of the tune. The improvisation was based, not on chords and scales necessarily, but often on unrelated melodies that seemingly emerge from the moment they're being performed, a spontaneous composition if you like. I have a few other theories which I often blather about in my classes and workshops at the college where I teach but they take more time than we have here."

"I'd love to hear them; your theories I mean." Naomi sips her wine and requests a third from the waiter. "Would you like something to drink, Mr. Farrell?"

"Please, drop the Mister. I'm Damon to everyone, friends and enemies alike. No drink thanks; I try to keep a keen head when I'm playing and I don't believe in needing crutches. I often have a couple at the end of the night though. You're not driving are you Naomi? The cops watch the area pretty carefully. I wouldn't want you to get into any trouble."

"Not to worry. I'm taking a cab home." Naomi changes the subject. "Is there any way that I could sit in on some of your classes at the college, formally or informally? I don't mind registering and paying for the course. I would really like to examine the possible relationship between the freedoms in both dance and in jazz. When you play your music here at The Concept, I feel like dancing, and because it's live, and not prerecorded, there's always an unknown, a risk factor if you like, about how I might approach it as a dancer; it's not predictable. I love it."

"Look Naomi. None of the courses at the college would work for you. First of all, they assume a level of musical theory and language. They're also so structured and regimented that there wouldn't be any room for you to try new stuff. Besides, these days at the college, they stuff as many bodies into the room as humanly possible. It's a wonder that any of them learn a damn thing."

"But what if I…"

Damon cuts her off. "How about this, Naomi? Every afternoon, five days a week between 2:00 and 4:00, I practice alone in the theatre next to the music department. Meet me there on Monday afternoon, and be prepared to do some dancing. This thing we do, this art, it isn't really about taking classes and reading books. It's about trying things and discovering how they all work out. Come to dance, and I'll come to play; if it works out, we'll do it again. But don't think of this as just playtime though; it's hard work, and I have very low tolerance for those who don't take their art seriously. I'm as curious as you are to see how this might all work out."

32

Damon rises from the table. "It's been nice talking to you, Naomi. Enjoy the music."

"I'll be there on Monday, for sure. Thank you so-o-o much."

05

Damon arrives at the theatre to begin his practicing at precisely 2:00. He fully expects Naomi to be waiting at the door but, when he enters, she is already on the stage, sitting in a lotus position with her eyes open but focused somewhere beyond, past where the empty seats are hidden by darkness. The only lighting is the mandatory minimum legal requirement; some red exit signs and a weak penumbral centre stage light that encircles Naomi.

Damon watches her quietly from the piano. He raises the lid and opens the keyboard without a sound. A soft movement of air from the ventilation system creates a barely audible din that is quickly lost as an ambient base fog, upon which all further sound will be created. Naomi remains acutely still, but for the slow expansion and contraction of her abdominal muscles as she inhales and exhales.

The small finger of Damon's left hand touches a D-flat in the bass region while his right foot rests on the sustain pedal; the tone resounds softly inside the piano before emerging out into the theatre and dropping like soft rain onto the unseen seats at the rear. Whether the D-flat provides any input into Naomi's consciousness is unrevealed by any physical movement. Her breathing remains constant.

Another sustained D-flat followed by its G tritone, triggers a subtle vibration in Naomi's ankles, which Damon follows with a D Major triad. Naomi transforms her lotus position into a scissor-like lever that slowly raises her body, seemingly without effort, until she stands tall and willowy in the softly shaded centre of the stage light. Her body vibrates in a constant motion, waving from her fingertips above her, to her toes against the hardwood, as she personifies the sound wave itself. As Damon alters the pitch and the timbre, so changes Naomi. The two muses blend together into a single harmonious entity, each aware of the other; Naomi listens attentively

34

to each subtle tone and variation; Damon watches Naomi's body writhe and waver.

Out of somewhere inside Damon's subconscious mechanism, his fingers jab a series of harsh dissonances that violate the serenity; Naomi maintains her calm exterior movements until Damon returns to a softer dynamic. Suddenly, Naomi drives her body into a contrapuntal response by forming jagged shapes and abrupt contortioned angles with her arms, legs and torso that defy imagination. After several athletic bouts of fugal interplay, Damon and Naomi find common ground that brings the experiment to a close.

Naomi stands erect. She places her hands together in praying fashion in front of her face while she focuses into the distance. Her breathing increases. Damon sits silent at the grand piano, staring into the strings that echo their final overtones against the soundboard. All remains quiet.

"Holy shit." Damon breaks the silence. "What happened here?"

Naomi closes her eyes, afraid that she may start to weep. 'He doesn't like this,' she worries. 'It didn't work.'

"My God girl. Where did you learn to dance like that?"

Still worried that he's being critical, Naomi is afraid to open her mouth. Finally, she offers some thoughts. "I was worried that I should have started to dance when I first heard the music, but then I worried that I should have waited a bit longer before starting. What do you think?"

Damon unleashes his enthusiasm. "You are phenomenal, Naomi. I mean it. That was something else." He runs his fingers in random sweeps across the keyboard. "Do you always meditate before dancing, Naomi?"

"Always, even when I'm just doing warm ups at home. Most of the time I meditate to purge any distractions from my mind, but sometimes I use it to focus on a specific emotion or thought that I want to interpret in my dance." She pauses before asking, "How about you? Do you meditate before playing?"

"Oh, I've tried to many times, but I don't seem to get much out of it."

"Maybe you're just going about it the wrong way, or trying too hard."

"Well, sometimes the music itself draws me into a meditative state, a trance-like space, almost a vacuum; I call it my Zone of Tranquility."

"Were you in your Zone of Tranquility a few minutes ago when I was dancing? What was your take on what we were doing? Did we accomplish anything worthwhile?"

"It's always worthwhile, Naomi. Always. The act of doing it makes it worthwhile. And yes, I felt like both the music and your dancing drew me toward my Zone of Tranquility."

"What about the freedom? Did you sense that we were free from any structure?"

"We can discuss that in a moment, but I wanted to point out that I was really impressed by the dialogue we were having between your dance and my music. It was like a conversation between the muses, where I offered a statement, and you answered it before offering your own new statement to which I could respond, and it happened several times over. It was a wonderful experience, something that I don't feel most of the time with other musicians. I think it happened because we're not pushing any egos around; we just wanted to find out what would happen, and wow, something did."

Naomi's face comes alive and her body relaxes with the knowledge that she was accepted; her talent was recognized, and it was free.

"It was free, wasn't it Damon?"

"You seem to be obsessed with the search for freedom. There is no liberty without structure, Naomi. I don't mean to burst your bubble of imagination, but that's my philosophy anyway. There are other schools of thought on the subject of course, but I firmly believe that we, as creative individuals, are bound by structures, whether formal or otherwise, structures that influence how we exercise our liberty. Sometimes that structure is found in theoretical boundaries, for

36

example, the so-called rules of composition. I guess, in the case of dance, they could be the rules of technique or of choreography. I've always believed that, if Bach or Mozart had chosen another approach to their structure, with a different set of mathematical parameters, we would still feel bound to follow their lead, even after so many years. Why is that? Why do we limit ourselves this way? One of my pet peeves with the students of today is that they're all looking backwards for some *retro* solution to their creative problems. It's all nothing more than copying. Most of them are so tightly wound that I swear they're going to snap if a truly original idea plucks at their strings."

"But Mr. Farr… I mean, Damon, we can't predict the future to find out what the next thing is going to be, can we?"

"First of all, I don't believe in *things*, like in trends or fads. Listen carefully, Naomi. There is no future tense when you create. Likewise, there is no past tense. The creative action can only happen in the present. In improvised forms, whether in music or dance, there is only the present tense. The only value it possesses is at the moment it's being created. For the creator, the final product is immaterial; it doesn't exist. Oh sure, if we record the work we're doing, there'll be some tangible evidence of the performance, but the act of creating, the real guts of it all, has already passed; the record will only be an historical document. Does this make sense?"

"I'm trying to translate what you're saying to my approach to dance. Even though you suggest that there is no liberty without structure, I strive for absolute freedom when I dance, and there are always references to the past that influence how I interpret things. My interpretation is therefore, totally free of structure, but linked to the past. I could also make the argument that I'm dancing the past away so I can enjoy more freedom in the future."

"When I talked about there being structure in every creative act, I was not only referring to the traditional theoretical or technical structures, but to the kinds of structures that exist already in our minds and bodies that cause us to create in specific ways. Pure knowledge gained from years of practice and performance, for example, build within us a distinct set of structures from which we draw our creative patterns; and they are patterns. Listen sometime to the evolution of the great John Coltrane; from his early days with Miles and Monk, through his Giant Steps period when he was extremely structured, and then on to his later, so-called free improvisation stage. There are distinct similarities to the structure of his solos throughout this lineage. Yet, most musicologists will agree that the latter stage involved a high degree of freedom. It just wouldn't have happened without his exploration into the earlier structures; that earlier material imbedded itself into Trane's creative zone, emerging when appropriate. Add to that, the basic influences of finger memory, or in the case of dance, limb and body memory. I would also suggest that we're influenced by our early childhood experiences, both physical and environmental."

"What about our emotional baggage? Do you consider that part of the structure?"

"Definitely."

"From what I hear you saying then, there really is no freedom whatsoever; our creative moments and improvisations are direct results of pre-conditioned structures."

Damon is amazed at Naomi's intellect and sincere desire to understand and to learn as much as she can.

"No!" he responds. "I disagree with that statement. Even considering all of the structural influences within us, we still manage to produce fresh material that is free and expressive, and extremely personal. In fact, it is our individual structural filters that we create, through which passes the freedom that is so personal and original."

"What happens when two or more individuals are creating simultaneously, either within one medium like your jazz quintet, or in mixed media situations like, for example, music and dance?"

"I believe that, in these situations, the creative product is a melting together of all the individual structures toward a single goal, and the infinite possibilities, if allowed to be open, will lead to enormous freedom. That was the greatest talent of Miles Davis. The product wasn't about any individual virtuoso, or any pre-planned sound, but the result of very talented individuals contributing without much direction. Do you follow?"

"It makes perfect sense to me. This is why I've been listening to your music. I feel something different each time I hear you play: profound but different. This is how I approach my dance as well."

"Why do you dance, Naomi? What stimulates you? What compels you? I'm curious."

"I love to dance. That's the short answer, but let me explain. I'm using my dance to explore some of my deeper secrets, issues that have been haunting me for years. Through my therapist, who has suggested that I employ my closest friend, *dance*, to explore these darker caverns of my past, I have had some minor successes. However, since I've been hearing your music at The Concept, I've been far more successful. I believe that it's because of the unpredictable nature of your music that has led me into areas I would otherwise be afraid to explore."

"My dear Naomi. That's a mouthful, for sure. Let me guess that you're a patient of Doctor Kinderman, the psychiatrist who specializes in the illusions and delusions of the creative mind. Am I correct?"

Naomi's mouth falls open. "How did you know that? I've never mentioned that to anyone."

"After our coffee-spilling episode, I watched you rush to your appointment across the street. Doctor Kinderman's is the only office in the house you entered. How do I know that? I also seek the assistance of the good doctor in solving some issues of my own. I had just finished a session with her when I went for my dark roast at the café. My appointment is every Thursday at 9 a.m.; I believe yours to be at 11:00."

"Wow, you're a real Sherlock Holmes, aren't you?" Naomi expresses. "Then you must have some issues that need sorting out as well, especially if you're seeing Doctor Kinderman. I'm not probing but maybe you should explore the use of meditation like I do to sort things out."

"I haven't talked to the good doctor about that. Maybe I should."

Naomi offers to help. "I could show you some things that might be useful; that is, if you're open to it."

"Why not. I still have the theatre for another hour. Go for it, but I should tell you, I'm a slow learner."

Naomi laughs. "Let's do something right now. Just repeat what I'm doing." She quickly adopts a lotus position.

"Are you crazy? There's no way in hell I'll be able to bend myself into a pretzel like that. I struggle to get myself out of bed in the mornings."

Naomi laughs. "There are no rules that say you must sit like this. Many people meditate while sitting in a chair, or even lying down on their back. Why don't you stay on the piano bench? Place your feet flat on the floor. If you wish, you may feel more comfortable removing your shoes. Now, stare openly ahead at some unimportant object in the distance; don't struggle to focus on it. You can even close your eyes if you prefer."

Before refocusing his eyes, Damon watches Naomi as she establishes her pose. She focuses beyond the edge of the stage, and out into the darkness of the theatre, her hands lightly placed on her thighs close to her knees, palms up. Her impeccable posture remains with her while sitting, her back absolutely perpendicular to the floor.

Damon places his focus into the bowels of the piano. He opts for closing his eyes and plants the soles of his shoes flat against the floor as suggested.

Naomi instructs, speaking slowly in a soft, consistent voice.

"Now, follow my suggestions. Breathe in deeply and exhale slowly and evenly until you feel the need for more oxygen. Repeat the process several times until it becomes natural for you, and then allow your breathing to assume its natural rhythm."

She allows some silent space before resuming.

"Breathing is the most natural function in the body. Embrace it, feel the air coming and going. Focus on the breathing and nothing else. Gradually you want to relax your entire body, starting with your toes. Now focus all of your internal attention on your toes and relax them; don't leave them until they're totally at ease. Once the toes have relaxed, move your attention upward to your ankles, and then to your calves, and your thighs, and so on, repeating the relaxation process with each region of your body until you've completely relaxed the brain. Allow all of the tension to leave your body as you exhale; also, watch the tension leave as it exits through your pores. This will take some time so be very patient. While you go through this process, always be aware of your breathing, but first, place your concentration on the relaxation."

Damon follows Naomi's instructions. She speaks with a soft, almost inaudible voice, a voice that, if he were not concentrating on his breathing and relaxation, would appeal to him as extremely sensuous. His mind wanders into visions of this exotic young woman who, until recently, was just a clumsy klutz who spilled his coffee. Now she's dragging him through some eastern ritual of mind, body and spirit.

Naomi's voice disappears, leaving them sitting in silence, with nothing but their breathing. Minutes pass, until Naomi's soft voice begins again.

"Place your fingers over the piano keyboard but don't let them touch it. Just let them hover there, maybe an inch above. Let your fingers move as if they're actually playing music, but don't think about any specific piece of music. Let several minutes pass. Remember to continue concentrating on your breathing, and gradually lower the fingers until they make contact with the keyboard. Don't try to make sense of the music; just let the fingers play. Don't even listen to the music. It will find it's own way into your body and start to fill up the spaces left from where the tension was expelled."

Damon's fingers produce sounds without any musical structure at first, but his years of training soon force them into forming a series of arpeggios based on common ii-V-I progressions that even Naomi recognizes.

"Stop right there," she states in a louder, non-meditative voice.

Damon stops playing and opens his eyes to look at Naomi. "What did I do wrong?"

"Nothing went wrong. It's a normal part of the process. You allowed your structure-based experiences to influence you. In other words, you relinquished control to your past. Just like you said earlier, you can only create in the present, but the demons from your past keep influencing whatever you're doing. The trick is to expunge the demons whenever they appear, or to use them as a contributing part of the current creative process."

"So what do we do now?" Damon asks.

"Anything we want. We can restart the meditation from the beginning, or we can call it a day. Whatever."

"Why don't we call it a day, a very interesting day, for sure? But please, show up tomorrow and we'll continue this. I'm here every afternoon during weekdays. And always be prepared to dance. You're not going to learn what you want out of this just by listening to me play and I can assure you that you're not the only one who'll be learning. Learning and teaching are the same process; they happen simultaneously. One doesn't exist without the other and nobody imparts knowledge on another without reaping the benefits. Besides, I find your motives fascinating; I too, would love to explore my own mysterious past through my muse."

Naomi adds a layer of loose clothing over her tights and walks to the piano. Damon stands.

"Thanks ever so much for the opportunity to dance with you, Damon." Her arms extend around him in a friendly embrace.

Damon reciprocates. "It's been my pleasure. I'm looking forward to tomorrow."

When Naomi leaves the theatre, Damon sits quietly at the piano. When he closes his eyes, visions of the tall, beautiful and talented woman occupy his mind. 'What happened here today?' he asks, recognizing that this day is one that will affect the remainder of his life.

In his solitude, he focuses his eyes into the bowels of the piano and slowly enters his Zone of Tranquility, while his hands shape fresh music from the energy that has entered the emptied regions of his body, forcing it out through his fingers and his pores and over the piano's soundboard until it filters through every thread of fabric in the theatre. The music is new, untested, and adventurous, unlike any that has emerged from Damon Farrell in the past; raw material for all that will challenge him in the days and weeks ahead.

To Damon, it seems like only yesterday since they met, Naomi and he, and yet so many enjoyable hours have passed. On subsequent sessions at the theatre they expanded their creative collaborations to progressively deeper regions. For a time, Damon started each session by establishing a mood with his music and Naomi responded. Gradually she adopted a more independent approach and became more fluid with her interpretations.

One day, after several weeks, Naomi enters the theatre early. By the time Damon arrives she is already dancing and firmly entrenched in her own zone. Damon sits quietly at the piano without touching the keyboard and watches as she moves so beautifully about the stage, confidant that she knows nothing of his presence. He feels it would be an invasion to introduce any music so he remains silent. Eventually, she gracefully returns to a meditative position next to the piano. Without abandoning her focus, she whispers, "Damon, I'm famished, please feed me."

Damon injects a series of arpeggios based on double diminished scales, ambiguous statements that can be interpreted with either elation or somberness. Naomi remains seated, inhaling deeply as if consuming a storehouse of sounds before she suddenly explodes into a frenzy of agitated motion, scurrying and leaping about. Damon hadn't witnessed such energy from her before. He has no choice but to follow her lead, wherever it takes him. She becomes his focus while he attempts to find his own zone; he senses the conventions and complacencies escaping through every pore of his body while her energy and his desire for fulfillment fill the void; they became one, as if the muses had fused them into a single expression. Sounds emanate from the piano that Damon has no control over. He becomes a soundboard, absorbing vibrations from the floor through the soles of his feet, and from the acoustics of the theatre through the pores of his skin. His eyes catch snippets of Naomi's body soaring here and flashing there, rolling as if in agony across the stage floor, and reclaiming her elation through orgasmic-like responses.

Without warning, she collapses. Everything becomes silent and still, leaving only a vacuum of emotions and mental activity. Damon has no idea how long they remain in that state. At some point they find themselves in each other's arms, exhausted, Naomi's perspiration saturating his shirt. On this day, they reach a point of no return, a summit that neither of them wants to retreat from, a pinnacle of emotions, which will make subsequent sessions very difficult, but also very exciting and rewarding, yearning as they do, to explore still further dimensions.

06

Several days pass, until they meet on Thursday at the café between their appointments, before Damon feels secure enough to ask Naomi about her amazing performance at the theatre.

Her response begins apologetically, "I hope you don't take offence at this Damon, but the reason I started early was intentional; I wanted to be in my zone and already warmed up before you arrived. In previous meetings, when we've practiced together, you've started the session with music of a specific mood, and I've adapted my dancing to suit the music. We've made tremendous strides doing it that way, but I wanted to see what would happen if I began dancing as freely as possible, so that you would then be forced to adapt your music to my dance."

"Why do your think I would take offence, Naomi? It was a marvelous experience, full of energy and emotion. It's the closest we've come to an ideal collaboration; we became one for the first time. What I really want to know is what was happening inside you, in your brain and in your zone that inspired that energy? And where did that incredible emotional outpouring come from?"

"Doctor Kinderman has been encouraging me to explore the horrific images from my nightmares using my dancing with the concept that, through my muse, I'll be able to explore and understand the images in more detail, and ultimately expunge them from my consciousness. The concept is based upon a theory that the more you know and comprehend about a subject, the less it influences you and the less fearful it is, mainly because it's been fractionalized to the point of insignificance. It's like taking a photograph and blowing it up until all you see are the pixels, which, one by one, you eliminate, until they no longer influence your thoughts. Then your mind is clear to do what's important. For me, I'll be able to dance more freely; that's the only thing that matters to me."

Damon suggests, "If that theory proves correct, then all the years I've spent studying musical theory and advanced harmonies could be fractionalized until they all become insignificant mush."

"I wouldn't put it in those terms, but…" she hesitates, "it could explain why your vast storehouse of information could be preventing you from breaking out into more liberating expression."

"Holy shit, Naomi. You can be blunt about things can't you?" Damon sips from his dark roast, keeping his eyes fixed on Naomi's.

"Oh, I'm so-o-o sorry, Damon. That's not the way I meant it." She places her right hand on Damon's arm. "Please forgive me."

"No!" He removes his arm from the table. "You are absolutely correct. Please don't apologize. In fact, you're being very honest, and I appreciate that. I've struggled for many years to break away from the rigidity of musical structure. The problem is that, once an entire body of knowledge is built upon theoretical dogma, one becomes bound to it; it's like a shackle of creative enslavement; like a religion."

They sit quietly for some time, each reviewing, in their own mind, the ramifications of their conversation, until Damon breaks the silence.

"So how have the sessions been going for you, the meetings with Doctor Kinderman, and the theory she proposed? Have you been able to dance some of the nightmares away as she suggests?"

"At home, I've been trying to focus on one of the images, a hand carved wooden cross dangling from a silver chain. I see that image every time I have one of my nightmares; it's the last image that appears before I wake up in a pool of perspiration. I have danced to that image in hopes of breaking it down into smaller components of understanding, but with little success. I know that the image is from a real event in my past but, until I can purge it from my memory, I will never eliminate that event, and it was a horrible event, I can assure you. My efforts at home haven't been too successful. I attempted to dance as if I was the dangling cross but it didn't go anywhere. It wasn't until the other afternoon in the theatre when things opened up for me."

"My God, Naomi, what kinds of nightmares are you having? I thought mine were bizarre. Please go on," Damon encouraged.

"During my meditation, my creative foreplay, as you so aptly call it, a small dot appeared in my toes while I was focused on relaxing and cleansing my body of distraction. As I concentrated on my ankles and calves, the dot increased in size, like a cancer, until it became a recognizable still image which continued to increase as my concentration passed through my thighs and my torso, eventually filling the void throughout my entire body and settling in my brain. It was the wooden cross, the same one that I've been seeing in my nightmares, fixed as a still image, as if a holographic photo had been exposed directly on the inner surface of my skin. The cross steadily expanded until it occupied every muscle, joint, organ, and cavity inside me. I tried to refocus my concentration beyond it but it occupied every dimension. Finally I searched for music, hoping to replace the image, but none was forthcoming. There was movement from deep inside of me; the cross twitched and bent, and started a dangling motion from its silver chain. I writhed and twisted to accommodate the cross' motion, its horizontal member filling my arms and hands and the vertical member occupying my torso from toe to head. It twisted, forcing me to follow its contortions until all the muscles in my body were drawn into a knot. A hand gripped my throat and a pain in my lower torso overwhelmed me. I retaliated with my legs and knees, the strongest muscles I have, and was able to partially fractionalize the hand until it release its grip.

Suddenly, just as in my nightmares, I was awakened wringing with perspiration. That's when I asked you to feed me; I needed your music to purge the ugliness that had overtaken me. Once your vibrations entered me I was rejuvenated. I writhed and twisted again to encourage the music through my body in an effort to replace the wooden cross. Pieces of the cross began to crumble, first the bits in my head, followed by fragments that had occupied my chest. Before long, the image of the cross was reduced to a small mound of dust on the stage below me, which I shuffled away with a sweep of my foot.

Once it was fully purged, I regained my composure and was able to dance with confidence, triumphant over the cross until I finally collapsed, exhausted."

"And that's when you approached me?"

"No, not quite. I was so spent that I couldn't move a muscle. I sat still, concentrating on my emptiness, that wonderful emptiness that follows fulfillment, until I realized that we had conquered the demon together. It wasn't just my dancing, but everything combined: the dancing, the music, and our sensitivity to each other's muses. That's when I came to you. I needed your arms around me to know that we're a team. I also needed to know that you received something from this, and I sensed that you did."

Damon couldn't disguise his enthusiasm. "Oh, I certainly did get something from it. I'm still shivering when I think about the energy, the electricity, and the emotion that dominated the entire performance. That's right, Naomi, it was a superb performance; it wasn't just some mere rehearsal. The problem is, I want to return to that space."

"I've thought about nothing else since then, Damon. I only managed to resolve one of the images that appeared in my nightmares. There are others. I know I won't reach the same intensity every time we work out, but I must try. I must know why these demons haunt me. I won't sleep until they're gone."

As with every Thursday's coffee break, time catches up with them. Naomi starts slurping down the last of her latte and Damon's dark roast is cold as usual. In the last minutes of their conversation, Damon ventures forth with an idea.

"Naomi, how would you like to go out for dinner? At a nice restaurant, someplace where we can talk for several hours and relax."

She stops slurping and stares into her cup before raising her eyes to his. "Are you asking me out on a date?"

"I don't want you to think of it as a date. After all, I'm old enough to be your father. I just thought that we never have enough time to talk about normal things. We're either dealing with philosophy or music and dance. How about just absorbing the ambiance of a nice restaurant and enjoying some real food. Besides, we both live alone in our small apartments; I'm sure you nuke more meals than you cook, just like me. This way we can relax while somebody else does the work; we'll have some wine and talk about anything that strikes our fancy."

Naomi laughs. "That's an interesting phrase — strikes our fancy — where does that come from I wonder?"

"That's exactly why I'm proposing this meal. I've never seen you laugh like that. We could just laugh over dinner, that'd be OK as well."

"I have to go to my appointment now, Damon. Can I think about it and let you know? I'll call you later tonight, OK?"

Damon retrieves one of his college business cards and hand-scribbles his home phone number on it. "Here, take this. Call me anytime, I'm always there, and I'll probably be awake."

As predicted, Damon can't force himself to sleep. His mind teeters between hoping that Naomi will call and accept his dinner invitation, and thinking that he must be an idiot for asking her out in the first place.

'What was I thinking? She's only 28 or 30, something like that, and here I am, ready to apply for senior citizenship. She was right; I was asking her out on a date. Hell, I haven't been on a date for… let's see… Christ, I can't even count the years. What do people do on dates these days anyway? When I was young, and Virginia and I went out before we were married, dates were just excuses to get laid, or at least, hope to get laid; well, in her case it was guaranteed. Come to think of it, I haven't had sex since… shit, I must be getting really old; I'm losing my memory. Oh, I remember. It was with Lydia, the week after Tiny hit rock bottom and she threw him out of the house. That was a tough time for all of us. He couldn't perform in the band worth a shit anymore; he was drinking so much I had to let him go. I told him that I'd help in any way I could, but he refused. He told me to fuck myself and he told Lydia the same thing. Nobody planned things the way they turned out, but a week later, Lydia knocked on my apartment door after the club closed. She had a bottle of CC in her hand and wanted to talk about how things had turned out. I poured a couple of drinks and, before we knew it, we were in bed. After telling Tiny I'd help him out in any way I could, and then I end up screwing his wife; some friend I turned out to be. I felt really guilty the next morning, but after a few more nights it happened all over again, and continued for the best part of a year.

Then one day Tiny showed up at the club, asking me for his gig back. He said he was working on his problem and needed some self-esteem, the kind he could only get from playing music. I understood that, and hired him back on the condition that he stays clean. I even let him sleep in my apartment for a while until he got settled. Shortly after that, Lydia opened her door to him, and he moved back in with her. I don't know whether he ever found out about Lydia and me. I could never tell him, and I'm sure she couldn't; it would set him off again. Sometimes, a secret is a better choice. He's still with the band and with Lydia, and she and I haven't touched each other since.'

Damon fades in and out of sleep. Finally he dozes off for a short period until the phone rings, but when he answers there is no one there, silence followed by a click and the dial tone. It's possible that it was a wrong number, or maybe it was one of those telephone sales bastards. Damon considers calling Naomi and apologizing for even suggesting a dinner date.

'No, she's probably sleeping, and even if she's not, she'll be trying to find a way to turn me down without hurting my feelings. She may even be in the middle of one of her own nightmares. Jeez, are her nightmares something or what? No wonder she doesn't sleep at night.'

In a state of semi-sleep he walks to the kitchen and pours a double of Canadian Club taking one swallow. He visits the washroom before returning to bed, but nothing registers after that, until he finds himself once again, reliving his horrific confrontation with death.

* * *

Powerful waves retaliate against our approach. The beach is still some distance away and the essence of seasickness puke blends with sea and salt smells: dead fish, kelp, and fuel oil from the landing craft. None of us can anticipate what lies ahead. The gate of the landing craft scrapes open with the full force of fingernails against slate, smashing into waist deep water. Like penguins we plunge into the dark sea toward our doom. Once in the water, the cacophony of war befalls us. One young lad trips and is immediately submerged under the landing craft, sent to his finish before even touching ground.

* * *

Damon struggles with his nightmare, the same one every time, it appears so real. He tosses himself about until the sheets are knotted and the pillow falls to the floor. As his inevitable death approaches, he once again faces the lure of the beautiful aquatic dancer.

* * *

She still comes to me, my beautiful Aphrodite, closer and closer, steadily dancing and swimming, alluring and sensuous and exciting. She touches me with her hair as she turns to leave. 'Follow me, follow me,' she beckons with erotic gestures.

* * *

The phone rings again, cutting Damon off abruptly from his rendezvous with Aphrodite. This time it rings three or four times before he can answer.

"Hello." His voice breaks as it rasps against his larynx.

"Hello, is this Damon? Do I have the wrong number? If so, I'm so-o-o sorry for interrupting you, whoever you are."

He recognizes the way she stretches out her apologies. "Naomi, is that you?"

"Oh, hi Damon. I apologize for calling you so late but I'm having a horrible night, and I need someone to talk to. I hope I didn't wake you."

"No, no," he fibs, "you called at the perfect time." He attempts to make out the numbers on his digital alarm clock, but his glasses are still on the night table. "What time is it anyway?"

"Let me see. Oh yeah, it's 2:46. Should I hang up and call in the morning?"

"This *is* the morning, Naomi. Let's talk."

"I'm having one of my nightmares, like the one I told you about earlier. Except now I'm seeing other images; they flash at me from the dark."

"What are the images like?"

"There's a lot of fire, like flames shooting upwards from below, and it's extremely hot. I see my mother inside the flames and I try to get closer to her but the heat prevents it. She looks like she's screaming at me, but there's no sound."

Before putting his brain into gear, Damon responds with an offhanded quip. "Maybe you should turn the volume up." He immediately regrets speaking.

"You're so-o-o bad Damon," Naomi says before adding some other images to the list. "You're going to think I'm crazy, or a pervert, or something like that, but there was also a separate image of a man's thing... you know... his penis... and it flashed at me; it was hard and erect and the man threatened me with it. This is getting too weird for me, Damon. I don't know where it's all leading."

"It sounds pretty weird to me as well. I don't know how much help I can be for you, Naomi, except to be a sounding board. Have you talked to Doctor Kinderman about these images?"

"Yeah, but tonight has been the worst yet. Yesterday morning I told her about our session last week, when it was so wonderful."

"Wait, hold it, Naomi. Does she know that you and I have been seeing each other?"

"Not really. I didn't tell her your name, just that you were a piano player from the college."

"I think she's got that figured out by now."

"Do you mean that you've never talked to her about our sessions in the theatre?"

"Not yet, but I suppose there's no reason to keep it a secret now."

"Oh jeez, I'm so-o-o sorry, Damon, I shouldn't have said anything to her, but I was so thrilled about the outcome of our sessions and about the breakthrough I had with the image of the wooden cross. She seemed happy about that too. She said that it was a giant step toward solving my problems."

"And it was, I'm sure. You should take a similar approach to solving the latest images." Damon tries to imagine how she'll dance away the image of the hard-on, and what music he could provide for that.

"Have you thought any more about our dinner out, Naomi?" Damon takes advantage of her pause to sip some CC.

"I've done nothing but that, well, except to have nightmares about erections and stuff. The answer is, yes, I've thought about it. I also talked to Doctor Kinderman about going out on a date, and how nervous I was about it all. You must know that I'm nervous as hell about going out with you, not because of you, but just about going out at all. I'm embarrassed to admit it, but I've never been out on a real date, can you believe that?"

Damon searches for the best answer and settles on, "Naomi, it's been at least 25 years since I was last out on anything that could remotely be considered a date; that would be around the time when you were five. So, it's been much longer since I've been on a date than for you."

Before she can become upset with his flippant response, he continues.

"Please don't consider this a date, Naomi. I'm just a friend who wants company over dinner, and you're the closest friend I have right now. Please join me for dinner. I'll pick out a nice spot that's close to your place."

"Deal," she says, "but I should tell you what Doctor Kinderman said when I told her about it. She told me that, for a first date, I should take a cab and meet my date there, and take a cab home, alone. She also said that I should only have one glass of wine and never go to bed with him on the first date. So, those are the rules, like them or not."

"It's a deal," Damon agrees. "I'll call you tomorrow with the details."

07

A steady drizzle creates myriads of puddles throughout the Village that reflect the lights and movement from traffic and commercial establishments, adding an air of excitement to the street. Most passersby opt to skirt the perimeters of the puddles while some boldly slosh through the middle like playful children with rubber boots in the first rainfall of spring. Damon waits patiently, umbrella at the ready, for Naomi to arrive by taxi as she promised. They had finally agreed on a small but upscale Italian restaurant located not too far from Naomi's apartment. Damon rode the subway from his apartment on Queen Street and walked the last four blocks in the rain beneath his black umbrella, dodging puddles and curbside creeks, and arriving earlier than scheduled to greet Naomi at the taxi door and, in a gentlemanly fashion, keep her dry between the taxi and the entrance. Something about the Oscar-red carpet runs through his mind when her taxi splashes into the curb. Inside the vehicle, Naomi struggles with the door while the cabbie remains seated counting his fare and tip. Damon steps forward, offering his umbrella.

Once inside, he helps Naomi remove her raincoat, shakes the raindrops off and offers it, and his own coat and umbrella, to the coat check attendant. He turns and immediately notices how elegant Naomi has dressed for the occasion. He's unaccustomed to seeing her in anything but baggy sweats and either trousers or tights, depending on the circumstances; she presents herself in a little black dress with matching small purse and medium heels that increase her already impressive height to meet Damon eye-to-eye. Her moderate eye shadow and enhanced lashes draw all of Damon's attention to her wide bright eyes that serve to disguise her nervous smile.

"I'm so glad you chose to come, Naomi. I was worried that you might change your mind at the last minute."

"The truth is that I've actually been looking forward to this for the past week, Damon. I even went shopping for this dress after I realized that I didn't even own a dress. Do you like it?"

"You look beautiful in it… I mean the dress is beautiful. No, I mean that you look beautiful as always, but even more so in that dress." He pauses. "How am I doing so far?"

"Thank you for the compliments, Damon. I'm not accustomed to being flattered, but I admit that I do feel beautiful in this dress, and in this restaurant. Do you have any idea how long it's been since I've been out to a nice restaurant? It's been years. Can you believe that?"

Not to be outdone, Damon adds, "I could easily match you year for year I'm sure. I find it deadly to eat out alone; it's like all of the other people are staring at me, or feeling pity on me. So, I just stay at home; sometimes I order out for a pizza or some Chinese, but that's it."

"I think that women have more anxieties about eating alone. I never know where to look. At first there's the menu, but once I've ordered, there's only the cutlery and the napkin to stare at until the food arrives. Once in a while I'll scan the room, but as soon as someone makes eye contact with me, I immediately look back down lest they think I'm coming on to them. It's embarrassing, don't you think?"

"Well," Damon proposes, "neither of us is eating alone tonight, so we should ignore everyone else, and take advantage of our freedom to talk between us about anything that tickles our fancy."

Naomi laughs again at the phrase.

The waiter arrives, lights the candle, and introduces himself as Kevin. He inquires whether a before-dinner aperitif is in order. Damon looks at Naomi; she approves with her eyes.

"A couple of dry Sherries please. And there is no rush Kevin. We have a lot to talk about this evening, isn't that right Naomi?"

"I've never had a dry Sherry before. Will it be very bitter?"

"I'm sure you'll enjoy it," he reassures. "Incidentally, don't you think that Kevin is a strange name for a waiter in an Italian restaurant? I would have expected a Mario, or an Antonio, but not a Kevin."

Naomi giggles at his attempt at levity before she poses the door-opening question, "Have you ever been married, Damon?"

He pauses to take a breath. "Yes, I was married many years ago. It didn't work out though."

"Do you have kids?"

Another pause. "There was one son, Graham, but I haven't seen him since he was nine years old. That's how old he was when Virginia and I split up."

"So, how old would he be now, Damon?"

She's a sly one, he ponders before answering. "Let's see, he was born in 1963; he'd be 39 now. I wouldn't even recognize him if he was sitting at the next table."

"So you could be a grandfather and not even know it."

Damon manages to deflect the conversation thread back to Naomi. "What about you Naomi? Have you been married, or do you have someone special in your life?"

"Heavens no. I've had too many bad experiences. I prefer to keep a wide distance from all people."

"Hmmm. I'm a 'people' and I'm sitting fairly close to you right now. Who does that make me?"

"You're different. I don't feel threatened when I'm with you, at least not so far. Maybe it's because you're a lot older than I am." She immediately realizes her faux pas. "Oh, I'm so-o-o sorry. I didn't mean it that way, Damon." She places her hand on his forearm. "That's not the main reason I'm not threatened by you; I enjoy talking with you. I don't get to talk with too many people these days, except for Doctor Kinderman of course."

Damon allows Naomi's slip of the tongue to pass without comment. "That's why I suggested we go out for dinner. I enjoy talking with you as well."

"What happened to your marriage? Like, why did it fall apart?"

"Naomi, you sound just like Doctor Kinderman and I've already been down this route with her. But I will tell you why my marriage ended. We were too young, and full of lust. One should never marry for such an unimportant reason as lust, not that lust isn't a wonderful thing; I strongly recommend it. However, when we're young, we often confuse lust with love. They are two completely different emotions. Lust is purely a biological phenomenon, a function of our existence as mammals, designed to keep the species alive; love takes more time to evolve, to learn to understand one's partner, to share both person's passions and to encourage each other in their pursuits. But, who am I to be giving such advice? I've never really been in love, except with my music that is; I am truly in love with her, my music."

"Aha. You do it too." Naomi points her finger toward him.

"I do what?"

"You refer to your music as a woman; a woman that you're in love with. Doctor Kinderman caught me referring to my dance, which I am truly in love with, as a woman as well."

"Is she? Is your dance a woman?"

"That's exactly what Doctor Kinderman asked me, and I told her that I'd have to think more about it. Back to the original topic, what was your wife like?"

"I didn't know that was our original topic, but I will address the question nevertheless. Here's the abridged version. She was attractive, sexy, and a dominant person who always got her way. I didn't know it at the time, but I was conned into marrying her when she became pregnant, fully believing that Graham was our son. We were certainly sexually active before the day she broke the news that she was pregnant. He was obviously her son, but I discovered later that he wasn't mine. In fact, he turned out to be the son of my older brother, Phil, whom I also haven't seen since 1972, when he and Virginia, and Graham of course, took off together. That was the end of my marriage and I haven't had any desire to repeat that mistake; I've been living alone ever since."

"Wow! That was 30 years ago; I wasn't even born then."

"That's exactly how Doctor Kinderman reacted, although that's not the main reason I'm seeing her. I've learned to live with my solitude."

"So why are you seeing Doctor Kinderman then?"

"You young people are definitely inquisitive, not to mention a bit forward."

"Sorry. I just thought that while we're talking we could get to know each other better, don't you agree? I don't mind telling you why I'm seeing a therapist."

"Go for it. I'm as curious about you as you are about me."

Naomi agrees to proceed. "OK. I'll go first. I told you a bit about the nightmares I have. Well, Doctor Kinderman seems to think that they're related to some of my missing past, although I can identify the sources of some of the images. I was adopted; I know that. I don't however, know who my birth mother is, or was for that matter. She may not even be alive. The people whom I know as my parents are Doctor and Rebecca Parsons. They adopted me very soon after I was born. For all I know, my birth mother might have been a prostitute, or maybe she died giving me life; who knows?"

"Have you ever tried to search for your birth mother? Apparently it's quite a common exercise these days."

"I think about it from time to time. I'd rather wait until I can at least sort out some of my demons. That's what I call my nightmares and those horrible images; I call them demons."

"That's a coincidence, because that's what I call my nightmares: demons."

Naomi starts to laugh. "That's a good one, Damon's Demons. That's what you should call your jazz group. You could all dress up in satanic costumes and have pyrotechnics surrounding the bandstand." She forms her fingers into quotation marks. "Damon's Demons, the jazz band from Hell."

"So Naomi, continue your story."

"Oh yeah. I almost forgot. Where was I? Oh yeah. So, the Parsons adopted me. I can only guess that their life together was a

58

disaster. From what I could gather, shortly after I arrived, my mother embraced a fundamental religious group that believed in the apocalypse and God's punishments. Apparently, that's when my father left us. I never got to know him; I can't, to this day, put a face on him. According to my mother, he just up and left for no reason whatsoever. She also complained often about how he left her with nothing and that she had to keep up the payments for the house and all the expenses, even my dance lessons. She went to church most days of the week and three times on Sundays. I was dragged to Sunday school and had to attend regular services as well. Every time there was a fundraiser, my mother and I went door-to-door selling chocolates or handing out pamphlets, all to raise money for the starving children in Africa. It was years later that I discovered the money didn't go to Africa at all; it went to print more bibles and other religious propaganda, which were then sent to Africa. Have you ever eaten a bible? I can't imagine that they're very tasty, and certainly not nourishing."

"I would agree with that." Damon offers. "So, you were a church-goer. Are you still religious?"

"Hell no!" Naomi answers emphatically. "But that's a story for another time."

"What kind of problems were your parents having? You mentioned that their life together was, how did you put it, a disaster."

"I can only guess that my father couldn't tolerate mother's religious fanaticism. Mother always complained about him, and there were no photos of him anywhere in the house. She said she was poor, but she gave a hoard of money to the church every year."

"Have you ever looked your father up?"

"Once in a while I think that I should try and locate him. It shouldn't be too hard, should it? He's a doctor; there must be records of where he is, maybe in the medical association records."

"Why don't you just Google him?"

"I'm just not ready to start anything yet."

"What about your mother?"

"On occasion I go to the hospital to see her, but she'll never leave there. Besides, she doesn't even know who I am anymore. She just stares into space. That's one of the reasons I'm seeing Doctor Kinderman. It's not the only reason, mind you, but I carry a load of guilt about what happened to my mother. Actually, there are several reasons I go to therapy; I suppose that they're all interrelated in some bizarre manner."

Naomi pauses to sip some sherry before continuing her story. Damon remains quiet.

"First there are the nightmares I have. There are several different ones, and Doctor Kinderman seems to think that they're related to some part of my missing past, possibly from before I was adopted, although I'm fully aware of the circumstances behind some of the nightmares. For example, I've been able to decipher the symbolism of fire and the falling baby in the one, but I'm afraid that I can't talk about that right now, maybe at another time."

"I thought you were adopted shortly after birth," Damon inquires.

"I know. That's the weird part, isn't it? How can there be anything for us to dream about from before we were born, or even at the time we were born? It beats me."

"You and I may share more than our muses, Naomi, but that's also a subject for another time, I suppose."

"There seems to be a lot of stuff that has to wait until later," Naomi offers. "Are we a couple of nutbars, or what?" Before she allows time for Damon to respond, she continues.

"There are some nightmares that I can tell you about though. In one nightmare that I can't figure out, a man and a woman are in bed and they're making love. Suddenly, the door bursts open and there's a lot of yelling and screaming in a language I don't understand. Then, some soldiers take the man away while the woman screams and weeps before my nightmarish vision fades to a black void, nothingness, a silent black vacuum that lasts for minutes until it's abruptly altered by a still image of an eyeball, all bloodied, a flashing image that is at first, extremely sharp and focused, but gradually, pixel by pixel, they morph into one of those kaleidoscopic images.

That's when I usually wake up, when all those broken pieces of the image move around in my head."

"Ugh!" Damon grimaces at the suggestion of the bloodied eyeball.

"Oh I'm sorry, Damon. I hope this isn't too grisly. Does it turn you off?" Naomi sips the last Sherry from her glass and wipes the edge of her lips with her napkin.

Before Damon can speak, Kevin arrives with salads and a bread plate. "Have you chosen a wine?" he asks.

Damon identifies interesting Chianti on the wine list, inquiring if that would be acceptable to Naomi; she nods her approval.

Damon returns to the conversation. "No Naomi, it doesn't turn me off. You seem to have an interesting dilemma. I don't mean to probe, but if you feel OK about it, I would love to hear more."

"Not now. The other stuff is much too personal, and it can be even more terrifying and gruesome.

"Oh Jesus, Naomi. I apologize for prying into your personal affairs. Maybe we should just concentrate on our salads and talk about the time of day, or the weather, or maybe our favourite colours. Here's one, how about this? What was the weirdest experience you've ever had on a city streetcar?"

"Not a chance, Damon. You're not getting away that easily. Besides, this isn't some kids camp here." Naomi smiles wickedly. "Now it's your turn. I want to hear about some of the mud in your backyard."

"Oh boy. That bit about my ex-wife and my brother wasn't enough, eh?"

Naomi shakes her head from side to side. "Nope. That was mild compared to mine. I want more."

Damon pauses to pull his thoughts together, sipping some Chianti before starting. "I too, have bizarre nightmares, although they can really happen at any time of the day or night. I'm underwater, bleeding to death, and I see corpses floating about me, staring at me while I'm drowning. The only saving grace in my visions is the appearance of a gorgeous unclad woman who dances and swims around me, beckoning me to follow her as she swims away; I call her Aphrodite, after the Greek Goddess of love, beauty, pleasure and procreation."

Naomi leans forward and whispers. "Now we're getting somewhere. Does she excite you, this Aphrodite of yours?" She leans back in her chair, sporting a wicked smile while waiting for his answer.

Damon chokes on his Chianti. "Wow, are you ever bold with your questions."

"Well, does she? After all I've told you about me already. Besides, I've also promised to tell you more at a later time; that should have piqued your interest. Surely you can reveal whether you had a hard on or not."

Naomi retains her wicked smile and forks at some salad, eager to hear his response. She observes the blush in Damon's face. "Did I make you blush? I'm so-o-o sorry."

"Actually… yes, you did… and yes, she does… excite me, that is. I mean, yes, you made me blush, and also yes, in my nightmares, Aphrodite has given me an erection. I often wonder if I'll ever have the fortitude in my dreams to pursue her, wherever she wants me to go, but I'm always reluctant, or unable, to do so. As a result, I'm left to drown with the rest of the pathetic corpses, although, so far, I've been able to wake up before I drown."

"I've heard it said that if you die in your nightmare, you really do die in life. I can't imagine how anyone would know that for a fact though, do you? It's like those nightmares where you fall over a cliff. Have you ever noticed that you never hit bottom? You just keep falling until you wake up. That's what happens to me in my flames nightmare; I jump into the fire and start falling toward Hell but I never get there before I wake up. Thank God for that."

Kevin arrives with the entrees and tops up the wine glasses before departing.

Damon raises his glass toward Naomi and proposes a toast. "To great conversation, and to the muses of music and dance. May they live in us forever?"

Naomi counters with, "And to our first date. May there be many more."

Conversation is quiet during the entrée except for occasional references to the meal. Across the room, a phone rings with a 'Hockey Night in Canada' bell tone, and is answered by an obese boisterous man with an equally booming voice who conducts business over the quieter din of the diners. Naomi leans across the table and whispers, "Don't those guys just piss you off?"

Damon leans closer to Naomi to agree, and raises his glass. "To the demise of modern technology."

Naomi reciprocates and opens her lips into a beautiful smile toward Damon. "That's something else we have in common."

"Excuse me, Professor Farrell," a voice addresses Damon from tableside.

He turns toward the voice; a stunning, shapely woman in her mid-30s stands beside him. She's poured into a skintight red satin dress split up the sides to where only imagination should go.

"Do you remember me? I'm Sandi. From your performance piano class."

"Sandi." He pauses. "Yes, of course. How could I forget? Sandi, with an 'i,' not a 'y,' right? What are you doing these days?"

"I perform here at the restaurant three nights a week. It pays the rent you know."

"So that's you playing. It's very nice. Sandi, allow me to introduce my good friend, Naomi. She's a dancer, a very fine one at that."

The two women shake hands. "It's nice to meet you, Sandi." Naomi says, her eyes securing contact with the pianist's.

Before she departs, Sandi asks, "Is there anything I can play for you two; any requests?"

Damon answers, "Sandi, could you play a couple of choruses of Giant Steps, just for me?"

"Whew. I haven't played that since my graduating year, and I didn't receive a very good grade for it. Is there anything else?"

"Then just pick anything else by Trane, maybe a great ballad. I've got it. Body and Soul... with the Trane changes. How's that?"

She agrees and departs for the piano. "It was very nice meeting you, Naomi."

While Sandi struggles through the bridge of Body and Soul, Naomi leans forward and whispers, "You don't remember her do you?"

"Not a chance. She couldn't have dressed like that in class, or I would remember her."

"How did you know that she spelled her name with an 'i'?"

"Take a good look at her, Naomi. Her mother named her Sandra, or maybe Alexandra, but her name was changed to Sandi the day she bought that red slit satin sheath."

Naomi laughs aloud and asks, "Do you find her attractive, Damon?"

"Yes, she certainly is an attractive woman, don't you think?"

"Yes I agree; she really is beautiful."

By the end of their dinner Naomi realizes that three hours had passed. They had added a chocolate dessert and a Drambuie with coffee to their already substantial meal.

"This has been the shortest three hours I've ever spent, Damon. It's also been the most enjoyable three hours. The time has just disappeared."

"Let me arrange a taxi for you, Naomi."

"I'd rather walk, if you don't mind. I live only a few blocks away, and the rain has stopped. Also, I must walk off some of these calories. It's such a gorgeous night. Look at the stars. Will you walk with me?"

Damon joins her. As they stroll through Yorkville, he points out landmarks from his past. "The Penny Farthing sat there; it was always busy. The police used to patrol the street and whenever a group of people gathered in one spot, they moved us on. And somewhere along here was a place called The Mousetrap, and over there was the Riverboat. As a jazz musician I spent more of my time along Avenue Road, particularly at The Cellar, and sometimes at The Night Owl." As they turn the corner Damon points to where The Purple Onion was located. "That's where Joni Mitchell performed, and I once heard this great gospel group called the Phoenix Singers at the Gates of Cleve next door."

"I had the distinct impression that you weren't a religious person, Damon. What were you doing listening to gospel music?" Unaccustomed to walking on heels, Naomi struggles with her balance by grasping Damon's arm and holding tight.

"I'm not religious at all; never have been. It was just the pure enjoyment and enthusiasm The Phoenix Singers demonstrated while they sang; they obviously loved what they were doing and that has to count for something."

They willfully prolong the walk to Naomi's apartment by strolling down side streets, sometimes stopping to look at an interesting building or to peer into the windows of an art gallery; it's an evening too enjoyable to bring to a close.

Damon's mind briefly considers the possibility that Naomi might hold some interest in him as being someone closer than just a good friend, but soon discounts the thought as wishing for something that could never happen. His mind switches to questioning whether Naomi might be thinking similar thoughts to his. 'Could she be considering inviting me up for coffee? Does she think of me as more than just companionship or as just some piano player?'

To change the subject in his mind Damon points across the street. "Do you see that large brick building there? I remember one night there were sirens everywhere; cops came from all directions. It turned out to be a massive drug bust."

Naomi, still holding Damon's arm for balance, places her head close to his shoulder so she can see the building he's pointing at.

Damon inhales the mild but sweet essence of her perfume; a feature he failed to notice earlier.

"You're wearing perfume," he voices.

"Oh, just a touch. I don't usually adorn myself with perfumes. Here, take a sniff." She turns her face askew, allowing him to more fully sense the perfume on her neck. "Do you like it?"

"It's divine," he answers. "I haven't been with anyone wearing perfume for years, but then I haven't been this close to a beautiful woman's neck for many years either. It's very nice, your perfume I mean... your neck is also very nice."

For the remainder of the stroll to her apartment, she leans her head on his shoulder. "This really is a date, isn't it, Damon?"

"It feels to me like it's turning into a date. I didn't really plan it this way. I just wanted us to enjoy something that we don't normally do, and it's evolving into a wonderful evening."

Naomi adds, "There are lots of things we don't normally do besides eating in restaurants."

Damon lets the suggestive nature of her statement pass without comment on the assumption that it might only have been suggestive to his current train of thought.

"Well, here we are. This is my pad. Well, not all of it of course, just the second floor on the right side." Naomi points up to her window. "Right up there. It's actually quite small, but it's just what I want." Damon senses that Naomi wants to ask him if he'd like to see her apartment, but she avoids what could become an embarrassing possibility.

Damon places his hand around Naomi's. "Thank you for being my guest this evening. I've had a wonderful time, and we've shared some incredible conversation, haven't we?"

"Well, it was great, but there's far more conversation that we avoided." She laughs a broad smile before stating boldly, "Is it appropriate for a 28-year-old woman to kiss a 60-year-old man at the end of a wonderful evening? That's assuming, of course, that they both want it to happen."

Damon answers, "Do you want it to happen?"

Naomi laughs aloud. "Why would I kiss you if I don't want to?" She pauses and stares directly into Damon's eyes, holding the palms of her hands against his cheeks. Adopting a more serious tone, she declares boldly, "Damon, I'm going to kiss you right now; please reciprocate with the same spirit."

They kiss for a short moment and withdraw from contact, dazed at how this could have happened. Damon pulls her closer and their lips reconnect. Naomi pulls back when Damon's excitement makes contact with her upper leg.

"This isn't right, Damon. Nothing good can happen from this. It wouldn't be right for me to lead you on. We shouldn't have kissed." Naomi turns toward her front door, key in hand.

"Wait, Naomi," he pleads. "It's the first time I've kissed a woman in many years. I'm attracted to you; I won't deny that. If you invited me into your bed right now, I'd follow you like a puppy. But you're not going to, I know that. And you shouldn't. I just want us to keep seeing each other, and to keep talking, and laughing, and getting together with our muses. We have something really special, almost mystical, something that most people will never have. Can we please keep it going?"

Naomi looks back at him, her eyes glossing over. She returns, wraps her arms around his waist and places her head on his shoulder. Without further movement, they embrace for minutes; nothing is said. Damon strokes his hand up and down her back as if consoling her. Finally, Naomi breaks the silence, "Please come up to my apartment, Damon. I promise that I'll close the bedroom door and keep my clothes on. Is that fair? I just want to keep the evening alive; I want us to keep talking. I'll put some music on, anything you want. Please?"

08

While Naomi prepares coffee in the kitchen, Damon sits on an Ikea sofa and takes notice of the furnishings: Ikea table and chairs with seating for two, Ikea bookshelves and CD cabinets, all with glass doors and very tidily arranged, Ikea kitchen utensils; none of it the economical student dorm version, all higher end.

"Do you own shares in Ikea?" he asks with an inflection of levity in his voice.

She laughs from the kitchen, "That's funny, Damon. I love the stuff. When I first moved in here several years ago I started with mismatched pieces of furniture culled from garage sales and flea markets, and from friends who dropped out of college: a red flowery sofa, a couple of beanbag chairs left over from the sixties, a futon that I slept on and almost ruined my back from, and what else? Oh yeah, a chrome and vinyl kitchen table with four randomly chosen wooden chairs with peeling paint. It was so bad I was having nightmares about it, and I have a lot of nightmares, as you know. One day I went to Ikea to find a CD cabinet and, by the end of the day, I had rented a van and hauled my new furnishings home. It took me two weeks to assemble it all. I paid for it over two years."

"Did you have to carry all those heavy boxes upstairs by yourself?"

"Oh, that was the easy part. I phoned the Salvation Army to pick up my old furniture, but I wouldn't let them take it away until they helped me move my new stuff up to my place. They were very obliging; there are some definite advantages to being a woman."

Damon scans the rest of her open concept kitchen/living room. "It's a nice cozy place you have here, Naomi."

"Cozy, eh? Isn't that a polite real estate word for small and cramped?"

"What more do you want? You have a place to eat, a place to sleep, and even a bit of space to dance in. Besides, you're close to everything you need. What else is there?"

"Here's your coffee, Damon. I hope it's not too strong. I tried to make it as close to your dark roast as possible."

He slurps to test the strength, "It's perfect."

Terpsie meows and leaps up onto Damon's lap. While Damon strokes Terpsie's back and under her chin, Naomi discreetly slips into her bedroom and exchanges her little black dress for more comfortable sweat pants without attracting Damon's attention. She sits cross-legged on the floor, her back rising straight as a pencil. Damon sits on the Ikea sofa at first, but when Naomi sits down, he joins her at floor level, but without any of the comfort she seems to enjoy in doing so. His legs jut awkwardly forward and his spine rests against the sofa for support.

"What's your pad like, Damon? I'm sure it's bigger than this."

"Not really, in fact, not at all. I live in a small two-bedroom apartment above The Concept overlooking Queen Street. One bedroom is filled with music gear and the living room is mostly bookcases and CDs, and my stereo of course. I couldn't live without my books and my music. Your kitchen is nicer than mine, more modern at least."

"What do you do for a piano? Obviously you need one where you live, right?"

"I have access to the grand piano in The Concept whenever it's not open for business and, as you already know, I use the Steinway in the theatre for practicing. In a pinch, I have a Yamaha digital keyboard in my apartment. Usually that only gets used when I have an idea in the middle of the night that I want to try out."

"Didn't you tell me once that your Aunt... what's her name again?"

"Lavinia."

"Right... Lavinia... that she has a grand piano in her cottage up north?"

"Yeah, that's right. She had it hauled up from the Steinway dealer here in Toronto, to her cottage on the lake up in Muskoka. She has a great place. There are several acres surrounded by old growth pine trees. The cottage itself is a grand old building that she had completely renovated and winterized when she started teaching school up there in the early 1950s. My grandfather originally bought it as a fishing getaway. When he died the cottage was left to Aunt Lavinia on the condition that she renovate it for year-round living and that my mother's side of the family could have access to it during the summer months as a cottage. My father was a bit upset that they didn't have joint ownership, mainly because he wanted to go fishing there, but Lavinia and my father don't get along too well, so he accepted everything the way it was laid out. Mom and Dad very rarely went to the cottage but they sent Phil and I there every summer. After a while, Phil stopped going so I was the only one there. I used to go as often as possible. Aunt Lavinia was great; we did lots of things together."

"Why do you say that in the past tense Damon? She's still alive isn't she?"

"Oh yeah, very much so, although she's getting up in years; she has to be in her late seventies by now. I haven't been there in a while, although we talk on the phone every few weeks. She called me last week and asked if I could arrange to go to the cottage for my birthday this year; I told her I would. She's always concerned about how I'm doing and whether I'm seeing anyone. I used to lie to her, telling her that that I was seeing this person or that person, when there was nobody at all. I don't really think she believes it, but she never challenges me."

"Does she know about me? Have you ever told her about when we get together to do our stuff?"

Damon pauses before responding. "Hmmm… What I did was stopped lying to her. I stopped telling her I was seeing all of these people; I just changed the subject whenever she asked."

"And you don't think she knows that something's up? You don't understand women, Damon. Do you know that? Of course she knows that something's up because you changed your modus operandi. You'd make a terrible criminal; the police would have you locked up in no time. Besides, what you're doing is still a form of lying; no woman wants to be lied to."

Damon's mind remains at the cottage. "You would love Aunt Lavinia. She's such a free spirit."

"Take me there, Damon. I would love to meet her."

"Then come with me for my birthday party."

"It's coming up soon, isn't it?"

"In about three weeks. I haven't been to the cottage for my birthday in several years. It would be great if you could come. I'm sure Aunt Lavinia would welcome you with open arms."

"It's settled. I'll come with you."

"Wonderful. Why don't we make a holiday out of it? We'll stay overnight at the cottage and maybe we'll have a chance to tour around the area a bit. I'll call her in the morning and confirm everything. I'll have to tell her that I'll be bringing a guest with me. Then she'll start asking me a pile of questions. Maybe I won't tell her, and just wait until we get there."

Naomi looks at him quizzically. "Do I embarrass you?" Before he has a chance to respond, she alters her tact, "Forget what I said. I had no right to say that. I sound like I'm your wife or someone like that." She changes the subject; "I bought some great olives yesterday. Would you like some?"

Damon watches her rise to her feet with no apparent effort at all, using her legs like scissors.

"How in hell do you do that?" he asks.

"Do what?"

"Get up the way you did. Your legs acted like scissor blades. You make it look so easy."

"Oh that. Here, I'll show you."

Naomi comes to where Damon is sitting with his back resting on the sofa. "Move over here Damon, so you're not being supported by anything." She pulls at his arm and drags him across the hardwood floor with little effort.

"Take it easy," he warns, "these muscles and bones could disintegrate at any time."

"Now, cross your legs in a lotus position, as if you want to meditate."

Not wanting to appear like a wuss, Damon accepts the challenge, and the pain, and after falling over several times, finally forms his legs into a simulated lotus position.

"Now, transfer your power to your lower legs and slide your feet along the floor, allowing them to lift yourself. This doesn't work on carpet by the way, so don't even try it."

"It doesn't work for me on hardwood floors either, at least not with my legs." Damon topples over after losing his balance, and rolls onto his side. Naomi starts laughing and falls on top of him. At first Damon doesn't share her humour, but she tickles his stomach to loosen him up. Before long they're romping and rolling around the floor like a couple of pre-school children.

When Naomi goes to the refrigerator, Damon struggles to pull himself up using the edge of the sofa as support. "To answer your earlier question, Naomi, no, you don't embarrass me at all. I must embarrass you though. You're so young and vital; look how fit you are. I'm at least 30 years your senior, and I groan when I stand up. You shouldn't even be seen with an old fart like me. My God, people will think I'm your father."

"There you go, using religion as a crutch again, and besides, why should I worry about what other people think? Here, try these olives." She holds one against his lips as if force-feeding him. "I picked them up at a deli a couple of blocks away. We should go there; they have wonderful Montreal smoked meat."

Their conversation lulls while they munch on garlic-saturated olives and Oka cheese from Quebec, until Damon asks Naomi to tell him more about her family.

"It's very complicated," she warns.

He urges her to continue. "In what way?"

"Are you sure you're into this, Damon? It's a bit of a downer."

"Go for it."

"OK. Where should I start? OK. I was an only child. My mother, my adopted mother of course, put everything she had into my success. I won't go into too many details about this, but when I left for university, she couldn't deal with it anymore, and she had a massive emotional breakdown that resulted in her being institutionalized."

Naomi stops to gather her thoughts before continuing.

"When I was very young my mother introduced me to dance lessons; she couldn't have been prouder. Whenever there was a recital or a competition, I was there, winning every ribbon, trophy, and award; whatever there was, I came home with it. Mother mounted every ribbon and award on a special wall, my wall, and the trophies were always on prominent display in custom-built cabinets. In no time, we ran out of space in the living room so my mother created 'Naomi's Trophy Room' in the spare bedroom; that's true, it even had a sign above the door. It became a shrine. My mother was heavily into shrines, just as heavily as she was into God."

"You did tell me that she was a fanatic born-again."

"Fanatic doesn't even cover it. The rest of this story leads to something that I couldn't talk about earlier. I hope you'll understand when I tell you, although I'm not sure how I feel about revealing this to you; it's extremely personal. I'm sure I'll be embarrassed and regret telling you."

Damon acknowledges. "Tell me only what you want to, whatever you're comfortable with. Or we can talk about music, or dance, whatever." He consumes another olive and some cheese.

Naomi inhales slowly and deeply with her eyes closed until her voice begins.

"When I was sixteen, I didn't have a lot of interest in boys, not like most other girls. I didn't want any of the boys getting close to me, and fondling me like they always try to do. Some of the other girls at school actually liked being touched all over; they'd act and talk sexy and con the boys into getting excited. It didn't take much encouragement of course, but their actions heightened the boys' anticipation. When the boys wanted to feel them up, they broke into two separate camps: those who chickened out, and those who let them do anything they wanted. You know where that leads, I'm sure. It's not easy being a teenager, but it's a lot tougher worrying whether you're straight or gay."

Naomi pauses to appraise Damon's response; there is none.

"There was a girl in my class at school, her name was Angelica, although she preferred Angel, who felt the same way as I did. I liked Angel a lot and she said that she liked me as well. At first we just hung out together and we started dressing the same way; often in baggy boys' jeans with button flies and sloppy shirts that hung out over our pants. Angel's distinction at school was that she had the largest bosom in the entire Grade 11 class, gargantuan compared to mine. Needless to say, she became the focus of the boys' attention; they all wanted to cop a feel from her. I even heard that some of the boys had a competition to see how many times they could fondle Angel's boobs. Disgusting, eh? Angel was also more outgoing than I, so when the boys started screwing around, she told them, in no uncertain terms, to fuck off, and they usually did. We'd laugh and continue on our way, arm-in-arm, sometimes singing the words to some pop song or changing the words to make fun of the boys. She always put on airs that it didn't bother her, the boys and their stupid fascination with her breasts, but I know that, deep down, she was embarrassed by it all."

"Angel knew about this park that had a small woodsy area, not too far from the high school. One warm May afternoon, she signaled me during class and I knew exactly what she had in mind. On the way to the park, we didn't talk much, but we both understood what we wanted to happen. That became obvious when we arrived at the woods. It was very private there."

"For the longest time we stood silent in the shadow of the trees, facing each other, eye to eye, with abstract thoughts passing through our minds. Our arms hung loose visually presenting a vision of total vulnerability to each other but inside, my entire body vibrated with the anticipation of what lay ahead."

"Finally, Angel reached forward and slowly unhooked the top button of my shirt while I stood staring into her eyes. I felt the movement of her fingers against my upper chest as they fumbled until the button released, allowing a wisp of cool air to touch my newly exposed skin. Without ceremony, and without moving my eyes from hers, I reciprocated. Slowly and methodically, button-by-button, our shirts fell open, exposing our bras; hers was massive and mine, diminutive, more like a training bra by comparison. In some distorted way, I could understand the fascination of the boys at school. We each peeled the shirts from the other's shoulders and allowed them to fall freely to the ground, still maintaining eye contact, as if daring the other into more adventurous untested territory. Not once did my rational mind query the reasoning behind our actions, nor did it plan any next moves or deduce the ramifications of such actions. This was not a time for the mind; only our bodies could determine the fate of that prolonged silence between us. When the moment appeared right, after staring at me and scanning my body with her eyes, Angel leaned forward and kissed my lips with a soft warm moist sensuality. My arms reached around Angel while we were kissing and, without any conscious direction, my fingers released the hook on her bra. It fell forward, exposing her breasts to me. In no time we both stood naked from the waist up, our hearts thumping from anticipation, until simultaneously we touched and explored each other. I can still remember the sensation that seared through my entire body."

Naomi pauses, reminiscent about her past. She inhales deeply before continuing.

"In all fairness, I must also admit that there were several incidents when I was younger, maybe 13 or 14, when I invited a shy boy at school to touch me on the breasts and I experienced the same tingling sensation, so being touched may not be exclusively a gender thing so much as it's a desire to be needed. I think that's also why women enjoy seeing, or especially feeling, a man becoming excited about them; they feel needed and the man demonstrates that they are wanted as well. Don't you agree?"

"You're asking me? I'm certainly no expert on how women perceive men. My track record has been abysmal. Besides, I haven't spent much time with women for so many years I forget what it's like. The disastrous experience with my former wife cured me of the need."

"Come on Damon. Loosen up a bit. First of all, what am I, a chimpanzee? I'm a woman, and I thought you liked being with me; we certainly spend enough hours together."

"Yeah, but..."

"There are no buts. I happen to know there are times when I excite you, like when I'm dancing and we're really into it. I get a sense of it through how you play and I feel your message when I'm dancing."

"Go on," he responds, not believing what she's saying, but flattered nonetheless. "You're just putting me on."

"Will you deny that you like being close to me? Of course not! There are other times as well, like earlier tonight for instance, when we kissed. You're actually quite sensuous, you know that?"

"No, I didn't know that." Damon laughs nervously at the thought, not sure about where the conversation is leading.

"According to whom? Is there a survey somewhere that rates sensuality? Probably one of those academic sociological studies that gets put on a shelf in some university library, never to be read again."

"According to me. I find you very sensuous." Naomi realizes that she's digging herself into a hole that may be difficult to escape from. "For an older man, I mean." The hole gets deeper. "That's not what I mean at all. What I really mean is..."

Damon finally interjects, holding his palms flat toward her. "OK. Before we get ahead of ourselves and arrive somewhere that we'll both regret, why don't you continue the story about your friend, Angel."

"Oh yeah, I almost forgot. So, there we were, Angel and I, we were smoking a joint to relax and fondling each other's breasts in the woods when, all of a sudden, our math teacher walked by. She caught us sitting next to each other on the grass; by that time we were both totally naked, if you can imagine that."

"I can."

"The look on her face is etched into my memory; she did one of those hand-over-the-mouth gasps that people do when they don't know what else to do or say. I tried to hide the joint but that didn't seem to bother her. It was actually quite funny. Here we were, naked, and I was worried more that she would see us with the joint. Once she regained her composure she started shouting at us to get dressed, and then marched us back to the principal's office where she phoned our parents. My mother freaked right out."

"What did your mother do? Did you get punished?"

"Punished? I wouldn't call it punishment at all. My life changed radically over that incident. As I've already told you, my mother was a fanatic born-again Christian. She didn't even give a shit about us smoking dope; she just ranted on and on about our latent lesbianism and how God would punish us."

"So, did your mother pray for your soul?"

"That and much more. She hauled me into her pastor's office first thing in the morning. He started out by praying for my wayward soul. Then he informed us that my behaviour was against all of God's teachings, and that Satan was behind my actions. He finally suggested that I attend a special camp for young people who *mistakenly believe* that they're homosexual, adding that there were experts at the camp who knew how to purge these unnatural evil thoughts from people like me. People like *me*, he said. Can you believe that? All of a sudden I became a member of some aberrant group of religious misfits because I was fascinated with my girlfriend's anatomy."

"I've heard about those camps. I think they're called conversion camps, or something like that."

"The term they used was conversion therapy."

"Did you go to the camp?"

"Not only did I go to the camp — it was three weeks long — but during the final night, I was accosted by an overly zealous counselor several times."

"Accosted… do you mean…?"

"Raped is the preferred word for it. This is what I couldn't tell you about at the restaurant. It's too embarrassing, and it really isn't dinner talk is it? Yes, I was raped repeatedly by this asshole who tried to convince me, while fucking me, pardon my French, that I would find God through this disgusting act, as he put it, this *natural* way of making love, the way God intended us to behave. How this asshole ever imagined that we were making love is beyond me."

"My God, Naomi. I had no idea. Look, we don't have to continue this. We can talk about something else."

"No. We've been very open with each other, Damon. I want to tell you the rest of the story. As my closest friend, you should know." Naomi pauses, realizing that she has escalated their relationship with one short phrase. "You are the closest friend I have, Damon, although I've never told you that before, have I?"

"Naomi, I want you to know as well, that I too, consider *you* my closest friend, and I will share anything with you."

"I was afraid to tell anyone about the rapes when I returned home, mainly because I was embarrassed, and I felt guilty about what had happened. I also didn't want to upset my mother, who believed that she did the right thing by sending me there. The shit really hit the fan several weeks later, when I missed my period. I was able to keep that a secret from my mother for a while, although she wondered why I lacked my usual energetic temperament. I wasn't keeping up with my dancing schedule and I was skipping classes at school. Finally, she took me to our family physician; he diagnosed my pregnancy immediately. My mother was livid; she blamed me for everything. I tried to tell her what really happened at the camp but she refused to accept the truth. A month later, I secretly went to a Planned Parenthood office at the university, lied about my age, and talked to a counselor about my options. After I insisted on the option of terminating the pregnancy, they referred me to a clinic and several days later it was over and done with."

"How did your mother deal with the abortion?"

"She was a fundamental Christian. How do you think she handled it?"

Naomi doesn't wait for his response.

"She marched me right back to the pastor, who berated both of us. My mother was called a whore for the devil, and I was Satan's bastard. He blamed my mother for introducing me to the evils of dance, suggesting that all dancers were queer, and forbade me from pursuing dance any further. My mother returned home and burned all the ribbons and trophies that I had won in competitions since I was four."

"Holy Shit! That's unbelievable. What ever happened to your girlfriend, Angel? Did you continue the friendship?"

"No, that's the real kicker. When I went to the camp, that little bitch immediately found someone else. It's the story of my life."

"So, how did you handle things after all that?"

"I turned totally inward, to my dancing; it became my sanctuary. All I ever wanted to do was dance, and that's the way it remains to this day. Dance is my life, and she's my lover as well. Whenever I'm dancing, I'm making love. I'll bet you find that pretty weird, eh Damon?"

"No I don't find it weird at all. I feel much the same about my music. Whenever I'm playing, whether it's in rehearsal or in a performance, my mind and my body are given completely to the process. When I'm not playing, I'm alone. It's that simple."

"What about now, Damon. You're not playing. Are you alone?"

"Ah. That's a loaded question. Let me answer you this way. When we do our stuff together we become one. I'm totally involved in what we're creating at that moment. I'm in love with that, and so are you. I watch you dance and it's an act of love. That's what makes it so beautiful. We respond to each other as if we're joined through our muses. Any move you make affects how I respond at the piano, and..."

"Any sound you play is felt inside me, therefore affecting every move I make. I feel that too, Damon, but I ask you once again. What about now? Are you alone?"

Damon feels tears forming on the edge of his eyes. In one great swell he's about to admit that, despite his claims about preferring to live as a hermit, he doesn't really cherish being alone; he needs Naomi in his life. It isn't like the lust he craved when he was young, that stupid biological need that is so often misconstrued as love. This is a far greater need. How can he explain this to someone so young and so vital, a beautiful woman who still deserves to experience those biological desires?

"No Naomi. I'm not alone. I'm never alone when we're together. That's why I invited you out on this date. Yes, I admit it; it really is a date. I need to be with you and to hear your voice. I love it when we sit and talk together."

"That's what I wanted to hear. I appreciate my aloneness too, but I also want to be needed by someone. Now I know who that someone is."

Naomi rises from her chair and goes to wrap her arms around Damon. Tears expose themselves under his eyes.

"That's one of the things I love about you, Damon. You're so sentimental." She leans over the table and daubs his tears with a paper napkin.

Naomi returns to her original topic. "I haven't quite finished my story, Damon. I've made it this far, so I'm going to continue. After the big blowup over my abortion, mother went into a severe depression. I think she felt guilty about forcing me into that camp, and she watched me return to my dancing without any assistance or encouragement needed from her. In fact, I danced in spite of her; I think that's what put her over the edge. She no longer had a purpose. I, at least, had my dancing. To my mother, I was her dance. She put everything she had into me, but I gave her nothing in return. After she'd taken ill, I had some things to deal with, not only her institutionalizing, but also some other issues that happened during my first year at university. It took me some time before I was able to refocus. When I finally did, I was determined to dance for a purpose. My dance became a vehicle for me to explore all of the guilt over my mother's condition and to delve into the nightmares that happen often while I sleep. I suspect that some of my mother's darkness' can be found through those nightmares and I intend to use my dance to shine some light on them."

"If you like, we could explore them when we get together at the theatre."

"We already have been. Since we started getting together I've been able to focus on the images from my nightmares when I dance, and I'm getting closer to solving them. I haven't told you this before, Damon, because I didn't want to influence how you played. I've been able to narrow the images down. The nightmare I have about the flames and the baby; that all comes from my guilt over the abortion, my mother's Christian fanaticism, and of course, the cross represents that zealous asshole who raped me in the name of God."

Naomi talks faster as the details become more vivid, but she stops suddenly. "He had a hand-carved wooden cross around his neck and it dangled back and forth in front of my face as he fucked me, that bastard. I'm sorry for using the f-word, Damon, but I can't honestly refer to what he did to me as 'making love,' or even as 'having sex.' It's fucking… down and dirty fucking. He's the father of that poor innocent dead child that I dive into the flames of Hell to save every other night."

Damon reaches out to console Naomi, who collapses against his shoulder. Her tears saturate his shirt but he holds her close, whispering into her ear.

"Everything is OK. Now that you know all of this you can start to heal."

"This is all too embarrassing, Damon. I hope you don't think I'm being crude or that I'm sensationalizing all of this. This really is the way my life has been; it's the way it happened."

"I believe you, Naomi. This is a big step for you. You don't have to say anymore."

"I do have something more to say, Damon. I've already told you how much you mean to me, but I can't let that go any further, without telling you the other reason that I'm seeing Doctor Kinderman."

"You already told me about the other nightmares that, once resolved, will hopefully connect you to your past, before you were adopted. I'm assuming that involves identifying your birth mother and father, right?"

"Right, but that's not what I have to tell you at this moment. I'm afraid to tell you this Damon, but I'm also a very confused woman. Remember the episode I told you about from high school that got me into shit with my mother and the pastor? Well, that wasn't just a passing phase. Angel and I believed that we were very much in love; OK it was puppy love, but it hurt me so much when she dumped me. Oh, maybe it was, as you put it, more lust than love. But the problem wasn't quite as simple as just declaring myself a lesbian and getting on with my life. I thought I knew who I was when I started university. All of my inclinations, my desires, drew me to other women. Besides, if there was any attraction to men, that bastard at the camp cured me of it."

"Men aren't all like that bastard, Naomi. Believe me, there are a few of us who are still OK."

"I know that. But please Damon, let me finish this up. I can't leave this unsaid. While in my first year of the dance program at university, I set out to meet other women, so I went to some meetings. There were posters on walls all over the campus advertising a social group, a gathering of like-minded women who wanted to meet others. During one of the meetings, an older grad student, also in the dance program, expressed some interest in me, and promised to help me with my dancing. I was flattered. She was extremely attractive, appeared to be very nice and friendly, and she shared many of the ideas I had about dance. One evening, after having a couple of drinks, she invited me to her apartment, on the premise that she would show me some exercises intended to help me with my warm-ups. When we

82

arrived there we had another drink. After some friendly conversation she asked me to demonstrate how I start my warm-ups. I positioned myself with my hands pushed against the wall to stretch my legs and she told me to hold that position. She touched my ankles, and then ran her hand along my calf where she stopped to squeeze. 'You have such wonderful strength right here,' she told me in a deep alluring voice, and then gradually moved her hand higher until settling on my thigh. Her grip tightened, squeezing my muscle until I felt pain. I asked her to ease up a bit, even though I was by now, enjoying her touching, and becoming excited by the anticipation over what she would do next. What happened next… became… unbearable."

Naomi struggles to finish her sentence. She pulls herself away from Damon's embrace and he respects her need for more space.

"She applied further pressure against my thigh which forced me down, my back against the floor, all along assuring me that she knew what she was doing and telling me to relax. Her right hand probed between my legs, at first tenderly, but gradually it became more forceful. I started to cry out but she only laughed, and continued to increase the pressure. Suddenly, an unbearable pain occurred between my legs; something hard entered me but I was already starting to lose consciousness. The room became fuzzy and started turning in a circular motion; there must have been drugs or something in my drink. I remember nothing else that happened that night until I awoke hours later in the parking garage below her apartment building; it was still relatively dark. I was only partly dressed and in incredible pain. Between my knees was a zucchini with a note stapled to it. It read, 'Thanks for the good time.' I struggled to walk; there was so much pain. When I returned home I stood in the hot shower for an hour."

"Didn't you report this to anyone; the university authorities, for example, or the police?"

"No. I dropped out of university and remained in my apartment for the entire year, rarely leaving except to go shopping, which I arranged to do early in the morning, or late at night."

"Shit. I can understand why you're so confused. You eventually returned to university I assume."

"The following September, when I was certain the grad student had left, I returned to start my freshman year all over again."

"Good for you. And you did well, I gather?"

"Dean's list every year. During my year off, I attended some workshops on yoga and read up on Buddhism. I learned to meditate and to focus my attention on what was important. My sexual desires, regardless of gender, were placed at the bottom of my list of important items; dance was at the top. For the following four years I thought about nothing but dance. Mind you, it was at the cost of any social interaction. It remained that way until I walked into The Concept one evening this spring and heard your music."

Conversation shields Damon and Naomi from the passing of time until morning light from the kitchen window brightens the edges of Naomi's hair and flares into Damon's glasses. Instinctively, he glances at his watch. "Are you aware that it's already after six? Can you believe that? We've talked the night away."

"Well, it's a lot better than losing sleep to nightmares, isn't it?"

Damon agrees. "I should really be getting along, Naomi. It's been wonderful spending the night with you." He grins as he speaks.

She slaps him softly against his cheek. "That's bad."

Naomi follows Damon to the door. "I've had such a great time tonight, Damon. I'd really like to do this again, soon."

They agree to another dinner in two weeks time. Naomi volunteers to choose a restaurant near Damon's apartment where they further agree to spend another night together. At the door, she kisses him once again as a friend would, and makes him promise to call Aunt Lavinia.

09

After several afternoons a week rehearsing at the theatre, a couple of nights at The Concept, and two Thursday morning coffee breaks since their Italian dinner and overnighter, Damon and Naomi are seeing each other more than most married couples. Most of their time together is spent either working on their muses, or talking about them. Little time is dedicated to personal discussions, relaxation, or to sharing laughs together, so they both look forward to their next dinner, their second date. Naomi chooses an upscale, but intimate restaurant specializing in Mediterranean cuisine, with most dishes from Northern Africa, but including some traditional Spanish and Greek fare as well.

Naomi prepares herself for an evening that, as she already knows, will include an overnight session at Damon's apartment. She packs a change of clothes and her toiletries, so she can be fresh in the morning. As her only dress was the little black item she wore for their first dinner together, she has doubled the formal outfits in her closet by purchasing a stunning blue sheath dress that is several classes above the slit red item that Sandi the Italian restaurant pianist wore, but with triple the allure, especially when Naomi's shapely body slides into it. Once fitted into the dress, she examines herself in the mirror, scanning her image from head to toe.

When she first spilled Damon's coffee at the café, their initial contact, her hair was shorter, randomly arranged into a denim cap. Since that first encounter, she has been allowing her hair to grow out, keeping it hidden from view with an assortment of caps or by combing it up, gathered into a short ponytail, or even a small bun, especially while she's dancing. Tonight it comes down. The image in the mirror reveals that her new style passes down over her ears in a bob, framing her face and emphasizing her dark, mysterious eyes. She splurges by employing the services of the exclusive stylist adjacent to the café they meet at every Thursday morning.

For several minutes while peering at herself in the mirror, she senses doubts about her new mission. 'What am I really trying to do here? Am I attempting to seduce Damon into a physical affair? Why would I do that? It's certainly not what I want. How can I want him as a man? I want him as a friend, in spite of the fact that he's a man? Is it even possible that I really want both? Dammit, sometimes I don't even know what I want. What if Damon was an equally nice, wonderful, talented and beautiful woman friend? Would I feel the same, or would it be a stronger desire? Will I ever know? Damned right I would. I'd wear this sexy dress for all it's worth.'

Her thoughts and concerns reassign themselves to Damon. 'How will *he* feel about all of *this*?' She points at herself in the mirror at the word *this*. 'Will he be excited? Will he still want to be with me as his closest friend or will he want to sleep with me instead, or will we spend the night talking like the last time? What if Damon thinks I'm being a bit of a tart? Is this dress a bit over the top, the way it accents every curve, every movement I make?' She moves provocatively to the mirror, admiring the reflectance of her newfound sexuality.

"My God, what am I becoming?" she asks aloud. Terpsie meows a response. "Do you really think so, Terpsie?"

'Goddammit no! It's not over the top!' Naomi struts herself with satisfaction, while struggling on one leg to fit herself into a new pair of moderately heeled pumps and taking a few minutes to primp the final details in her new hairstyle. She speed dials the cab company and proceeds down to the front entrance with a soft leather jacket strewn over her shoulder.

Before he leaves to meet Naomi's taxi, Damon has already spent several hours cleaning and vacuuming his apartment, even rearranging some of the furniture. For a last inspection, he calls Lydia up from the club to see it through a woman's eyes.

"Wow, Damon. You never did this for me when I used to visit. This girl you're seeing must be special. And I emphasize the word, *girl*. You're really robbing the cradle this time, aren't you?"

"Ah come on, Lydia. I just don't want her to think I'm some kind of a bum. What do you think? Does it look OK?

"You did well, Damon. Why don't you head out now and I'll make some minor adjustments to the place while you're gone. Don't worry; I'm not going to mess you up with this. Your date will love it. Away you go. Good luck. Should I check in on you later?" Lydia laughs as she starts shuffling some cushions around on the sofa. "As a matter of fact, it looks so good that I may start to visit you again, maybe even move in. How would you like that?"

Damon calls back to her, "I don't think Tiny would take to that very well, do you?"

He arrives at the restaurant only moments before a taxi pulls to the curb. Naomi slides out using Damon's hand as support. He relieves her of the overnighter and her toiletry bag.

Damon is struck by the change in her appearance and can't remove his eyes from hers. "Where did all that hair come from? Is it all yours?"

"Of course it's mine. I just had it styled, that's all; at that yuppie hair place next to the café."

Damon's scanning eyes are drawn to the colourful woolen shawl that Naomi has wrapped around her, triangularly covering some of the black tights underneath but still showing enough to accent her figure.

"Do I look OK, Damon? How do you like the shawl? I picked it up at one of those import bazaars last year. I just love the colours. I think it's Guatemalan, but I'm not certain."

"Who is this gorgeous woman that I behold before me; this actress, this model, this beautiful dancer, this goddess? You are absolutely stunning, Naomi."

She hugs him, and places her arm through his for their entrance, confident that she made the right decision after all, and thinking that, if she'd worn the body-tight blue sheath dress as originally planned, Damon might have had a heart attack.

"Oh, Damon, do you mind checking these bags? I thought I should bring a change of clothes with me."

The coat check woman casts an acknowledging wink to Damon as he places the overnighter and the toiletry bag on the counter and drops a fiver into the dish before he winks back.

After being seated and introduced to Ali, their server, they order dry Sherries, only because Naomi has adopted a fondness to them.

"This is really a cool place, small and intimate, but fascinating." Damon observes. "I've lived in this neighbourhood for a number of years and I've never seen this place before. I should get out more, spend more of my time checking things out."

"That's what I said the night I decided to check out The Concept, and, *voila*, look how things turned out."

The Sherries arrive and Naomi starts the conversation. "Last time, at the Italian restaurant, and especially afterwards at my apartment, I revealed to you some of my most intimate secrets."

"That you did, and I haven't forgotten one of them. I say that just in case there'll be a test tonight on what I've learned."

"Tonight, right here in this restaurant, I'm giving you the floor. It's your night to shine, Damon. I want to hear all about your life, particularly more about your marriage and your family. I realized over the past two weeks, that you just scratched the surface the last time, like passing out some crumbs and avoiding the main course."

"OK. I agree, albeit reluctantly. Where would you like me to start?"

"How did you meet your wife? How's that for a start?"

"Here we go. Promise to stop me at any time if you start to fall asleep, please. I first met my wife when I was only 13 years old. She lived in the town near Aunt Lavinia's cottage. Her father ran the Lodge there, and she was the younger of two daughters. It was the day of my 13th birthday and I had just arrived by train from Hamilton, where we lived. Aunt Lavinia picked me up at the train station and we went down the main drag for an ice cream at the Dairy Bar. Some kids were acting up and causing a disturbance in the Dairy Bar, so Aunt Lavinia chastised them for being hooligans. I remember that one of the kids made a farting sound with his armpit in response. Isn't it strange, the things we retain in our memory banks? Aunt Lavinia had an appointment to get her hair done, so I wandered down to the pier to watch the boats coming and going. Several of the hooligans from the Dairy Bar followed me and started to harass me about being a sucky tourist. I didn't respond so they grabbed me and bound my hands and ankles with ropes. Another boy wrapped a blindfold over my eyes. I tried to fight back but there were too many of them."

"I'm sorry, Damon, but I'm having trouble relating this to your wife?"

"Bear with me, Naomi. The best is yet to come. Besides, we have all evening. They stood me up on the pier and I felt someone's foot in the small of my back. It shoved me off the pier and into the water, which was deeper than I was tall. I must tell you now, I was petrified of water, and still am to this day. I once took swimming lessons but failed miserably at it. So there I was, sinking into the deep water with my hands and feet bound; I couldn't even kick my way out of it. I immediately went into my terrible visions, the same as the nightmares I have about dying underwater, with corpses staring at me as I drown. It's the same nightmare where Aphrodite pays me a visit and wants me to follow her."

"And… ta da… she gives you a hard on, right?"

"You have a good memory. Right, I was excited. Give me a break; I was only 13 and a naked woman wanted me to follow her. Of course I was excited."

Naomi breaks out in uncontrolled laughter. "Oh Damon, you are so-o-o funny." She sips some Sherry.

"So, finally someone dragged me up on the beach so I could breathe again. I was still tied up and blindfolded, when I sensed a person close to me. I could feel her breath against my skin, that's how close she was."

"How did you know it was a she?"

"She was wearing perfume, very similar to the lavender perfume that Aunt Lavinia wore, and still wears, I would assume. The girl kissed me on the lips and was acting very precocious for someone only the same age as me as it turned out. I remember that she stuck her tongue between my lips and it felt exciting."

"How old did you say you were? Thirteen? Weren't you a bit young for that?"

"Let me say that I remained excited even after the nightmare was over. What do you think about that?" He pauses to sip some Sherry and watches Naomi's response.

Naomi bursts into laughter that catches the attention of other diners until she starts to choke on the final drops of her Sherry. When she regains control, she asks for clarification.

"Let me get this right. A 13-year-old girl gave you a hard on, correct?" She starts to laugh again. "Damon, before you continue, may I have another glass of Sherry, please."

Damon finds it difficult not to join Naomi in her laughter, but manages to place the order before continuing.

"So there you go. That's how I met Virginia, the woman who became my wife. She saved my life that day; saved me from certain death by drowning."

"Something must have happened after that. One doesn't fall in love at the age of 13, and decide to get married right away, does one?"

"Of course there's more to it. But first, I think we should at least look at the menu, don't you?"

Damon calls Ali over for assistance. "What can you recommend here, Ali?"

"For a start, my friend, I suggest the Lentil Soup, with some Khobz on the side." Ali speaks precisely, with a combined Arab-British accent.

"Hold it Ali. What is Khobz?"

"Ah. This is a Moroccan flatbread. You will like it very much, I guarantee. Now, for the main course, I suggest our specialty, Mrouzia." Before Damon or Naomi can ask what it is, Ali continues, "Mrouzia is a sweet dish cooked in the tagine. It is lamb with raisins, honey and almonds. Very, very delicious."

90

They accept Ali's suggestions. Damon adds, "Would you also bring us a bottle of this Merlot please, Ali?"

"So Damon, what happened next? How did you go from an erection at 13 to getting married? That's what I want to know." Naomi sips some Sherry and adopts her wicked smile of expectation; her penetrating eyes fix on Damon's while he struggles to find the best words to begin again.

"Two years later, let's see, that would be in 1957, I spent my usual summer vacation at Aunt Lavinia's cottage. Phil, my older brother was also there, but he was working at the Lodge, and he was dating Virginia's older sister as well. He borrowed Aunt Lavinia's Studebaker for the afternoon and he and I went cruising into town. He introduced me to his new girlfriend, Samantha, but everybody called her Sam, and then Virginia joined us at the Dairy Bar. She reminded me that she had saved my life on the pier two years before, as if I had forgotten. Phil and Sam left us alone so we talked for a while, and then she asked if I wanted to take her to the movies. I said yes. The movie was The Incredible Shrinking Man. It was about a man..."

Naomi is now hysterical with laughter. Damon doesn't quite understand why until she repeats the title of the movie.

"Anyway, at the movie there were some scary moments, and Virginia grabbed my arm and pulled it around her shoulder. One thing led to another, and we started to kiss, which led to some petting. Before I knew it, we weren't watching the movie at all, but we were touching each other and enjoying it immensely. We had a great time after the movie as well, mainly kissing and fondling each other on the beach in front of her family home, until her father called her in at 11:00. Before she went into the house she assured me that she loved me and wanted to see me again on the following Wednesday."

Naomi makes a joke over the word *fondling*, and Damon responds, "Let's call it *exploring* each other; I think that's the word you used to describe your experiences in high school with Angel. At any rate, I was convinced that I had fallen deeply in love and I looked forward to seeing Virginia again, with anticipations of what would follow our *explorations* of the night at the movies."

Ali arrives with their orders and Damon and Naomi suddenly discover their hunger. Few words are exchanged while they eat, except for some *m-m-m's* and other accolades about how delicious the food is, until Naomi reintroduces the topic before a fork of couscous passes through her lips.

"So Damon, did you see her again as planned? And, if so, did your explorations prove to be fruitful?"

"Not really. My impatience in waiting for Wednesday caused me to go by her house on Tuesday; I couldn't wait another day before seeing her. She was there all right, but with another guy, some Elvis clone with his own car. When I saw them on the beach outside her house, his hand was inside her unbuttoned blouse and she was giggling while he felt her up."

"So, what did you do?"

"Like a jerk, I confronted them. Elvis removed his hand and walked away. While attempting to adjust her bra straps and button up her blouse, Virginia reminded me that our date wasn't until Wednesday, and that I shouldn't have come by on Tuesday. I told her where to go, and then left, and I didn't see her for several years after that. Instead, I attended high school and concentrated on my piano studies to prepare for the music program at U of T, where I completed my freshman year with honours."

"Did you have any other girlfriends in high school, or while you were at university?"

"Not a one."

"Oh, surely there must have been someone who turned your crank."

"No, I honestly wasn't attracted to anyone. I set my sights on my music, and pretty much avoided any outside social contact. I became a hermit, except for playing gigs when they came up, and there were lots of those: dances, weddings, clubs, and house parties."

Damon pauses to consider another thought, and then continues. "Incidentally, I have a theory about the false sense of personal satisfaction that young musicians have when they base their success on the number of gigs they're able to get. Aside from the occasional serious gig when there's an opportunity to play jazz alongside older, more experienced, musicians, young players rarely learn anything from gigs. Besides, it's inversely proportional; when they have lots of work, they usually practice less. In other words, the more you gig, the less you learn. Gigging is not the road to talent, although it may lead to a bigger bank account. They are two different things, as different as love and lust; love being the talent while lust is merely the commercial satisfaction."

"Wow! That's heavy, but I do follow what you're saying. I'm sure that applies to dance as well. However, you still haven't married Virginia. What happened next?"

"You are a bear for punishment. Here we go. During the early part of the summer after my freshman year, I received a wedding invitation from my brother Phil; he and Sam were tying the knot in a ceremony up in Muskoka. I was asked to be his Best Man and Virginia was to be the Maid of Honour? Honour, there's a misnomer if there ever was one. I went to Muskoka on Friday for the rehearsal and stayed over at the cottage until Sunday, when I had to return to Hamilton for my summer day job. The rehearsal offered a chance for Virginia and I to renew acquaintances. She was friendly but at arms length. We completed the rehearsal, which was followed by a short reception for the families and the bridal party, and then we all dispersed. On Saturday, I met Virginia at the church; she was dressed to kill, and she looked amazing. Later, following the wedding reception, we walked along the beach to where I last saw her at the age of 15. She walked me to a more secluded area of the beach where she stood facing me, lit only by the moonlight. Before I knew it, she was naked and she asked me blatantly if I wanted to… you know… have sex with her. Well, she said it more bluntly than that, actually."

Naomi leans across the table and whispers, "Are you trying to tell me, in so many words, that Virginia said, "Do you want to fuck me?"

"Yup. That's exactly what she said. You're very perceptive, Naomi."

"And did you?"

"Of course I did. What Virginia wanted, Virginia got."

"Oh come now, Damon. Don't blame that all on her. My God, man, you were ready with baited breath to have sex with her since you were 13, the sooner the better, right? Oh wait. I get it. It just occurred to me. Oh my God!" Naomi covers her mouth with the palm of her hand. "That was your first time, wasn't it?"

Damon feels the heat on his face. "Thank you for pointing that out. It was indeed my first time. It was also my second and third as well. We spent the entire night on the beach together."

"You're a devil, Damon Farrell. How old were you by then?" Naomi's wicked face leers at him over the table. "What did you do after that? Did you propose to her?"

"First of all, the age at which I lost my virginity is a matter for you to calculate for yourself, if it's really that important to you. Did I propose? Of course I didn't. But I had fallen totally under her spell. I couldn't think about anything else, day or night. I had a dull pain in the pit of my stomach. I returned to my pad on Sunday night and called her as soon as I got home. We talked for hours."

"After returning to my routine, the brief encounter started to become more of a memory than something I wanted to repeat again. Once again, I became totally wrapped up in my music and spent all my waking hours preparing for my second year at university. One Wednesday night, about a month later, I was playing with my band at a club in The Village, when the waiter said that someone was asking for me. There she was, Virginia, sitting at a candle-lit table in the corner. She told me that she had just moved to the big city and had rented an apartment close by. I pretty much moved in with her and, of course, we became very active sexually. A month later, she informed me that we were expecting a child. Two months later a minister married us in a family-only ceremony; the minister called it a *special circumstance* wedding and would only allow us to use the small side chapel, not the main church. Phil was my best man and Sam,

Virginia's sister, was the Maid of Honour. Just before Virginia and I left the reception, Phil pulled me aside. He told me that the only way my marriage to Virginia would survive is if I were to let her know who wears the pants. 'Slap her around from time to time. She'll love it,' he told me. So there you are, the complete, but slightly abridged version of Damon and Virginia's love life."

"Oh that's a wonderful story, Damon." Naomi feigns applause. "But there's still more I want to hear, like how married life treated you, how it was raising a child, and how it all ended. I'm really curious to hear how your brother ended up with your wife and son. There must be some gritty bits to that part of the story. Oh, and one other thing. You didn't really follow Phil's advice did you?"

"No, of course I didn't, but in a strange distorted way, it cost me my marriage in the end."

Both Naomi and Damon take a few minutes without conversation to complete their entrée and sip the last drops of wine.

"Before I even try to continue, Naomi, I suggest that we call Ali over and order something from the dessert tray, or possibly an Irish coffee. What's your preference?"

"I'm stuffed; there's no room for any dessert. Besides I have to watch my weight; I am still a dancer you know."

Damon interjects, "Surely you're not one of those anorexic dancers, are you?"

"No Damon, don't worry. I'm not one of those stereotypical *anorexic* dancers. Why is it that people always identify dancers as anorexic and gay?" Tears emerge.

"Oh shit, Naomi. I am sorry. I didn't mean anything like that. Please accept my apology."

"That's all right. I hear that kind of crap all the time. I get used to it. It's like water being swept off a windshield by the wiper blades; it always comes back."

"But you shouldn't hear that kind of thing from me, not from your best friend. I am really sorry. How can I make it up to you?"

Naomi wipes the tears away with the corner of her napkin; a smile raises the edges of her lips, which in turn, increases the dominance of her cheek structure and adds emphasis to her beautiful eyes.

"Apology accepted. You can make it up by ordering me an Irish coffee, even though I've already had far too much to drink, and you can continue telling me your life story. It hasn't been gritty enough for me yet. Get on with it, we haven't got all night." She pauses before adding, "Well, actually, we do have all night, don't we?"

Damon signals to Ali and orders two Irish coffees and a pair of Baclavas for dessert.

"After the wedding, with a baby on the way, I was forced to drop out of university. Aunt Lavinia was livid. She had spent most of her years nurturing my music, paying for all my lessons, buying two pianos and covering the cost of my university tuition; she had a huge stake in my musical success. Besides, when I told her I was going to marry Virginia, she hit the roof, saying, 'You've gone completely mad, you can't really be marrying that trollop.' While I understood how Aunt Lavinia felt, I couldn't let Virginia raise our child by herself, could I? It wouldn't be the *honourable* thing to do. Everything finally blew up when I dropped out of university. It was a long time before Aunt Lavinia and I talked again."

Naomi licks some of the whipped cream from her Irish coffee and it spreads to the tip of her nose. Damon chuckles while she raises her tongue to retrieve it.

"So," Damon continues, "married life proved interesting. I was fortunate to find a regular day job at a recording studio, where I accompanied different artists and worked on their arrangements. I was also able to work some night gigs, taking everything that came along. I did maintain my after hours gig at the Cellar one night a week which was great because it kept me in touch with the jazz people. Virginia was becoming less and less happy with herself as the baby grew within her; that's a normal thing, I guess, because she was feeling less attractive and losing her self-esteem, and I was busy most of the time getting my shit together and earning a living."

96

"When Graham arrived in early April, we were both ecstatic. He was healthy and so was Virginia. I thought that, once Graham was born, Virginia's outlook would improve, but it became worse. She became insanely jealous of other women; not just some women, every woman I came in contact with, at work, on the gigs, even walking down the street. If a woman passed on the sidewalk while we were driving, she would accuse me of checking her out in the rear-view mirror. One day, I was in the middle of a recording session backing up a new singer. There was a full band and a trio of backup singers, all being paid; the studio was packed to the walls; it was a big production. Virginia arrived, walked straight to the vocal booth and opened the door. She started shouting at the woman, calling her a bitch and a whore; it was so embarrassing that the engineer called the entire session off. Do you have any idea what her idiocy cost the studio? The boss told me that, if I didn't get my wife sorted out, that he'd find someone else."

"She was insecure," Naomi offers. "Were you ever jealous of her?"

"Listen to this. One day a letter arrived for me at the studio. When I opened the envelope there were all these letters from the alphabet cut from magazines and pasted onto a sheet of paper telling me that my wife was having a steamy affair with another man. It was signed 'a concerned friend' in the same cut out letters. Several months before, Virginia and I had seen a movie where a similar letter had been part of the evidence in a murder trial. I decided to ignore the letter. Weeks later, Virginia started a conversation about the weird things that people receive in their mailboxes. Before long she asked me whether I had ever received anything weird. I answered that her pasted up letter was the only thing I'd ever received. She went silent… and stayed silent for days afterwards."

"Definitely insecurity; a bit over the top, but insecurity nonetheless. She wanted you to admit your jealousy, but you essentially told her you weren't jealous of her at all. Bad move,

Damon. You should just have played along with the scheme. It would have bought you some time, at the very least."

Ali arrives with the bill and a tray full of mints. Damon and Naomi are alone in the restaurant.

Naomi whispers, "I think were getting a message, don't you, Damon?"

"My story isn't quite finished. Over the years the jealousy continued to be a problem. Virginia decided that she didn't want to be a stay-at-home mom anymore, so she got a part-time job. We shared the parenting except when there were conflicts; then we hired a sitter. At one point she even accused me of trying to have an affair with our baby sitter, a 14-year-old student and the daughter of our next door neighbour."

Naomi jokes, "You do have a thing about young girls, I must say."

"One January afternoon, I had some tickets to a jazz concert for children. I suggested that we all go, but Virginia wanted to stay home because of a headache or something like that, so Graham and I went by ourselves. A heavy snowstorm blew in, and by the time we arrived at the theatre, a full-blown blizzard had brought the traffic to its knees. A sign on the theatre door announced the concert's cancellation, so we headed back home. When I opened the front door, I heard screaming from upstairs. I ran to our bedroom and was confronted by my brother Phil, choking Virginia on the bed; his hands were wrapped tightly around her throat. I grabbed him and pulled him back, separating them until I saw that they were both buck-naked. Virginia yelled at Phil to run for it and then she started chastising me. She asked me what I was doing home so early. Then I remembered Graham, who had followed me up the stairs and was staring at his naked mother. I finally asked what the hell was going on, and she started verbally pulling me apart. In her rage she informed me that I wasn't Graham's father at all; that Phil was. Graham heard everything. She blasted out a litany of detail about how she and Phil had been getting it on well before Phil married Sam, and that the only reason she started having sex with me was to cover her bases, in the event that she might become pregnant. In fact she admitted that she was pretty certain about her pregnancy by the time she arrived in town and showed up at the club. I was completely bewildered and taken by surprise. She then informed me that she was leaving with Graham to live with Phil up in Muskoka and that Sam had already left Phil months ago when she found out about everything."

"Ah. That's better. I feel sated now. The gritty bits have been revealed. Now we can proceed with the rest of our evening. By the way, don't forget my bags at the coat check.

10

With their appetites more than sated, Naomi and Damon stroll along Queen Street from the restaurant toward Damon's apartment, but choose to pass his front door, which he shares with The Concept, for more walking time. The night's atmosphere is alive, with traffic hustling in both directions and other walkers taking in the west end ambiance. Sections of the street struggle to become the Village of the new millennium, with clubs, restaurants and trendy cafés opening at a dizzying pace. The old Queen Street still maintains some of its presence with used furniture shops in transition from junk to antiques, a smattering of hamburger joints and diners, and a suspicious storefront offering 'Satisfaction Guaranteed to Members Only.' 'Coming Soon' signs appear on a variety of closed shops with newspapers taped over the windows, promising a new Tat Boutique, a Cuban Cigar and Chocolate Emporium, and, 'Penetrations,' a boudoir shop for erotic lingerie and accessories.

"Have you ever noticed how neighbourhoods come and go?" Damon queries. "They start out as a vital area with new housing for first-time buyers, until the original owners sell to go to a more upscale burb. Within a couple of years, the new owners turn the units over at a profit after painting the walls a different colour. The next ones, to make ends meet, break the houses up into smaller apartments and rent them out, not spending a dime on the places before they sell them off at a profit as income producers. Gradually, there are more and more vacancies available, so they become cheap housing and the so-called artists move in. For a while, the area caters to the creative types like us, until there are hoards of curiosity seekers wandering the streets at all hours. The more people attracted to the area, the higher the rents become, drawing a new wave of investors, until the artists can't afford to stay there anymore. Custom kitchens with granite and marble countertops replace the old, and a new generation of high-income folks move in who, in their Audis and Infinitis, drive for an hour across town to the newest trendy neighbourhood of quasi-artists and rundown tenements for their excitement."

"And so it goes," Naomi responds. "Is that what we are, Damon? Are we quasi-artists, or as you also eloquently put it, so-called artists?" She senses one of Damon's rants ready to boil over.

"Artists! Who in hell are artists anyway?" Damon emphasizes with his hands, palms up, in front of him. "It seems like anybody who wants to can become a self-proclaimed artist: a kid in high school who finger paints semblances of her self-portrait from a mirror becomes an abstract artist; some guy who sits in his basement with his guitar and a 20 dollar stereo recorder becomes a recording artist; an auto body mechanic who welds remnants of his trade into wheel-headed, muffler-armed robots to decorate his front yard becomes a sculptural artist; a restaurant advertises their minimum-waged help as sandwich artists. Artists should be creative people who, after a substantial period of incredible work that makes a statement, become recognized by their peers as an artist. One doesn't proclaim one's self an artist; one becomes accepted by others as an artist."

"So, are we artists?"

"I'm a musician; I play the piano. I'm also a composer; I compose music. I teach at the college; I'm a teacher, although they officially call me a professor. You dance; you're a dancer. You choreograph; you're a choreographer."

"So. I ask again. Are we artists?"

"I can't answer for myself; that's up to others to determine, and I don't just mean record producers who put labels on CD covers like 'Jazz Artist,' that kind of thing."

"What about me?"

"I knew you'd get around to that. Do I think you're an artist? Absolutely! Not just because you dance, but also because you do it with your soul, with your life, with every fibre of your body. You don't merely follow the instructions that come with the occupation of 'dancer.' You don't even dance because you *want* to. You dance because you *have* to. You explore your inner self with your dance, and through that, you discover things that make you need to explore more. That's what I call art, and that's what makes an artist."

"So, by those parameters, you are also an artist, Damon."

Damon avoids further complications by relating the discussion to another rant. "People calling themselves artists are sort of like what being a hero is these days. When I was a young kid, in the years immediately following World War II, I remember hearing about this hero and that hero, guys who had done amazing things on the battlefield. Maybe they had saved an entire platoon from certain death by volunteering their own life, or possibly they had put their life on the line to rescue an injured buddy. Whatever their deed was, there were very few heroes. Dying in battle did not make one a hero; exceptional deeds did."

"But what about those who…?"

"I know where you're going with this. I'm not in any way denying that being at war is a tough grind, and I'm not proposing that we should ignore those who go, but heroism is one of those titles that should be reserved for the exceptions; just like acknowledging only the exceptional creators as artists."

They arrive at the door to The Concept and enter. Recorded jazz wails through the sparsely populated darkness. Lydia wipes the bar clean with a large rag and talks to two men about the price of gas at the pumps.

"Listen to her carry on, Naomi. Lydia doesn't even drive anywhere in a car. In fact, her car hasn't been out of the garage in months. Why does she care about the price of gas?"

"Welcome home, you two. How was the dinner?

Naomi responds, "Fabulous, but we're filled to the brim with Moroccan food."

"I'll pour you a drink."

"No thanks, Lydia," Damon answers, "we've had enough for tonight."

Upstairs, Damon offers to brew Naomi a coffee. She prefers green tea, something that, until he met Naomi, would never find a place in Damon's apartment. "Green tea it is." He pours some water in the kettle. "I think I'll join you in that tea."

While Damon prepares the tea, Naomi saunters around the apartment, stopping to pick up a small, framed photo for closer examination. It's the only photograph in the room. "Is this your mother, Damon?"

Damon answers without looking up. "No, that's Aunt Lavinia in Muskoka, at the cottage where we're going next week. I hope you two get along."

"She's very pretty. You must get your eyes from her side of the family."

Books are neatly arranged on shelves according to author and subject with a just-cleaned-up-because-company's-coming appearance. Naomi wonders if Damon cleans his own apartment, or if he hires someone.

"Sorry about the mess everything's in, but I rushed around to get the place cleaned up." He stops, and then clarifies. "Actually, Lydia gave me a hand rearranging everything earlier today."

"You did a good job, Lydia and you."

Damon switches the stereo on and selects some Charles Lloyd. "Would you like to sit in the living room, or at the kitchen table?"

"My mother always told me that acquaintances sit in the living room; close friends sit in the kitchen."

"The kitchen table it is, then." Damon pours two cups of tea. They sit facing each other across the table.

Finally, Damon speaks, "Alright Naomi. I've been spilling my life out to you all evening. What's been on your mind this past few weeks that you'd like to tell me? Anything juicy?"

"Well, let's see. Recently I've been thinking about the components that make up males and females, and what the ratios of those components are in each of us." Naomi corrects herself, "Each of us doesn't just mean you and me, but all of us; everybody. Life isn't just black and white; we aren't just male or female, but many different shades of each. For example, why was I attracted to Angel in high school? Should I conclude from that, that I'm a lesbian, only attracted to other women? If so, why am I also attracted to you?" She looks directly at him for some response. His eyes brighten, raising his eyebrows in the process. She clarifies, "I am, incidentally, attracted to you just in case you don't realize it?"

Damon listens quietly with a great degree of interest and a hint of a smile. "Go on," he urges. "This could lead to something very interesting."

"Don't read that the wrong way, Damon. I don't believe that I'm bisexual. I'm not really drawn to wanting sex with both males and females. Often, I'm not even sure that I want sex with anyone for that matter. It's just that I find myself being attracted to certain people; some of them are males and others are females. Is it possible to be attracted to someone for the mere desire for friendship, or must there always be a sexual component? Maybe, because I've been alone for so long, I just want companionship, some form of social intercourse, and I shouldn't confuse this with sexual desire. Yet, there are times when I find myself wanting to be intimate with someone. Mainly I want someone touching me, to feel his *or* her warmth against me, and to know that someone else cares about me. Is that sexual desire, Damon? Or, is it some pathetic need for friendship?"

"Before I even try to answer that, Naomi, I must first declare a conflict of interest."

Naomi sets her elbows on the table, places her chin into the palms of both hands and stares directly into Damon's eyes. "I'm waiting for your answer with great interest."

"I've had quite a bit to drink this evening, so please consider that my answer to your question is affected by that, as I'm quite sure your question was also. First of all, please don't call your need for friendship pathetic, because that makes my need for friendship almost suicidal. The moment you spilled that coffee in the café my life changed. For most of the last 30 years, I have lived alone with the only social interaction being the guys in the band, and the students in my classes. Do I think of you as a friend? Yes. Do I want to be with you as much as possible? Yes. Am I attracted to you? Damned right I am. Do I want to have sex with you? My God, yes. But, do I want to have sex with you at the risk of losing a much-needed friend? Absolutely not! Now, here's the real kicker. Could I spend the night in bed with you, keeping you warm and close, knowing that I would not have sex with you because it would jeopardize our friendship? That's a tough call, and I won't even try to come up with a definitive answer."

"Let me back up a few steps, Damon, because what I was leading to was more of a discussion about how we're all constructed. Like, some men have more maleness than others, just as some women have more femaleness than others. Each person is not just straight or gay, one extreme or another. Aside from our physical construction, we all contain varying degrees of both genders, just the same as skin colours are not just black or white, but so many shades of white, tan, brown, black; you name it, we're all represented. I think it's the same with gender."

"I believe that's already been well documented, Naomi, going all the way back to the Kinsey Report in the mid-1950s. Didn't they come up with some kind of chart to represent the varying degrees of sexual orientation?"

"Yeah. I looked that all up, and there are dozens of other charts too, but I'm referring to our emotional variations like how I feel about you at the same time as how I responded when that Sandi with an 'i' bimbo came to our table in the red slit sheath dress. Both are attractions with different needs and desires attached. By the way, Damon, I'm pretty sure that your Sandi is a lesbian."

"Oh shit! Now you've done it. You've managed to destroy the faith in my own sexuality."

"What I want to know is, does each person's individual ratio of male-female construction determine what his or her needs and wants are when it comes to other things in life, like occupations; science versus the arts, for example? Why are more gays attracted to dance than to engineering, or to figure skating than to transport driving?"

Damon waits, but Naomi knows, from his body language, that he's preparing a response.

"How do we know that? Maybe that's not the case at all. It's entirely possible that there are more gays in engineering, but the environment isn't as tolerant. Artistic genres probably have higher degrees of allowance for self-expression than in commerce or the construction industry. Maybe that's where the line is drawn, in how self-expression is tolerated."

"Are you suggesting then, that the more gay a person is, the more self-expression they exhibit? What about the masses of gay people who are deathly afraid of being exposed for fear of some retaliation by the public?"

"Not at all. I am suggesting however, that in some areas, like for example, the arts, one might feel more at ease in expressing their openness than, let us say, the construction industry, where there's always a predominant machismo attitude. My God, even in politics there's a current movement toward public figures coming out. There is some progress being made, is there not?"

"I guess the bottom line for me is, where in hell do I stand? Sometimes I'm so confused. I actually made sexual eye contact with Sandi, and she confirmed my curiosity with her eyes, but she is so not-my-type. It was pure lust, that's all. At the same time, I was having a great time with you and actually thinking of what the night would bring if I invited you up to my apartment. I think I was open to almost anything at the time."

"Now you tell me."

"Sometimes I still have difficulty answering the question, 'Who Am I? Who the Fuck am I?' It's so god-damned confusing." Naomi throws her hands in the air and turns her head away.

The discussion, which has gradually been heating up, brings Damon closer to Naomi. He walks over to her side of the table and, from behind her chair, wraps his arms around her to show his complete understanding.

"Why don't we move into the living room, Naomi? The sofa's much more comfortable."

106

"That sounds like a great idea, but before I settle in I'm going to change into something more relaxing. Do you mind if I use your bedroom?"

A few minutes later, Naomi emerges wrapped in a heavy dressing gown. She sits next to Damon on the sofa and pulls her feet up into the warmth of the gown. Damon wraps his arms around her; she lays her head against his chest and listens to his heart beating.

"How are you coming with solving your nightmares?" Damon asks. "Has there been any more progress?"

"In some of the images, I've made real progress. Just the other day, Doctor Kinderman expressed her satisfaction with how I'm doing. But my success has mainly been with images that I can easily identify in my memory. The ones I'm really struggling with are those of the couple in bed making love; I have no idea who they are supposed to be or what is represented there. There are even sounds, voices in some other language that, because they're whispered between each other, I can't decipher. Likewise, I can't understand the soldiers, nor does the bloodied eyeball in the box make any sense to me."

"There must be some bloc in your memory, Naomi, some period of time in which these images are contained. Possibly the missing time frame is from some traumatic event that you're refusing to accept."

"No, I don't think so. I believe that they're from some event prior to my birth. I know that medical science denies this as a possibility, but it's the only thing I can think of. I have a full command over my memory from the earliest events; there are no holes in it."

"I can even remember my first dance lessons. Mother took me to some gymnasium, possibly in a school, or even the basement of a church. It was a class of about ten little kids and there was one teacher. In fact there were exactly ten kids because we all had a number pinned on us and I was number ten, the last kid in the line. She told all of the mothers to sit at the edge of the room and remain quiet, and then she told us what she wanted us to do. I remember all of us kids walking around her in a circle, while she clapped her hands in some kind of a rhythm. At first, the rhythm was slow, and gradually she sped it up, hoping that we would respond to the change in tempo."

"You told me that your father left your mother shortly after you were adopted, right?"

"That's right. I don't remember anything about him, and mother never mentioned him. Whenever I brought the subject up, she always said that he'd gone away, abandoned us; that's all I knew while I was growing up and I don't know any more about him even now."

"Is it possible that your father was a soldier, and he was away at some war? Maybe he was injured and that's why the eyeball appears to you in your nightmares. What if he was killed in action somewhere? That would explain why he never returned home."

"If that was the case, why wouldn't my mother tell me the truth? There's no shame in a father being killed in battle, is there? She could even have made him out to be a hero, someone to look up to. No I don't think that's what happened. I think there's something more sinister than that. But my mother can't tell me the truth anymore, not in her state of mind, and that isn't going to change for the better. I may never know the truth. I just wish these nightmares would end forever."

Coltrane's 'Ballads' fills the room with soft warmth.

"I can feel your heart beating, Damon." Naomi places the palm of her hand against Damon's chest. "Right here."

He pulls her closer. She's aware of his increasing pulse and snuggles tighter. They lay in quiet enjoyment of each other. Damon inhales the sweetness of Naomi's hair and the fragrance on her neck and behind her ear. She relaxes into the safety of his arms until they both succumb to slumber.

11

Damon settles into a bizarre, but vaguely familiar, dream.

We have just made the most wonderful love and shared our moment of ecstasy. I wrap my arms around her and feel her warm breath against my skin. All the anxiety and excitement of a few moments ago are now calm. The night is still; a cicada sings outside the open window. Her body snuggles closer, her lips press against my ear and she whispers, "Te Quiero."

* * *

Naomi accepts Damon's arms tightening around her while her sleeping mind wanders into unfamiliar territory.

I tumble about in the surf; it sucks me seaward from the rocky beach into deeper water. The salty brine burns my eyes. Ogling cadavers float past me in a parade of the dead as the finned carrion of the deep nibble at their carcasses. A small light in the distance catches my attention. The longer I stare at it, the larger it becomes, until it reveals the shape of a woman, a naked dancing woman surrounded by an ever-flickering aura. She beckons me to follow her. My body tells me that I want to.

* * *

Damon feels Naomi attempting to release herself from his arms but he holds her tighter.

There is a banging on our front door before it comes crashing inward. Soldiers force their way through to the bed where we lay. I have just told my wife, "Te Quiero tambien," when the soldiers seize my arms and pull me from her loving grasp. She screams as I am led toward the door, still naked from our lovemaking. A rifle butt slams behind my knee and I stumble to the ground. A boot kicks against my buttock. The soldiers drag me outside, and push me into a waiting vehicle. Before they blindfold me, I see others in various stages of night clothing; some covered in blood, one other as naked as I. The last strains of my wife screeching my name pursue me from the doorway as the vehicle speeds away.

* * *

Naomi watches the aura fade as she struggles with Damon's arms.

The corpses, all uniformed, begin to dance as a chorus. One approaches me to be his partner and I rise to the occasion. His eyes stare blankly beyond me. I feel his limp arm around my waist. The watery space above is infinite and my dress balloons outward like a jellyfish as I dance. We go higher and higher until I see my mother's face screaming at me from behind a barred window. Soldiers run in and steal my husband away from our bed. I scream his name, and my mother screams at me, "You bastard of Satan, you murdered God's son."

* * *

Damon vibrates as Naomi turns restlessly against him on the sofa.

Flames shoot upward as the dancers soar above me. While they dance, an eyeball drops from one of the dancing cadavers. He has a beautiful partner in a billowy white dress. While she dances amid an aura of changing hues, she beckons to me. I try to follow her but am blindfolded and held captive in an army vehicle. It stops with a jolt and we are all forced to leave. Other soldiers laugh at my nakedness as I'm forced through a gauntlet of rifle butts and kicking boots. I fall many times but am dragged by the arms to continue the forced march. There are many voices surrounding me, murmuring and weeping voices, crying out names with no responses.

* * *

Naomi pushes her face into Damon's chest to hide from the horror.

My mother holds a baby in her hands and the flames rise higher and higher. The surf tugs my weakened body seaward and a soldier strikes my kneecap with his rifle butt. I'm in a soccer stadium with thousands of other people. There are screams everywhere. My mother drops the baby into the flames and I pursue the child. The woman in

110

the aura appears and a large wooden cross stands between us. There is pain throughout my body. My mother screams.

* * *

Damon is drawn from one nightmare to another, no longer able to distinguish between them.

Everybody is screaming. Injured soldiers on the rocky beach scream from the pain; officers scream orders at their petrified charges; soldiers wearing fascist helmets scream in Spanish; a woman screams when they take away her husband and screams again when they return with his eyeball in a cardboard box; throughout the stadium people are screaming the names of missing and murdered loved ones; Rebecca Parsons screams from her barred window in the insane asylum; a fanatic, demented, born-again screams Old Testament rhetoric while he forces sex into his victim in the name of God, and she screams from the pain; everybody is fucking screaming.

* * *

Naomi screams aloud, pulling Damon immediately from his nightmares into reality. Her skin ripples with perspiration. Her hands tremble with fear. It's dark but for the reflections of Queen Street traffic passing across the ceiling. She awakens in an unfamiliar place enveloped within the grasp of some man's arms.

"What's the matter? What's happening?" Damon shouts as he awakens from his own conflicting nightmares. He feels the sweat of his own fears saturating his clothing, blending with Naomi's perspiration.

"Damon? Is that you?"

"Don't worry, Naomi, I'm here. What happened?" He switches on a table lamp next to the sofa.

"Oh thank God." Naomi crosses her hands over her face; her chest heaves from hyperventilation. "I just had the most confusing and horrible nightmare. Actually, it was a combination of many nightmares, all compressed into one. There were soldiers, flames, screaming, dead people, even an eyeball."

"We must have been having the same damned nightmare. There were snippets from my usual visions like the rocky beach, the underwater stuff, and the dead-eyed corpses, and they were interspersed with some of the things you described from your nightmares like the eyeball in a box, the lovers in bed, the soldiers, and even your mother screaming from the barred window. It was horrible."

"I saw your Aphrodite. She tried to make me follow her into the aura. You're absolutely right; she is beautiful."

"Did you follow her?"

Naomi pauses, uncertain about how Damon will respond. "I wanted to. I really wanted to."

"It would be interesting to see where she'd lead you to. I've often wondered what would happen if I was able to continue my nightmares and follow her to wherever she leads me."

"No Damon. I mean that I wanted *her*. I felt something deep inside that told me I wanted her to be close to me, to touch me. Can you understand that?"

Damon avoids a response. "Would you like something to drink, a whisky perhaps?"

"Heaven's no, just water please, I'm parched," Naomi answers, and then ponders aloud. "How could we have been seeing each other's visions in our nightmares? How can that happen?"

Damon speculates. "Probably because we've been talking to each other about the weird things we experience during our nightmares. We're so familiar with both of them that we're now dreaming them together."

"That's true, but they're all mixed up. Your soldiers are beating up my people, and my mother is screaming at your corpses. This is all just too weird for me."

"And then there's the bit about the stadium. What's that about? You've never told me about that one before."

"I was going to ask you the same thing. I don't know anything about a stadium. It's never appeared to me before. I thought it must be from one of your nightmares."

"Sorry. The stadium doesn't ring a bell. Maybe we're also seeing another person's visions as well, like some third party nightmares we're pulling in from Queen Street, as if there's a wireless connection from a stranger's personal hard drive." Damon points his forefinger at the side of his head. "This hard drive."

Naomi breaks into a fit of laughter as if in shock. "That can't be possible. No way. Are you putting me on? No! That can't happen. Can it?"

"Hell, how do I know? I'm witnessing horrible things from some war; which one, I have no idea. You're experiencing events from some foreign country where they don't speak English and where they smash people's kneecaps with rifle butts. I even heard your lovers speaking to each other in… shit… I think it was Spanish, or Portuguese, maybe even Italian. You're absolutely right, Naomi. This is all too weird."

"What can we do about it?"

"Well, we could bring it up with Doctor Kinderman during our sessions on Thursday, but that would just complicate any successes either of us has accomplished so far. We could just try to forget this night, and hope that it doesn't happen again."

"Aren't you curious, Damon? Like why it happened?"

Neither could sleep for the remainder of the night. Damon put on some coffee and diverted the course of conversation to details of their trip to Muskoka for his birthday with Aunt Lavinia the following week.

In the morning, Naomi showers and leaves Damon's apartment early to attend a scheduled rehearsal with the dance company. Damon showers against a backdrop of Jazz Abstraction, humming along with Ornette Coleman's erratic alto solos.

Reflecting on the strange events of last night, Damon takes the first step to solving the mystery. 'There are things in Naomi's past that she knows nothing about; events that can only be answered by her adopted mother or father, and her mother is no longer capable of logical communication. That leaves only her father. Who is he, this missing Doctor Parsons? Surely there must be some record of him. What about the medical association? If he's a physician, he must be a member.'

Damon places a call to his own physician, but must leave a message with his service. While waiting for the return call, he decides to search the Internet for Doctor Parsons, a futility that reveals many potential candidates from around the globe. He starts to edit through them when the phone rings. He outlines what little he knows about Naomi's father to his physician, and provides a time line, his wife's name, Rebecca, and informs him that they adopted a daughter in 1974 or 1975.

Damon adds, "That should make him at least 50 years plus. He may even be retired by now. Do they have an archives section in the association's membership list? What about a golf registry?" Damon laughs at his own joke.

His physician accepts the humour. "That's where I'm heading this afternoon so don't get sick. It would help my research if you could tell me in what area of specialty he practiced."

"I have no idea. I do realize it's a long shot, Doc, but I welcome anything that might help. It's for a very dear friend who really needs to find her parents."

"That very dear friend wouldn't be the young woman I saw you talking to at The Concept a while back, would it? If it is, you'd better come in and have a complete physical, Damon; you're going to need it."

"Sorry Doc., it's nothing like that, believe me. She's just a good friend who needs some help. That's all."

"It's not much to go on, Damon, but I'll ask around. You do know that we can't reveal some information due to privacy considerations, don't you?"

"Of course Doc. Thanks for checking this out for me."

"Oh, one other thought worth considering, Damon. What if he's not a medical doctor; could he be a chiropractor or a naturopath, or possibly an academic doctor? Check the universities as well."

"Good thought, Doc. Thanks again."

Damon calls some colleagues at the University of Toronto and at York. He also sends an e-mail inquiry to the dental association and to all faculty associations across Canada.

12

If the amount of time one spends with another is any measure of the dedication and closeness of a relationship, then Damon and his car are as far apart as Toronto is from Moscow; they have become complete strangers. Since he located in central Toronto several years ago, he has rarely driven his car, using public transit for most of his urban travel. It's a miracle that he coaxes it to start on this beautiful August 19th morning.

The air is cool when he arrives in front of Naomi's apartment at precisely nine as promised, an exception from the recent wave of heat and humidity, but the sun is shining with much promise. She's waiting at curbside with her travel bag and a cooler sack containing Montreal smoked meat on rye for lunch. They hug before she enters his vehicle, a silver-grey non-descript Toyota something-or-other hatchback that hasn't seen a carwash for at least a year. The specific name of the model actually meant something to Damon when he purchased it, but his interest in cars has waned considerably over the past ten years.

"Happy Birthday, Damon. According to the weatherman, it's going to be a great day." She gives him a short kiss on the lips. "I also have a card for you, but I'll save it for a more opportune moment."

"Oh thank you Naomi. It's just a birthday, it's no big deal, really."

"What do you mean it's no big deal? This is your 60th birthday, a round number, one of the big ones."

Damon had already started driving. "There'll be lots of time for birthday celebration once we arrive at Aunt Lavinia's, I'm sure."

"I hope your aunt doesn't expect me to dress up for the occasion. I'm more comfortable in my hoody and track pants, with the cool air and all."

"Hey, we're only going for a couple of days and one night. I just brought the jeans I'm wearing now. Don't worry; she prefers comfort as well and abhors formality."

Once north of the city, Naomi sheds her hoody for the tee shirt she sports underneath; the one that reads, 'I'd Rather Be Dancing,' in huge letters spanning across her chest, accompanied by a silhouetted figure.

"Than what?" Damon asks, nodding toward her tee shirt proclamation.

"Almost everything," she answers without further elaboration. "By the way, you did tell your aunt that I was coming with you didn't you?"

"Yes I did. And she started asking me all kinds of questions, like who you are, how old you are, whether you're a musician or not. I told her the truth, just like you said. I told her you're a dancer, that you live in the Annex, and that you're 25."

"You're a liar, but thanks for telling her I'm only 25, Damon; she must think you're a kidnapper, a child molester, or just a dirty old man. Didn't she ask you whether we're a couple, you know, like, whether we're involved, that kind of thing?"

Damon hesitates. "Yeah, she did ask that, and also how I met you, and for how long we've known each other."

"And?"

"I told her that if I answered all of her questions on the phone, we wouldn't have anything to talk about when we arrived, and I left it at that."

"You're such a chicken shit, Damon." She punches him on the shoulder. "I didn't realize until this week, that you were born on the same day as the Dieppe invasion. I found out when I checked out your birthdate on the Internet, on one of those 'look what happened the day you were born' websites."

"Yeah. That's when I was born, in the Mount Hamilton Hospital, August 19, 1942, the same day as many other Hamiltonians were dying on the beach."

"Well, I got thinking about something. It sounds really weird, but is it possible that your nightmares are connected to Dieppe? They're all about a stony beach, tanks, uniforms and rifle fire, not to mention the corpses you see underwater. It sounds an awful lot like a war scene to me, and the coincidence of your birthdate and the invasion at Dieppe made me think that maybe there is some connection."

"You could be right. It is pretty weird, but I can't see any connection other than that. A similar thought occurred to me when we studied the war in high school, that maybe something was said at home about Dieppe that might have triggered my nightmares, but my father never went overseas; apparently he failed his medical due to flat feet. Now I ask you, what do flat feet have to do with going to war?"

"What about any newspaper clippings, magazine stories, or TV programs?"

Damon starts to laugh. "Naomi, I have to tell you that there was no TV when I was a kid, not in our home at least. We got our first TV in 1955; I was already 13 at the time. The only reason we got one then was because my father wanted to watch the World Series. The Yankees and the Brooklyn Dodgers were playing. The Dodgers won the series in seven games, the only time they won under the Brooklyn banner."

"Wow, I'm impressed. I thought you were a typical artsy-fartsy guy. How do you know so much about sports?"

"Not all sports, just baseball. It's the only sport I ever played, and I was pretty good at it. I was a pitcher, but I could also hit. In those days a pitcher had to be able to hit as well as throw. My favourite team was the Brooklyn Dodgers and Jackie Robinson was my childhood hero. I stopped following the game in 1958, when the Dodgers moved to LA; it just wasn't the same anymore. When I was a kid in Hamilton, I played hardball for the Panthers at Inch Park on the mountain. I think I still have one of my jerseys from back then. How about you? Did you ever play any sports?"

"I wanted to play ringette at school. That's a version of ice hockey played mainly by girls. But my mother wouldn't allow it. She said my dancing was too important and that I would probably screw up my knees, and there was always a chance that I might have fractured an arm or leg, which would finish me as a dancer. I guess in retrospect, it was good advice, but I was mad at her at the time. I told her that all the other girls in school played ringette, and she answered, 'But none of them are dancers.' I never became interested in watching sports on TV. To this day, I don't even own a TV."

"Is that because Ikea doesn't make a TV?" Damon laughs and she responds with a challenging leer. "Seriously though Naomi, I'm the same as you. I can't stand staring at something that's so bland and repetitive. I'd rather listen to some new music, or play something myself."

Their conversation slides into a topic that has been challenging Damon for some time.

"The college has offered me a package for early retirement, a subject that I've been trying to avoid, but their deadline is running out; I have to respond by the end of this year."

"Do you have to accept it, or can you stay on until you turn 65?"

"Hell, I can stay on as long as I want, within reason of course. If I choose to retire, what will I do with myself? I have nothing else. Well, not quite true. I have the gig at The Concept, I guess."

"Do you enjoy teaching, Damon? My guess is that you do."

"I enjoy it in principal, let me put it that way. There are times when I could easily walk away from the place and never return, but most of the time I look forward to going into work. I love seeing all those fresh young faces every September; they appear so eager to learn and to experience this new life they're buying into. It's later in the term when they show their true colours. There are those who have the desire and ambition to dig in and those who don't give a shit, or are too lazy to care."

"Or too busy with their social lives to have any time left for school," Naomi adds.

"That too."

"What are the up sides of early retirement?"

"First there's the cash incentive. If invested it will add a few dollars a month to my already mature and adequate pension. I'm not one of those people who fanatically grabs as much money as I can get my hands on and negotiates to the last drop of blood left in my veins; if there's enough to live on with a few bucks left over for the finer things in life, then I'm happy. My car is paid for, although it's probably closer to retirement than I am. I have no debt, except that I don't own a house, and as long as I keep the gig at The Concept, I have a roof over my head. In other words, I'm financially ready for retirement. It's the mental part that I'm not sure about."

"You would have more time to explore your music, Damon, unless you'd like to spend the extra time on something else; maybe you could find a hobby, like sailing for example, or travelling to exotic places, or maybe even stuffing model ships into bottles, if that's what turns your crank."

"I don't know. I'm on the side of not deciding anything and letting the deadline pass. By doing that, I'm effectively turning down their offer of an incentive, but I will continue to teach, until I, not them but I, decide to terminate my employment. Sure, I'll be sacrificing the incentive package, but who says there won't be another offer in a few more years, maybe a more attractive one at that?"

"It sounds to me like you've already decided, but we have another, more immediate, decision to make. Where would you like to have lunch? I have some great Montreal bagels, smoked meat, some cheese, those great olives, and a fine bottle of Merlot."

"That's decided. We'll stop in the next town and find a quiet park with a picnic bench, preferably by a stream or a river. It's during the week so there shouldn't be too many tourists around."

They settle on a picnic area along the river in the next town where they can watch pleasure boats motoring leisurely by. Naomi waves at the hobby sailors from the picnic table and they wave back to her. She lays a tablecloth down.

"You never know what people do on picnic tables so it's always a good idea to cover them with something. I once watched a couple changing their baby's dirty diapers on a table down in The Beach and

120

I'm almost certain that lovers use them at night as well. It always pays to be safe."

Damon can't add further wisdom to her statement so he wastes no time in pouring a couple glasses of wine while she opens the bagels and slices some tomatoes.

"I wonder how you and Aunt Lavinia will get along; she has a knack of being crusty and difficult with people she doesn't like, you know."

"Thanks for the warning Damon, I'll be on my best behaviour."

They laugh together. Damon is confident Naomi and Aunt Lavinia will hit it off wonderfully. To change the subject he asks, "Naomi. What's more important to you, the journey or the destination?"

"Are you talking about this journey, Damon? Obviously our destination, meaning our time with your aunt at her cottage for your birthday, is the main purpose of this trip. Therefore, the destination is more important."

"I'm thinking more of the big journey, our travels through life. Do we spend too much time looking forward to reaching goals and to arrive at destinations that may, or may not, ever be realized?"

"You're the one who advised me to concentrate on the present tense, that there is no past and no future. Remember? And I follow your advice daily, to the letter. I now live only for the present. Oh, I still have a few remaining pieces from my past to sort out, but I no longer concern myself with the future. Life is too short."

"For you? Not a chance. You still have more than two-thirds of your life ahead of you. Me? There's almost nothing left. Statistically, the average life span for a Canadian male born in 1942 is 63 years. I'm already 60. According to the stats, I only have three years left before I croak."

"But you said that we should only concentrate on the present."

"That's for art, the act of creating. It's only important while it's being created."

"You also told me that 'Art is Life and Life is Art.' So therefore, whatever is good for art is good for life. Besides, life is being created each moment we exist. So there." Naomi takes a huge bite from her bagel and chews with a smug look on her face before they both break into laughter.

"We should get moving. I told Aunt Lavinia we'd arrive around two, and life is passing us by; even in the present tense."

Aunt Lavinia is walking along the road picking wildflowers when they arrive. She approaches the car and feeds a bouquet through the car window to Naomi who accepts gracefully.

"Thank you so-o-o much. No one ever gives me flowers." Naomi directs an aside toward Damon, who makes a mental note to include flowers for her at their next dinner date.

Aunt Lavinia welcomes Damon with a hug and chastises him for not visiting more often. Before he has an opportunity to introduce Naomi, Aunt Lavinia takes charge.

"I'm Lavinia, Damon's crazy aunt." She offers her open arms to Naomi and they put their cheeks together.

Naomi reciprocates, "Hello Aunt Lavinia, I'm Naomi. It's so nice to finally meet you. Damon always talks about you."

"I'm sure he's told you many stories about me; most of them are true. Damon tells me you're a dancer, Naomi. You must dance for us later."

Naomi glances at Damon quizzically and mouths the words, "*must* dance?"

He smiles and nods toward the cottage where they drop their bags on the porch.

"It's beautiful here," Naomi observes.

Aunt Lavinia responds, "It's home. I wouldn't live anywhere else. Do you swim, Naomi?"

"Yes, I love to swim."

"Later we'll go swimming together. There's no point in asking Damon though; he hates the water."

There is afternoon tea on the porch with scones and raspberry jam, followed by a walk about the property, starting at the lake where

122

they all sit on the dock watching a pair of loons and listening to their haunting calls.

Aunt Lavinia offers an observation. "Did you know that, contrary to popular opinion, loons do not mate for life, Naomi? I've been very lucky here; every summer there's a pair of them in my little bay. Their calls are wonderful at dusk, when I'm usually reading quietly on my bench under the ancient pines."

For Damon, it seems different from previous visits. Is it because Aunt Lavinia is getting older, or is it because he's not the only visitor this time? He surmises that it's probably the latter, because she directs all of her conversation to Naomi, as if he isn't there at all.

As they walk toward the area of her property she affectionately refers to as 'the ancient pines,' Aunt Lavinia assumes an air of reverence, especially compared to her levity down at the lake. "Do you believe in spirits, Naomi?"

"Well," Naomi allows a pause so she can gather the most appropriate words for her host. "I'm not a religious person Aunt Lavinia but…"

"You don't have to be a religious person to be spiritual; that's just a load of bunk, if you ask me. And you don't have to call me Aunt Lavinia; I'm not your Aunt. Just call me Lavinia. Now, what were you saying?"

"I often feel spiritual; the very nature of being creative is a spiritual experience, don't you think?"

"You don't have to ask me, girl, you're the dancer and you're doing just fine by yourself. Keep talking."

"I've come to believe that the spirit is within me; in fact, I am the spirit of my own creations. I view the spirit and the muse as the same entity. When I perform satisfactorily, I can take the credit for it because I created it but, on the other hand, if I screw it up, then only I can be blamed. Before I start dancing, I try to encourage the spirit inside me to emerge through meditation and focusing; when it does, I'm ready to dance. Usually I know when that happens, and it happens often whenever Damon plays the piano for me."

Naomi smiles in Damon's direction before turning back to Aunt Lavinia. "He's a wonderful pianist; he understands the sensuality that results when the muses of dance and music are blended. We work very well together."

"Sensuality? Damon? Are they being used in the same sentence?" Aunt Lavinia asks jokingly. "I can't believe it." Everybody laughs and she continues, "I'm being serious now. Damon is a wonderful musician and he's certainly sensuous and sensitive. I'm overjoyed that the two of you have found each other; you seem so well-suited."

Naomi gives Damon another one of her glances.

Aunt Lavinia introduces Naomi to the ancient pines. "This is where I spend most of my time, sitting right here. From this bench I can see the entire property and it's so quiet most of the time. There's a small clearing in the pines above the bench. Do you see it there?" She points toward the clearing. "On a cool clear night the Milky Way often lights up the sky, and if we're lucky, the northern lights will paint the sky with their magic. During the day I read here and at night I dream. This, Naomi, is my spiritual place, where everything in my life is resolved without any conflict whatsoever."

"I'd love to have a place where all my conflicts would be resolved," Naomi wishes.

Aunt Lavinia pats her hand on the bench, "Come, Naomi, come and sit next to me." Naomi joins her.

"Sometimes I just sit here, close my eyes, and listen to the call of the loons from the lake. It's magical. Try it, Naomi."

Naomi adopts her familiar lotus position and closes her eyes. Damon watches her abdominal muscles regulate her breathing into a steady pattern. Everything remains silent; several minutes pass.

In a soft, ethereal voice, Aunt Lavinia speaks to Naomi. "What do you feel?"

"I feel like dancing." She answers.

"Then dance, girl, dance."

Damon steps back to allow Naomi some room. Silence prevails; even the loons remain quiet. Naomi maintains her stillness; Damon assumes she's searching for her muse. Gradually her legs unfold from the lotus, her left foot touches the retired pine needles that blanket the ground; her right leg soars skyward, forming a vertical straight line from one toe to the other. The left leg bends and she catapults outward. Her movements are for the most part, graceful and predictable, as she circles the area, but they're interrupted by occasional unexplained jolts that cause her body to tremble before regaining her composure.

From the bench, Aunt Lavinia watches her intensely, as if attempting to understand the purpose behind each of Naomi's movements. Damon seems worried that the sudden jolts may indicate that Naomi is experiencing some pain; he has never seen her dance quite this way before. However, she seems to return easily to her more confident posture without any signs of pain or grimacing. After dancing for a few minutes she returns to her seated position on the bench next to Aunt Lavinia, who gives her a brief embrace.

"Thank you so much for this impromptu performance, Naomi. You're a wonderful dancer. Maybe later you could dance to Damon's music."

"I'd love to, if Damon's up to it." She waits for Damon's approval, which he provides by nodding his head in the affirmative.

"But first," Aunt Lavinia asserts, "we must have something to eat. Come; I'm going to treat you both to a nice dinner in town."

Before Damon can say anything, Aunt Lavinia continues, "I don't cook at home anymore, I'm getting too old for that. Sometimes friends drop by with something they've prepared, or they bring a pizza, or we order some Chinese takeout. But for an occasion like this, we go out. Consider it your special birthday dinner, Damon, but don't expect a cake at the restaurant. We wouldn't dare sacrifice our late night cake ceremony, would we? Besides, I know very well that you detest those stupid public displays of birthdays when they're sung by a chorus of out-of-tune waiters."

"We're on the same page, Aunt Lavinia." Damon answers. "But, you're not taking us to the Lodge, I hope, especially now that Phil and Virginia are managing it."

"No-o-o. Not on your life. We're going to a new family restaurant in the village. By new, I mean that they opened maybe 10 years ago. In the front it's a hamburgers and fries operation, but they have a nice dining room in the back where the food is quite acceptable."

They arrive and settle at a table for four adjacent to a large bay window overlooking a park; the view is quiet and serene. There's a family of Canada geese strolling about the grounds and two children blowing soap bubbles and following the geese. The waitress serves water and distributes menus to all four settings. That's when Aunt Lavinia announces that a friend of hers will be joining them.

"Ah, speak of the devil." She stands and points toward the entrance. A woman, possibly 10 years younger than Lavinia, which makes her only seven years older than Damon, arrives at their table.

Aunt Lavinia introduces everyone. "Damon and Naomi, this is a dear friend of mine, Betsy McGinnis. She's the chief librarian at the town library where I spend a lot of my time and she's a lover of contemporary literature. Betsy, I'd like you to meet my nephew, Damon, and his new friend, Naomi."

Betsy, as it turns out, is an intellectual equal to Aunt Lavinia, and their conversation over dinner is stimulating. Both express interest in Naomi's dancing and Damon's music, but more fascination is invested into how Damon and Naomi manage to blend the two muses, especially as they have no written music and no choreographed sequences. Betsy is particularly interested in the creative act of simultaneous improvisation, and is vaguely familiar with the free jazz experiments of Ornette Coleman, Eric Dolphy and even Paul Bley. 'Who would have guessed that from a small town librarian?' Damon ponders to himself. He is able however, to check his stereotyping before opening his mouth, a technique he perfected since meeting Naomi.

Following a mediocre dinner which was improved tenfold by the stimulating conversation, Aunt Lavinia convinces Betsy to join them back at the cottage where, she promises, they are to indulge in some fine music and dance, and of course, Damon's special birthday cake. Betsy follows them in her own car.

13

Once back at the cottage, dusk eases toward darkness as the last light of day disappears under the horizon. Drinks are served and Aunt Lavinia ushers the women to the bench under the pines. Damon is directed to the piano where he's expected to accompany Naomi while she dances in a command performance for the ladies. There's a direct line of sight from the piano bench to the clearing under the pines. The outdoor porch lighting sprays a portion of its luminance across the area where Aunt Lavinia often reads and communes with the spirits.

Damon knows that Naomi will want to meditate before starting so he begins by playing lightly on the keyboard, spacious little statements that will allow her to find her direction. He's reminded of the many occasions over the years when he was obligated to perform, both here at the cottage and at the lodge during his summer visits. He can still hear the introductions from his childhood prodigy days, 'Ladies and Gentlemen, Little Damon Farrell will tickle the ivories for your listening pleasure.' This time, however, he isn't the focus of any attention. Both Aunt Lavinia's and Betsy's eyes are trained on the movements of Naomi's lithe body as it draws images across the lawn, loosely interpreting Damon's music. He wonders which of her nightmarish visions are consuming her this time as she balances her performance between long graceful strides and abrupt muscle-tightening tension. She is the ideal student, the caliber of which, if there were even 10 to call a class, Damon would never consider retirement. There is nothing more he can teach her about improvisation or freedom, but there is everything they can learn together; as teacher and student they become one. Their muses connect once again. Is it the location, the weather, this particular evening, the audience, the spirits, or is it that special affinity that embraces them whenever and wherever they perform together? The oneness is becoming stronger with each of their collaborations, leaving only their imagination as a future destination. What ever happened to creating only in the present?

Betsy McGinnis points toward Naomi during one of her more acrobatic maneuvers and Aunt Lavinia offers her agreement by nodding. By default, Damon's music intensifies into more dissonant intervals and obscure syncopations that Naomi responds to with tenderness and sensuality. Naomi's performance fades into a clump at the feet of the two ladies who politely pause before applauding. The women gather to return to the cottage while Damon plays several choruses of Sophisticated Lady.

Betsy applauds softly to acknowledge Damon's playing. "You play wonderfully Damon, and you and Naomi are such a marvelous fit."

"We're taking Naomi for a swim, Damon," Aunt Lavinia announces, "I hope you don't mind. We'll be back in an hour."

"We didn't bring any bathing suits, Aunt Lavinia." Damon proclaims.

She replies, "Don't be such a prude, Damon. We're going skinny-dipping."

Damon continues playing, moving through a series of turnarounds before his left hand falls into a Latin-sounding vamp that leads into several choruses of Green Dolphin Street. After a short pause, he delves headlong into McCoy's Passion Dance, from which he has no difficulty in removing himself to a freer space.

As time passes he pores more heavily into his personal music. During rests and pauses he hears the women laughing and joking as they swim together in the lake; Naomi's laughter can be heard above the others. Damon hopes that, with any luck, they're not sharing jokes at his expense. After all, Aunt Lavinia knows more intimate details about him than anyone else, probably more than even he knows. 'Surely she won't tell all to Naomi,' he wishes. What else could they be having so much fun about? They just met each other a few hours ago, and Damon hadn't told Aunt Lavinia anything about Naomi before then. His aunt is in her late 70s, Betsy must be in her mid-to-late 60s, and Naomi is only 28. What could they possibly have in common?

Damon's attention is drawn back to the piano, where his fingers begin creating fugal interplay with their laughter; he jokingly considers it to be a new composition: Concerto for Three Wet Hysterical Women and One Dry Pianist. 'Surely I could sell that proposal to the Canada Council,' he jokes to himself.

When the women arrive back at the cottage, each of them wrapped in a towel, they are still giggling like young teenagers. Naomi stops by the piano, "Damon, we had so much fun, I could hardly contain myself from laughing. It's so-o-o beautiful at the lake. Betsy is a truly funny woman, and so is your precious Aunt Lavinia. She's a sweetie."

Damon reflects, "I'm surprised there are any loons left in the bay, considering the racket you were all making."

Lavinia delivers an announcement from the dimly lit porch. "Attention, attention, everybody." She stands on the porch with Damon's chocolate cake; there are enough candle flames to light the entire yard.

"Happy Birthday to you, Happy Birthday to you…" the three women sing more or less together in a chaotic attempt at unison. The candles are arranged with 10 blue candles circling the perimeter of the cake, another inner circle of six blue candles, and a single white *good luck* candle in the middle.

"This is a very special birthday, Damon." Aunt Lavinia reminds him. Sixty years, imagine that. Did you notice that I also included a special good luck candle like I always used to do?"

"Yes Aunt Lavinia. Thank you so much. And, I have a special surprise for you. Because you always sang it on my birthday when I was young, I want to play it for you now."

Damon sits at the piano and starts playing. Aunt Lavinia immediately begins singing, "We'll meet again, don't know where, don't know when, but…" Tears stream from her eyes as she sings and Betsy places her arm around Lavinia and sings along.

From where Naomi is standing, she overhears the tearful Lavinia whispering to Betsy, "It's 60 years ago today; such a long time, but I can never forget." Betsy rubs her hand over Lavinia's shoulders in consolation. Naomi thinks it to be an odd statement to make in a celebration of Damon's birthday, but files the thought away when she approaches Damon with her own special birthday kiss. She hands Damon an envelope. It contains a 'Peanuts' studio card with a picture of Linus playing the piano; Lucy admires him from the side with a dreamy look on her face and Snoopy sits grinning in the corner. A balloon above Lucy's head asks, 'What do I have to do to get your attention?' The card is signed, 'Happy Birthday to my dearest Damon, with all my love, Naomi,' and an inscription that reads, 'August 19, 2002, at the cottage.'

He ponders the meaning behind the message. "Thank you, Naomi," adding, "I love you too." He pulls her toward him and kisses her meaningfully. Naomi moans softly from deep within and he feels the vibration against him.

"This is the first card I've received from anyone besides Aunt Lavinia in many years; even my mother and father don't send me one anymore."

Further kisses are exchanged and substantial slices of cake are distributed.

After much celebration and memories of past birthdays are discussed, Damon finally announces, "I'm beat. I think it's time I retire for the night. We'll see you all in the morning." He leans toward Naomi, kisses her on the lips and starts up the stairs to his room.

Aunt Lavinia pursues him and whispers, "What *are* the sleeping arrangements for you two? I thought you were a couple?"

"Oh shit, Aunt Lavinia, I should have straightened all that out with you earlier. Naomi and I, we're not a couple, like in the biblical sense I mean. Our friendship, while very close, is purely a platonic affair. In other words, we don't sleep together; she'll need one of the spare guest rooms. I'm sorry."

"So am I," Aunt Lavinia responds, somewhat tongue-in-cheek, with a strange glint in her eyes that questions Damon's sanity. "Just for the record, Damon, I would have assumed, from conversations we had during our swim, that Naomi might be thinking differently about everything than you are. She didn't say anything outright, but that would be my casual observation and I'm never far from right. Goodnight, and sleep well. Give your old auntie a kiss. If I were she, I'd be climbing right in beside you. Sweet dreams."

Naomi is placed in a room two doors away from Damon's. The sign, 'Damon's Private Room,' still hangs above his door. Before they depart in the upstairs hallway, Damon and Naomi embrace.

"Thank you so-o-o much for bringing me here Damon. I'm really enjoying Lavinia and Betsy; they're so-o-o much fun. Goodnight." They peck their lips together.

Despite his exhaustion, more from the northern air than anything else, sleep comes slowly to Damon. His mind wanders from subject to subject, from Aunt Lavinia to Naomi, and to Betsy. Aunt Lavinia had never mentioned Betsy to him before now, yet they act like they've known each other for years. Damon assumes they must belong to the same reading club, or some such organization. His thoughts turn to Naomi, 'she danced so beautifully among the pines tonight; the women obviously enjoyed her performance. I certainly did.'

Cottages reveal their age more when the creaks and moans of the old wooden structures can be heard against the silence of the night. A loose-fitting window frame rattles from a breeze, a rafter and roof joist fight for position as the evening coolness relaxes the tension at their joints, floorboards shrink in the dissipating humidity, and stairs weep under the weight of ascending footsteps.

Out in the yard, Betsy's car starts and rolls slowly and crisply along the gravel driveway until it reaches the main paved road and fades away. Damon looks at his clock; it reads two-something, more than an hour since he came to bed and he remains caught in limbo between the land of nod and conscious awareness.

'What is Naomi thinking at this time?' his half-awake mind ponders. 'Did she fall asleep immediately, or is she having similar thoughts to mine? Do those short kisses mean more than I give them credit for? Why do I always imagine things that aren't possible, or at the most, very unlikely? Because there is a difference between impossible and unlikely, that's why. Oh Christ, I'm answering my own questions now.'

Following a brief respite, his mind wanders back into questioning mode. 'Is it possible for two people to be close, as friends, without resorting to the lustful thoughts that I seem to be having more often? What if we stop having any physical contact whatsoever, no kissing and no embracing? No, no, no, that would only feed the flames of desire. I always believed that these thoughts dissipated when a man reaches my age, but she's not my age; she can still have her thoughts. So what is she thinking? Does she, like I do, entertain some idea about visiting during the night? We're only two doors apart. I even hoped, for a brief moment, that the creaking might have been her footsteps coming to visit me but my door remains shut. Did she think the same about the creaking floorboards? What if I take the initiative and pay her a visit? How would she respond? Would she welcome me into her bed or would she be so upset with me that everything would crash in on us?'

Damon is awakened by the smell of fresh coffee. Upon opening his eyes he's treated to another chorus of Happy Birthday, sung by Aunt Lavinia and Naomi, who wear matching aprons imprinted with some cottage country motif. His first impression is that he has awakened in a swank hotel in some exotic location. Both of the women, one on either side of the bed, kiss him on the cheeks simultaneously.

Naomi hands him his dark roast in a large mug. "This should be just what the doctor ordered," before kissing him more enchantingly on the lips. Did you sleep well?"

Before Damon can answer, Aunt Lavinia explains why they are still celebrating his birthday the following morning.

"It's been so long since you and I have spent some quality time together that I don't want it to end. So, we're extending your birthday for another 24 hours. That will give us some more time to talk and to laugh."

Aunt Lavinia returns to the kitchen, leaving Naomi and Damon alone. Naomi sits on the edge of his bed.

Without revealing details about his nighttime thoughts, he tells Naomi about his difficulty in getting to sleep, and she admits to having similar difficulties. "I think it must be the silence up here."

"You must be very special," Damon informs her. "Very few people get to spend any time in my private room. Didn't you read the sign? This is 'Damon's Private Room,' after all."

Naomi laughs.

"I've never heard you laugh so much as you have here, at the cottage, Naomi."

"I'm so-o-o relaxed here." She moves her shoulders back and forth in a gesture of coziness. "Maybe it's just about getting away from the city; maybe it's the fresh air, or the silence, or it's Aunt Lavinia's wonderful hospitality, but I feel so free here. It's like I don't have anything to worry about."

From the foot of the stairs, Aunt Lavinia's voice calls, "Break it up, breakfast is being served."

Naomi jumps from the bed. "I'll go downstairs and help Lavinia with breakfast. You'd better throw some clothes on." She kisses the tip of her forefinger and touches Damon's lips with it, gesturing a 'bye-bye' with her fingers as she departs his room.

Damon is filled with mixed messages, not knowing whether to pursue her casual kisses and embraces further. He has reached a stage where he wants to pull her close to him, to kiss and touch her passionately, but is afraid that he could destroy the illusion. 'What if she backs away? What if she doesn't share my passion? What if I just make a fool of myself? It might send her away from me, and I couldn't bear that. I've come to need her around me, to have her as a close friend, which has become far more important and desirous than making physical love with her, but there are many times I want her with me in my bed, if just to feel her warmth next to me.'

Downstairs, a hearty breakfast of eggs, ham, home-fried potatoes and toast awaits, much more substantial than Damon's usual bowl of Corn Flakes.

Aunt Lavinia inquires, "Do you two have any plans for the rest of the day?"

Damon wanted to say that they hadn't made any plans, but his mouth was occupied chewing on some toast.

Naomi speaks for both of them. "We were thinking of going into town and wandering about before we start heading back to the city. I've never been to this area before and the town looked kind of quaint when we drove through it yesterday. Why don't you come into town with us? We can drop you off back here before we leave."

"You young folks don't need me around," Aunt Lavinia answers. "I'll find a good book and settle down on the bench."

To be referred to as one of the young folks is welcome and flattering, but reality strikes as soon as Damon considers the source of the statement, proving once again, that everything is relative.

Naomi responds, "Nonsense Lavinia. You know the town; you can show us around. Please come with us. We can have lunch in town before we leave. Is that alright with you Damon?"

Before Damon can answer, Aunt Lavinia reclaims her dominance. "No, I'm going to stay here for the afternoon. I have some things I must do and I'm sure you both want to be alone."

Damon whispers into Naomi's ear, "I know that voice. Don't push this any further."

After breakfast, Naomi and Damon pack their belongings into the Toyota. Betsy arrives just as they're about to say their goodbyes. Hugs and kisses abound and they leave the two women waving at them from the porch.

"That's where the Dairy Bar used to be." Damon points at an empty lot where several vehicles are parked. "That's where Aunt Lavinia chastised the hooligans who tried to drown me."

"Isn't that also where you met your wife, Virginia?" Naomi recalls from what Damon had told her.

"I try to forget that," he laughs.

"There's the pool hall; I'm surprised that it's still here. The façade of the old movie theatre still stands, but it hasn't operated as a theatre for many years."

They walk down to the pier and watch some young boys fishing from the dock. A small motorboat arrives and two men reel it up on their trailer.

"There's something so simple and peaceful about small towns," Naomi offers, placing her hand in Damon's. "I've always thought that someday I'd like to move out of the city and find a place like this to live in. Maybe I could teach dance classes to the kids. Have you ever had those thoughts, Damon?"

"I don't know. Jazz doesn't happen in places like this. Where would I play and with whom?" He pauses. "I'll bet there isn't one other jazz musician in town."

After strolling from one end of the main drag to the other, Damon suggests they have a quick bite to eat at the restaurant they ate in the previous night. "The burger part," he emphasizes.

Damon orders a coffee and the greasiest mushroom bacon banquet burger on the menu with fries on the side; Naomi opts for a garden salad and green tea. They both have the homemade apple pie with a slice of cheddar.

It's in the middle of eating the apple pie that Naomi remembers leaving her bag on the bed at the cottage. "We'll have to go back," she says. "I can't survive without it, I'm afraid."

They return to the cottage, only a couple of kilometers from town, to see a car leaving Lavinia's driveway; a distinguished looking man is behind the wheel. He waves at them as they drive in. Betsy's car sits in the driveway, next to the garage. As they approach the cottage, they notice Lavinia lying down on the cot with Betsy sitting on the porch by her side. She sips on a glass of lemonade.

"Hello Betsy," Naomi starts. "Is everything OK?"

"Oh yes. Everything's just fine. Lavinia is having a rest. I guess the visit tired her out."

"No need to waken her. I just forgot my overnight bag. I'll run upstairs and get it, and then we'll be off."

On the way out, Naomi hugs Betsy while running for the car. Damon waves at her from the driver's seat.

"Aunt Lavinia is sleeping already. We must have tired her out." Naomi tells Damon.

"Well, she is getting up there in age. I guess that's what happens the older one gets."

"Is that what you'll be like in a few more years; falling asleep all the time?"

Damon laughs, nodding his head to the side and feigning a snore.

14

Aunt Lavinia died this morning. Damon's mother called an hour ago with the news. She didn't have much to say about it, except, "I think you should know that Lavinia died at the cottage early this morning. I'll call you back when I have more news." Then she hung up.

Damon sits, staring blankly into his morning coffee, bewildered by the news. 'Of course I should know. What can my mother be thinking? She didn't even ask how I felt about it. And why didn't she say *Aunt* Lavinia died? She always did before whenever she talked to me about her; she always referred to her as 'your Aunt.' Besides, she's my mother's younger sister after all; of course she's my aunt, and of course I should know that she died.'

Once the initial shock of the phone call passes, uncontrolled sobbing replaces the numbness. Aunt Lavinia was the most important person in Damon's life, 'the only one who gave a shit about me,' he remembers. She was far more nurturing than his own mother, and certainly more than his father, who always wished he were somebody else entirely; more like his older brother Phil, a real man who goes hunting and fishing. Damon? According to his father, he's just the sissy who learned to play the piano well enough to eke out a living.

It's only ten in the morning and Damon feels a sudden urge to pour a rye. He raises his glass to Aunt Lavinia and balls his eyes out. 'God, did we have some memories, she and I? Everything in my life that I value started with her.'

Damon's mind searches for memories, and there is no shortage. At every twist in the road that became Damon's life, Lavinia was there, guiding him around the jagged corners, helping him through the labyrinth of obstacles, and being the only one to listen when the bricks and mortar started to crumble.

Her cottage was his refuge, a place to hide, and to seek advice. 'I love going to the cottage, although it won't be the same without her.

What will happen to the cottage now? It'll be tragic if it's sold to some stranger. So much of my life is there.'

'It's been several years since I spent any amount of time there, except of course, for the overnighter in August when I took Naomi there to introduce her to my wild and crazy aunt and to celebrate my 60th birthday. Shit, that was only a month ago. Naomi and Aunt Lavinia hit it off immediately; they even went swimming together in the lake while I stayed in the cottage playing the grand. I love the sound of that piano, especially when the doors and windows are open to the woods and the pines. It's like performing in a natural concert hall with the sound filtering through the trees and echoing across the lake.'

Damon recalls listening to them talking and laughing down at the lake, hoping all along that they weren't sharing jokes about him. Aunt Lavinia knew everything there was to know about him because he always confided in her so he had crossed his fingers that she wouldn't reveal any of the juicier bits to Naomi. He remembers when Aunt Lavinia tried to teach him to swim. Swimming is one of those talents Damon was never able to master. He just sinks; floating isn't in the cards for him at all. To this day, he maintains a healthy respect for any water that's deeper than he is tall. To be blunt about it, he admits that water scares the shit out of him. So many memories rise to the surface that he's having difficulty processing them. The phone rings. It's his mother again.

"Damon, I just found out that the funeral is this Saturday. They're holding it at the cottage. Why would they do such a thing when they have a perfectly good funeral home there? And, get this; there won't be any minister there either. Can you believe that?"

"Mom. That's exactly what Aunt Lavinia wanted. The cottage was her special place, and she didn't have a religious bone in her body."

"Oh Damon. Everybody becomes a Christian before they die. You should know that. How else will they get into heaven?"

"For Aunt Lavinia, her cottage *was* her heaven. She lived in heaven every day of her life."

"Not every day, I can assure you of that, but now isn't the time to talk ill of the dead is it? Besides, the cottage was supposed to be a special place for the *whole* family, not just for her. Why my father ever left the cottage to *her* is beyond me. Charles warned me at the time that there were bound to be problems and suggested that I should have contested the will. After all, it was the *family* cottage for so many years while your grandfather owned it. Charles used to go fishing there, but as soon as Lavinia took it over, she told Charles he couldn't fish from there anymore. She was a bit strange sometimes, your aunt."

"From what I remember, mother, the cottage was left to Aunt Lavinia because she started teaching fulltime at a school in Muskoka, and she needed a place to live in permanently. The conditions mentioned in Grandpa's will stated that she had to look after all the winterizing and the renovations herself, and the rest of the family, meaning all of us, got to enjoy it during our summer vacations. But, the title to the cottage belonged only to Aunt Lavinia. What she chose to do with it was entirely up to her. From what I've heard, the cottage was in shambles when she acquired it and it cost her a fortune to fix everything up. Besides, mother, you received the equivalent value from the estate in cash and investments."

"You never heard that from us; Lavinia must have brain-washed you. But why did she ban your father from fishing there? Tell me that."

"There are thousands of lakes in this province for him to fish in."

Suddenly Damon is struck by the banality of their conversation. "Mother, why are we still talking about father and fishing on the day Aunt Lavinia died?"

"I suppose you're right, Damon, but you must admit, she was a strange one, that aunt of yours."

"I assume that you and Dad are going up for the funeral. Are you staying at the cottage?"

140

"No. Your father says he won't step foot in the cottage, so we're staying at the Lodge. Phil is looking after a room for us. Do you want to come in the car with us?"

"No. I'll drive up on my own. Who knows? I may stay up there for a few days after the funeral."

Damon was determined not to subject himself to the ranting and bullshit from his father and, as he has managed to stay clear of Phil for much of his adult life, there's no chance he will stay at the Lodge either, even though he knows that he'll have to face Phil, and Virginia as well, at the funeral. Damon pours his second rye and his thoughts return to his beloved aunt.

'Oh shit!' Damon sputters between sobs. 'I'm going to miss you Aunt Lavinia. You were one of the only friends I ever had. Well, you were *the* only friend I had until Naomi came along. Naomi, thank God for her. Jeez, I should call her and let her know.'

"Hi Naomi, it's Damon. I have some terrible news. Aunt Lavinia died early this morning."

Naomi's end of the phone is silent.

"Naomi, are you there? I know that you liked her, and she liked you as well."

"I'm so-o-o sorry, Damon. It's so weird; I really can't believe it."

"Are you OK, Naomi? What's weird?"

"Damon, you won't believe this, but I had one of my terrible episodes last night when I couldn't sleep. I considered calling you but decided against disturbing you. It was the usual nightmare with my mother screaming at me from behind the bars of that institution she's in. Then the flames began, and the baby appeared in my mother's hands. While the wooden cross was dangling in front of my face, Lavinia appeared from the darkness and ripped the cross from the guy's neck. She threw both him and the cross into the fire, causing a huge blaze before it was suddenly extinguished. Then, she lifted the baby from the fire and handed it to me. At that point I wasn't sure whether I was inside the nightmare or if reality had taken over. At any rate I was lying in my bed, in my own room, when Lavinia walked over to my bed and sat down beside me; she handed the baby to me and touched me on the shoulder. She told me that, pretty soon, everything will be resolved, and then she vanished, out the window. Now, you tell me that she died last night. Isn't that weird? What does it mean, Damon?"

"I have no idea. I just phoned to tell you about Aunt Lavinia's death, and to ask if you'd like to go somewhere for supper tonight; I really need someone to talk to and I want to get out of my apartment. This is hitting me hard, and obviously it's affecting you as well. This really is weird."

"Come to my place, Damon. I'll cook something up."

"At your place? Are you sure you feel like cooking? What time? Six? OK, but I should warn you, I haven't slept all night. You will excuse me if I doze off while I'm there, won't you?"

In the middle of Damon's shower, the phone starts ringing. Thinking it may be Naomi calling back, he wraps a towel around his waist and answers it after the fourth ring.

"Hi Damon, it's me again."

"What is it this time mother?"

"I received more information about Lavinia's death. Apparently she was out in the yard, sitting on that teak bench under the pines, the one she liked so much. She used to spend a lot of time out there, just reading. Now I ask you, what in the name of God was she doing out there in the middle of the night? From what I was told, she died at around three o'clock, *in the morning*. She couldn't have been reading at that hour, could she? So I ask you, what was she doing out there at that time?"

"Mom, how would I know? I don't even know how she died. All I know is what you've told me so far, and that isn't much."

"Well, I can tell you how she died; she had a heart attack. Apparently, she wasn't ill and she wasn't taking any special medications. So many seniors these days take far too many pills; I don't know why doctors prescribe so many. There's a woman down the street from us who takes 12 pills a day. Can you believe that?

There was a show on the TV just last week about seniors and how they abuse…"

"Mother, for crying out loud."

"Anyway, as far as I know, Lavinia didn't take any prescriptions. At least that's what he told me, the man up there who called to let me know she died, and he said she just fell off the bench onto the grass. Her heart gave out. That happens to old people like us. I can only wish for the same myself. So, that's about all I know at the moment. I'll make some more phone calls. If there's anything I can add, I'll call you back."

"Don't worry about calling me back, mother; I won't be here for the rest of the day. I'm going out and I won't be back until late tonight."

Damon arrives at Naomi's apartment just before six; they embrace at the door. She quickly recruits him to slice some tomatoes and dice onions and green peppers for the salad. Naomi had prepared a shrimp quiche figuring that something light would be best under the circumstances. She hands him a bottle of his favourite Merlot and a corkscrew. "Here, this is your department."

Occasionally, the meal is interrupted by thoughts of Aunt Lavinia. Naomi shares some of her experiences from her recent visit, only a month before during Damon's 60th birthday party.

"Lavinia was so funny while the three of us girls were swimming"

"Girls?" Damon asks. "Aunt Lavinia was in her late 70s, and Betsy must be getting close to that."

"Betsy is only 66. I only know that because we were talking about the differences in people's ages, like yours and mine for example."

"I can imagine that would have been one of the topics that Aunt Lavinia brought up."

"Yes, I think you're right. She did start the conversation, right after they threw me into the water from the dock."

Damon recalls a conversation he had with Doctor Kinderman.

"She once asked me whether it's possible that the beautiful woman in my nightmares, the one I call Aphrodite, represents the woman I've always wanted, or could she even represent a real person, maybe even someone I've already met and have been fantasizing about."

"And what did you answer?"

"Although the beautiful woman in my nightmares doesn't represent anyone I can identify, there were a couple of times when Aphrodite transformed into Aunt Lavinia. When I told Doctor Kinderman that, she asked whether I experienced wet dreams or had erections after I realized it was Aunt Lavinia, and I had to admit to the erection but told her that I felt pretty weird about it all."

He clears his throat and continues. "I used to wonder why Aunt Lavinia appeared in my nightmares until I recalled an incident many years ago when I was staying at the cottage. I was probably only 17 or 18 at the time, well, maybe 20 or 21. I know it was before I was married because Aunt Lavinia and I didn't communicate for several years after that. One night I couldn't sleep so I walked down to the lake. It was totally dark but for light from the Milky Way. I heard something splash in the water; I thought at first it was a muskrat or a beaver. I looked closer and discovered Aunt Lavinia swimming; she was in the nude and I saw everything. I do admit to feeling awkwardly excited and I continued to stare at her for some time until I realized that there was another person there as well. I left before finding out just who the other person was. I assumed that Aunt Lavinia had a secret boyfriend, and why shouldn't she; she deserved someone else in her life. Aunt Lavinia was a wonderful caring person. But I admit; the image of her naked became indelible. You know, even though she was my aunt, she was a beautiful woman. I feel odd about saying this now, but she had a fantastic body when she was younger. Ever since that time, I've reacted differently whenever she's hugged me or kissed me, but not in a perverted way or anything like that. It was more like I felt embarrassed because I knew more than I should have known. I don't think she was ever aware that I saw her that night and I never mentioned it to her, or to anyone else for that matter. I suppose it's possible that what I witnessed that night has affected my nightmares."

Damon's voice breaks. He pauses, sips some Merlot.

"And now she's gone. How can I even think about that image of her naked? Besides, that was years ago. But, I still can't erase it from my mind. And who was the other person? Aunt Lavinia never mentioned a man in her life, and we used to talk about everything, she and I. Of course, I never told her about seeing her swimming that night; maybe she kept secrets from me as well. With her gone now, I assume that any secrets will be taken to the grave with her."

15

It is a simple, but joyous, celebration of Lavinia's life. She had lived without religious convictions of any sort and she abhorred pomp and circumstance. Her only wishes... no, they were demands... were that she was to be cremated and her ashes distributed across the cottage property under the ancient pines, where she savoured life through her books, music, thoughts and deeds. Some ashes were to be saved for the lake where she swam and bathed.

The celebrants who gather about the lawn and the porch of Lavinia's cottage are many and diverse: students of all ages who, over the years, attended her classes, other teachers, business leaders, local politicians, members of the Little Theatre group, artists of all media, and of course, her immediate family: Damon and Naomi, Helen and Charles, Phil and Virginia, Graham, and a 40-something woman, whom Damon assumes to be Graham's wife or partner.

There are tears of sadness and loss because everyone here misses her friendship and compassion, and there are tears of joy and laughter for her outgoing personality and inescapable humour.

Damon is the first to speak. "Aunt Lavinia was the closest friend I ever had." His voice cracks and his throat tightens against the arrival of tears, but he continues. "She was the one, the only one, who inspired me to pursue my greatest love and passion, my music, and she encouraged me every step of the way, from my first lessons to my most recent concerts. The most wonderful times of my life were spent right here at this cottage, Aunt Lavinia's home. It is where my life began, where I first experienced the joy of feeling independent, and where I learned that life is what you make it."

From his pocket, Damon withdraws a white candle and a lighter borrowed from one of the smokers in attendance. Upon lighting the candle, he begins singing a Capella, "We'll meet again, don't know where, don't know when, but I know we'll meet again some sunny day." Once again the tears choke him. "This white candle is for good luck. That's what Aunt Lavinia always told me before she started singing that song. With this white candle I wish her luck wherever she may travel." Damon's eulogy is followed by sporadic applause; his eyes sting with tears.

The peak of the celebration belongs, however, to the powerful, adoring words from her friend, Betsy McGinnis, the demure town librarian and beloved wife of Daniel McGinnis, the school principal and Aunt Lavinia's former boss.

"For those of you who don't know me, and I expect that constitutes a very small number, my name is Betsy McGinnis, and I'm a longtime, very close friend of Lavinia Hope, whose life we are celebrating today. For almost 40 years Lavinia and I have shared a secret that we have kept from all of you. On this very significant day, I am proud to reveal that secret."

There is uneasy shuffling among the celebrant mourners.

"Lavinia and I shared a wonderful relationship, one that has survived these many years, despite the trials we went through and the daily anxieties that our love for each other would be discovered and turned into the laughing stock of this shallow-minded community."

There are gasps and coughs from several of the gathered, and a few snickers from others. Damon snatches a glimpse of his father gesturing rudely toward Phil.

Daniel McGinnis, Betsy's husband, abruptly storms from the celebration to avoid embarrassing comments, the rear wheels of his Oldsmobile spraying gravel from the driveway toward the coach house.

Betsy charges on in spite of her husband's display. "Today, moments like this are referred to as, 'coming out of the closet,' but there was no such opportunity when Lavinia and I first found each other; the closet door was locked: by society, by common misbeliefs, by blindness and bigotry, and by religion."

"Lavinia Hope was my teacher in Grade seven, when I was merely 12 years old. She taught me that literature was the door to knowledge and a better understanding of the world, a lesson that would shape my entire life from that moment on. After completing high school, and subsequently college, I returned to Muskoka with my new husband, Daniel, whom you all know as the former Principal of our beloved elementary school, to continue with my love of books as the new Town Librarian."

"Because Lavinia was still considered an outsider, or as the locals called her, a cottager, she faced the jeers of the original settlers like those from my own family. Her fresh, innovative teaching methods were met with vocalized apprehension and severe criticism. Her name was bantered about in disgusting language in the pool hall, the dairy bar, and even the council chambers."

"Lavinia used to come into the library to talk and to discuss the world of literature with me. She asked me to order books we didn't have, and we were struggling with a budget of zero dollars, so she contacted some of her friends in the city to send us any books they were finished with, and we started to stock the shelves of our meager collection of board-approved books with more contemporary volumes. Catcher in the Rye comes to mind."

Suddenly, Betsy's courageous exterior begins to crumble. She stops talking to allow a bevy of tears to dissipate before resuming.

"Lavinia Hope and I, Betsy McGinnis, were lovers. We promised each other, that when one of us dies, the survivor would publicly declare our undying love for each other. I loved her more than life itself. To stand here, under these giant old pines, where she and I spent so many hours together is extremely emotional."

Betsy pauses again to cry openly; she makes no effort to hide her tears. The other celebrants sit patiently and silent, except for a young woman, a former student of Lavinia's, who approaches Betsy with a handkerchief and wraps her arm around Betsy's shoulder in an act of moral support.

Betsy turns to the young woman and whispers, "I'm alright; really I am. There are just a few more things I want to say, then I'll step down."

The young woman returns to her seat. Betsy wipes more tears away. Damon can't help but think that poor Betsy is compressing 40 years of anxiety and secrecy into a ten-minute release like the pressure from a teakettle, whistling out through a small spout as steam.

"I know that many of you, as soon as you heard that Lavinia and I were lovers, imagined all sorts of behaviours that to you, are aberrant, immoral, and at the very least, socially and religiously unacceptable to your diminutive minds. To satisfy your imaginations, yes, Lavinia and I had physical sex and we had it often, right here by the way, here under the pines where we're all seated now. I might add that it was magnificent sex; we were made for each other. But there were so many more wonderful moments here when we were not having sex. We took midnight strolls around the grounds arm-in-arm, we sat on this very bench together, feeling the warmth of each other against us, we read the most intelligent and inspiring literature and talked for hours about our discoveries, we swam in the lake together; yes we were naked, weren't we Damon?"

Damon breaks down, half crying, half laughing, and feels Naomi's arm around him while patting her consoling hand against his shoulder.

"In closing, I want to challenge everyone present to open your minds and your hearts; to accept a wider diversity into your lives. Love is so much more than climbing into the sack with someone. I know this is not what many of you expected here today, but I owe this to Lavinia."

Betsy raises her wine goblet to the urn that's placed next to a photographic portrait on their special bench. "I love you so much Lavinia."

Some of the celebrants do the same. There are among the mourners, those who choke back tears and those who just choke. One of Lavinia's former students, young enough to have been in one of her final classes before she retired, stands up and offers a brief, but quietly noticeable applause at the finale of Betsy's eulogy. Others seize the opportunity to leave or to refill their glasses. At any rate, the celebration of Aunt Lavinia's life comes to a close.

Damon is initially surprised, although not shocked, at Betsy's delivery. By the time Betsy steps down, Naomi is smiling discreetly in a gesture of solidarity. She turns to Damon and whispers, "What a courageous woman Betsy is, to publicly declare her love after all those years." She leans her head on Damon's shoulder and squeezes his hand. He feels her tears drop onto his neck.

Damon whispers to Naomi. "It was her; it was Betsy. She was the one swimming with Aunt Lavinia that night when I saw her naked. And, they both knew all along that I had seen them. Why did she keep that a secret?"

"For the same reason you did, I'm sure." Naomi replies.

There are no further volunteers to offer their thoughts after Betsy's proclamation. She is too big an act to follow. Some people leave, but a few stay on to share their memories with each other. Most of the conversations begin with, "I remember the time when Lavinia and I were…" She was very much a member of the community, which made it all so bewildering that she and Betsy had been able to conceal their relationship from all of them.

A short stout man approaches Damon, introducing himself as Oberon Claxton.

"As her attorney, I have taken care of your aunt's… um… Lavinia's… affairs for many years. You are probably eager to return to the city after the affairs are completed so I thought it would be more appropriate if I presented these documents to you at this time."

He produces a brown envelope, addressed, 'Damon Farrell, on the event of my death.' Elsewhere on the front of the envelope, in large bold letters, is the word, 'PERSONAL.'

The attorney continues, "I can assure you that all of the information contained herein has been handled with the utmost in discretion and secrecy. Not even my secretary has any knowledge of these documents."

Damon accepts the envelope. "Thank you Mr. Claxton. After the events of this afternoon, however, I can't imagine there being anything more that would surprise me."

Mr. Claxton raises his eyebrows. "Hmmm. Before you peruse the contents of this envelope, I suggest that you find a quiet spot to reflect upon your findings. Please feel free to contact me at any time concerning these matters." Oberon Claxton hands Damon one of his business cards. "My office is in my home. I repeat, call me anytime." They shake hands before the attorney departs the premises.

Damon opts to wait until everyone has left before examining the envelope so he deposits it, for the meantime, into a drawer in Aunt Lavinia's desk. A black and white framed photograph of she and Betsy McGinnis stares up at him from the drawer; both are laughing, their arms wrapped around each other's waist and their heads touching. Damon stands the photograph on the top of the desk and places his envelope inside the drawer.

Betsy, who has been watching Damon since Oberon Claxton handed him the envelope, enters the cottage.

"Damon, I have a request. If it's alright with you, I'd like to be here when you scatter Lavinia's ashes under the pines."

"I would have it no other way, Betsy. It seems that you know my aunt better than any of us ever did. I should warn you however; it may take some time before I get around to doing that. I'll have to be in the right frame of mind, I'm afraid."

"I don't think that I'm ready to set her free yet either, Damon. Just call me whenever it's time." Seeing the photograph displayed, she adds, "Thank you Damon, for bringing the photo out. Usually it stands proudly on Lavinia's desk, just where you placed it, but I thought it better, under the circumstances, that it remain hidden, at least until I delivered my eulogy this afternoon. I hope I didn't shock you too much."

"Well, I must admit to being surprised, but shocked? No, I wouldn't put it that way. Aunt Lavinia was always doing something that others found difficult to accept. I'm certain that your declaration today has had a similar effect on some people."

"Oh I know it has." Betsy pauses to study Damon's facial expression. "I will probably be looking for a new place to live after Daniel's reaction to my news." There is another short pause.

"Damon, may I speak to you about some other information. I'm sure you will soon be reading the material in the envelope that Oberon Claxton presented to you, but there's something that won't be in there, and I think you should know about it. You must agree not to tell anyone else about what I'm about to reveal. There are only three others beside yourself, who currently share this information. One of them is myself, of course, and Mr. Claxton. The third person is Doctor Flanagan, Lavinia's personal physician."

"What information can there possibly be that demands such secrecy?" Damon asks.

"Lavinia didn't die of a heart attack, Damon. Oh, sure, her heart stopped beating, and I don't doubt for a minute that's what finally killed her. But what you don't know is that she had terminal cancer, and has known about it for more than six months. Doctor Flanagan has been looking after her, and has made sure that her pain was kept under control. You see, Lavinia wanted to die with dignity, and with all of her faculties, so she refused chemotherapy and radiation. She didn't want to become reliant on anybody else; you and I are the only close friends she had, although she had many friendly acquaintances. So, she arranged her own death, even choosing it down to the final moment."

"How can a secret like that be kept in such a small town?" Damon asks.

"Lavinia and I have been living in a secret world for many years. So have Oberon Claxton and Doctor Flanagan, if you follow my drift." Betsy winks. "Doc Flanagan and Oberon were both avowed bachelors, and they often accompanied Lavinia and me to social events, and occasionally we went out to dinner as a foursome. The townspeople just assumed that we were double dating, Lavinia with Doc Flanagan and Oberon with me. I always thought it strange that the community could accept that I might be having an affair with a man outside of my marriage. Of course, once those evenings came to a close, I came here with Lavinia and the Doctor spent the night with Oberon. It was a perfect ruse. "When you have secrets to keep; it is much easier to keep secrets."

Damon reflects, "I was here only a month ago, for my birthday. She didn't seem ill at the time; in fact, she was livelier than I'd seen her for years. When the three of you went swimming in the lake, it sounded like you were having an orgy; you told jokes and laughed. I thought you were all drunk, or doing drugs or something."

"That was a façade in a way, and Lavinia was taking some heavy medication. Oh, don't misunderstand me; Lavinia really had a great time, but she also put on a magnificent show. You know how she is with theatre and drama. That was her best performance ever, even better than Stella. When you and Naomi returned to retrieve her overnight bag, Lavinia wasn't merely sleeping; Doc Flanagan had just left when you arrived. He had given her a strong sedative that put her out almost immediately. She was under enormous stress that day. First, there was her cancer, which she was trying to hide from you, and, as you know, it was your 60th birthday, and she wanted everything to turn out special. It was also an important day for her in another way but, until you read the documents Oberon Claxton gave you, I'd rather reserve comment. Lavinia never stopped talking about your last visit, until the night she died. She also loved Naomi; they got along wonderfully. It's truly unfortunate that she didn't last longer so she could get to know Naomi better. They could have been such good friends."

"Naomi loved Aunt Lavinia as well. That's why I invited her to come to the celebration today."

"I'm so glad she came." Betsy's eyes suddenly fill with tears but she insists on continuing. "I must tell you the whole story. Earlier on the day Lavinia died, Doctor Flanagan came to the cottage. I was here with her when he arrived, and I stayed with her on the bench until the very end, in the wee hours of the morning. It was very peaceful and emotional for us both. We sat with our arms entwined. Lavinia made me promise that I would watch over you to make sure you were OK with everything and, I might add, to do whatever I can to keep you and that beautiful Naomi together. Lavinia just loved that girl. Whatever you do, don't let age differences, nor any other differences keep you apart. She always used to say to me when things appeared dark, 'Love is more important than any details that threaten to get in the way,' and the way I see it, Damon, you two are deeply in love. Do whatever it takes."

Betsy finally gives Damon a well-intended embrace and leaves him alone in the cottage, where he succumbs to weeping. By the time he returns outside, Betsy and many of the other celebrants have departed. He locates Naomi wandering alone under the pines. She carries her shoes in her hand and stares trancelike at her bare feet, walking gingerly in a dancing manner, as if contemplating every step she takes to be interrupting consecrated ground.

Damon decides to leave her alone with her thoughts and returns to the brown envelope. Inside, there is a smaller white envelope labeled, 'Damon,' and another packet titled, 'Last Will and Testament.' He opens the small envelope with his name imprinted on it and begins to read. 'My dearest Damon,' it starts. As he reads further, his eyes swell with tears; his body trembles. There is already more than he can handle in the first paragraph but he reads on regardless.

> *My dearest Damon:*
>
> *The time has come when you are entitled to know the truth. I am your birth mother. I was barely 17 when you were born. The day was August 19, 1942; I have remembered it every day since. It was an otherwise dark and somber day in our lives, with the only exception being the brightness you brought me when you entered this life. Your father, George Farrell, the younger brother of Charles, died that very day on the beach at Dieppe.*
>
> *I was left alone with you. The news that George had died caused me to plunge into a severe depression, for which I required many months of hospitalization. George and I had a*

special relationship, one that we could never discuss with others. On one level we were so much in love, but I also had other feelings that went beyond loving him alone; feelings that society could not tolerate at the time. Everything was so different then. A single mother was faced with extreme difficulty having to balance some kind of a menial job with raising a child, not to mention my additional problems with depression.

Charles and my older sister, Helen, insisted that I permit them to adopt you. They agreed to raise you and to allow me as many opportunities to be with you as humanly possible. On some occasions it was extremely difficult to bear, especially on your birthdays, with the joy of having you with me conflicting with the sadness of missing my beloved George, but I always looked forward to seeing you and to share those precious moments together. Your father's memory was wrapped up in those white candles, the good luck candles that I lit and shared with you each birthday. This will help explain to you why Charles and Helen never attended your birthday parties; it was to be our special day together, just the three of us. I have done everything possible to provide you with an education and to allow you to pursue the life you most desired. I'm so proud of you, Damon. You have brought me such joy. Please be kind to Betsy and give as much love as you can muster up to that new friend of yours, Naomi. She's a wonderful person, definitely a keeper.

I will love you eternally.
Mother

Damon places the letter down on the desk next to the photograph and weeps openly, first from the shock of reading the words as if they were being spoken directly to him by Lavinia's own voice, then in a fit of anger. He storms out of the cottage, passing Naomi in the doorway.

"Where are you going Damon?" She pauses, recognizing the change in his manner. "What's wrong? Are you OK?"

He grunts something to her about going to the lake and being alone for a while. She knows something about wanting to be alone so she lets him leave without further questions.

His intention to be alone at the lake is suddenly altered; he turns abruptly toward the main road where his mother and fath... no... where Helen and Charles are staying at the Lodge. On his approach, he recognizes Charles' laughter emanating from an open window facing the parking lot.

"Wasn't that the cat's ass, Helen? Your little sister was a lesbo all the time. I should have known, the way she pampered Damon and all. Can you imagine how he would've turned out if she'd raised him all by herself? Heh-Heh-Heh!"

Damon hears Helen trying to get a word in edgewise, "That's not fair, Charles, she looked after all his lessons, she paid for Damon's university and..."

"Yeah right, in a sissy program like music. There's no way I was going to support that. It's a miracle he ever earned a living. He could've come directly into the business with me, or gone into his own business like Phil did, but no, he had to listen to that sister of yours and all her crazy ideas."

Damon's rage forces him to burst into their room, slamming the door behind him.

"You bastards," he shouts before realizing that Phil and Virginia are there as well. He turns to them. "Did you know about this all along too?"

"Don't be stupid Damon," Phil starts. "We all just found out about it today, the same as you, when that stupid bitch went on about them being queer and all."

Damon's face turns scarlet. "I don't give a shit about that. I'm talking about me being adopted, and you all knew about it."

He turns to Charles. "And you... you were responsible for it by insisting that she — my mother — give me up to be adopted and raised by you assholes. You son-of-a-bitch."

156

"You're the son-of-a-bitch, not me." Charles snickers toward Phil before continuing. "Lavinia went out and got herself pregnant to that little prick of a brother. He was hardly old enough to tie his own shoes."

"If he was old enough to serve and die for his country, then he was old enough to be a father. You were already a father. Is that why you chickened out and stayed at home?"

"I was being a responsible father, not only to Phil, but then I took on the extra responsibility of you as well. The least you could have done to pay me back was to be a man."

"What were you doing when my father was dying on the beach?"

Helen quickly interjects. "Please, both of you. Stop now. This is leading nowhere. I don't think we should pursue this any more."

From the tone of Helen's voice, Damon realizes there is more that he hasn't been told. He plunges headlong into his last unanswered question. "Where were you, and what were you doing, when my real father was dying on the beach at Dieppe? Tell me that."

Charles' mouth moves to answer but no sounds emerge. He mutters and stammers incoherently for the right words.

Helen speaks out on Charles' behalf. "I think it's time to put everything on the table, Charles. He's going to find out about it eventually."

Damon questions Helen. "About what? I can hardly wait. It's not like I haven't learned a few new things already today. Go ahead. Hit me again."

At this time, Phil forces his two cents worth. "Why don't you get the hell out, Damon? Can't you see that…?"

"Phil, fuck right off. You're not my big brother any more. You're nothing but a distant cousin and the bigger the distance the better it'll be."

Helen, who has never heard language like that from Damon, starts again.

"Please be calm, Damon, at least as calm as possible under the circumstances." She inhales deeply before starting the story. "When every young boy was enlisting, Charles and George went together to sign up. Charles convinced George that it was the best thing to do, although George never wanted to serve. Charles did, and he convinced George to sign up by telling him that everybody would laugh at him and call him a coward if he stayed home. I remember the day before they were to report for their medicals, they got drunk together and talked well into the night about how they were going to single-handedly end the war. They said that the world would remember 'The Farrell Brothers.' Well, they went to their medicals and when they came home, I could see the look on Charles' face. When I asked him what went wrong, he said that he hadn't passed the medical. 'Flat feet,' he said."

From the sofa, Charles interjects, "What the hell did it matter whether I had flat feet or not?"

"Charles, please don't interrupt me," Helen advises. "George was accepted, he passed with flying colours."

Helen stops; tears flow freely down her cheeks. She weeps openly, struggling to utter her final words; "Charles was devastated when we heard the news about George. And poor Lavinia, she just lost it. It was only a couple of days after you were born when the names of the dead started appearing in the newspaper. We had to do the right thing, and that was to take care of her new baby. When Lavinia kept having problems, we talked to her about adopting you, and she finally agreed that it would be the best thing for you. We tried to do the right thing always, but Charles, you see, he had to correct what he felt guilty for, the death of his younger brother George at Dieppe. He wanted you to be a man, so you would have the strength that he never had. The bravado, that was just a smokescreen to help him keep his sanity. And that's all I'm going to say! Don't ask me another question, and Charles; I don't need to hear any more crap from you. The same goes for you Phil, and for that disgusting little tart you call a wife."

Damon holds the woman who posed as his mother for 60 years and allows her tears of shame to rain over his shoulder. He pats her gently on the back. "It's all right Mom. It's OK. I understand everything now."

Charles remains focused on the floor, avoiding eye contact with everyone. Virginia looks at Phil, and he ignores her, staring instead at some obscure spot elsewhere in the room.

"Enough said," is all Damon can utter. He leaves the Lodge. It's time for him to spend some time at the lake.

16

Sitting quietly on the bench at the end of Lavinia's wooden dock, Damon peers over the lake; small wavelets wash under the dock and splash like clockwork against the rocks and pebbles. If only his life could be as simple as the waves, he thinks, steady and unwavering. In one day, his entire existence has been turned inside out, overwhelming him with layers of bewilderment. While sitting alone, he questions more than ever before, just who in hell he really is. Every new answer introduces a plethora of fresh questions.

Naomi arrives toting a picnic basket. She sits next to him. "Isn't it about time we have something to eat? I brought some fresh bagels, a wonderful cheese I found in the cottage, and a pair of wine goblets just waiting for a creative man to uncork this... Abracadabra... bottle of fine Merlot." She extricates the bottle from the picnic basket as a magician produces a rabbit from his top hat. "Ta-da!"

Despite his overloaded mind, Damon manages a smile, before uploading his thoughts to Naomi. "I had parents this morning, who have become a somewhat estranged aunt and uncle; a much-beloved aunt who became my mother upon her death; an older brother who is now my despicable distant cousin, and..." he hesitates, turning to look directly into Naomi's eyes, "a beautiful, intelligent, talented companion who understands my every thought and deed."

"You flatter me. I don't deserve that."

Damon pulls the cork on the Merlot, and pours two glasses. He offers a toast, "To Lavinia. May her spirit live forever in our memories."

Naomi reciprocates, "to Lavinia."

Damon looks directly, and meaningfully, into Naomi's eyes, "to us."

After their initial toasting, Naomi suggests taking a stroll along the shoreline. "We'll take our wine with us, and then, when we return, we'll have our picnic, right here." She removes her shoes. "The sand feels so sensuous underfoot. I love it when it sifts between my toes."

They lock their arms together leaving one free hand for the Merlot. Little is said between them as they stroll the sandy shore but their minds churn with thoughts, the kinds of thoughts that must eventually become words to share.

Once back at the dock, Naomi spreads a brightly coloured beach blanket large enough for two. In the middle of the blanket she places the picnic basket and starts rummaging through it.

"I hope you don't mind, Damon. I found this envelope on Lavinia's desk, next to the letter you left open there." She hands him the folded letter and the envelope containing the Last Will and Testament. "I thought you might eventually calm down enough to read these so I brought them along."

"What do they say?" Damon asks.

"How do I know? I don't read other people's mail."

Before he pries open the envelope, Damon passes the already opened letter to Naomi. "Here, why don't you read this letter while I'm looking at the will? You'll find it very interesting." He scans through the document, reading specific passages aloud. "To my son and sole heir, Damon Farrell, I leave my entire estate." Damon gazes, with a blank stare, toward the water.

Naomi reads the letter but remains silent, waiting for him to utter something. Minutes pass; nothing is said.

Damon straddles an emotional fence between anger and love: anger for spending his best years believing that Lavinia was his aunt when he could have lived here with her as a family and known the truth about his real father; love for the many years of encouragement, beauty and enjoyment given him by Lavinia who was the only family supporter of his passion for music and the only person he could go to when there seemed to be little hope at home.

Damon finally speaks, "Life is too damned short, Naomi. You're too young yet to appreciate that but, at my age... well, there's not enough left to make it work."

"Believe me Damon, I do appreciate everything you're saying, even at my tender age of 28. There's been a lot of discomfort passing through my years as well, and I don't want to waste any more of them."

"Would you mind replenishing my glass, Naomi? I need some emotional fortification, and wine always seems to serve the purpose well."

"There's more than just wine, you know. I'm here to help as well. I'll do whatever I can; whatever you want."

"I know. Believe me, I know. You're the best and closest friend I have, in fact, probably the best friend I've ever had, and now, you're my only friend. You're always there for me. Thank you so much." He touches her glass in a toast, "To best friends."

The sun eases closer to the horizon painting a magenta coating on the few clouds above and transforming Naomi and Damon into a warm evening glow. They dine on bagels and cheese, quietly soaking up the last light of the day, and pondering the changes in their lives over the past 24 hours. Damon stretches back, his eyes close, the miniscule waves trickle into his mind's ear as steadily and predictable as a Vivaldi season.

"I guess I'll soon own the cottage. I wonder if I'll spend much time here, or whether I'll eventually sell it."

"Don't ever think of selling the cottage, Damon. You'll need it someday, if just to get away from the chaos of the city and of work. Besides, you have some wonderful memories here."

"The *only* good memories I have *are* from here," Before waiting for a response from Naomi, he corrects, "I'm wrong. I've also had many great memories with you."

"I sincerely hope that we can have many more great memories. Maybe we can have some of them right here, at the cottage, what do you think about that?"

"That'd be nice… yeah, that sounds really nice."

"This has been a tough day for you, Damon. I have an idea that may help, but you'll have to trust me. You do trust me don't you?"

"Of course I do. If I can't trust you, who can I trust?"

"Good!" Naomi jumps up from the towel, smiling. "Because I want you to go swimming with me, right now. It'll do us both some good." She begins to undress.

"Swimming? Here? Right now? I'm a terrible swimmer, did I ever tell you that?"

"The water is calm. Look at those little wavelets. It's not that deep. Come on, Damon. It'll help you get rid of your fears and anxieties. This is as good a time as any. Appreciate today as a day of change; or as the saying goes, get back on the bicycle."

"I don't even own a bicycle, and I certainly don't own a bathing suit."

"So what?" Naomi contests. "It's going to be dark soon, there's nobody here but the two of us, and besides, I've seen you naked before."

"Go on. Where have you seen me naked?"

"I'll never tell. It's my secret."

"Get out of here. You're just putting me on." He presses her for an explanation. "Where have you seen me naked?"

"In my dreams."

Naomi finishes undressing and starts walking down the dock toward the water. Damon watches her hips and buttocks rise and fall. Before diving into the water she turns to see if he's following. He reluctantly sheds his clothes and joins her, opting for the ladder instead of diving in. She takes his hand in hers to lead him past waist-deep water, before releasing her grip. Damon stands alone; he feels the wavelets splashing against his armpits. Naomi dives under, disappearing for a moment before resurfacing further away, where she treads water, looking back at him.

"Come on Damon. It's wonderful out here. There's nothing to be afraid of. Look" She stands up; the water only reaches her waist. "Look, I'm standing on a sandbar."

Damon's eyes become fixated on her breasts. Water from her hair cascades down over them. He allows the image of this beautiful woman, his closest friend, to fill his body.

"I'll get there. Just give me a chance. I'm pretty slow." Damon finally submerges and attempts to dogpaddle toward her but she disappears, only to resurface once again, reminding him of a loon avoiding a pursuing canoeist, submerging and reappearing in another unexpected location.

Damon attempts to stand up, but discovers there is nothing tangible to set his feet on. He dogpaddles but can't maintain the momentum and slips under the surface, his feet scrambling for a footing and his lungs gasping for oxygen, inadvertently inhaling some water. Darkness surrounds him, sucking him through to another reality. He returns to the demon that has haunted him his entire life.

* * *

There is the usual cacophony, the sounds and smells and pains of battle. Tanks grind through the rocky shore going nowhere but burrowing deeper into the rocks. Rifle fire and shells zip and blast away while comrades fall all around me. Suddenly a flash of light penetrates the side of my head and takes a piece of it away.

I cry out for help, but there's no response. I can no longer breathe. Blood oozes from my wounds. Open-eyed corpses, the flotsam and jetsam of man's most aberrant behavior, float beneath the surface like jellyfish, brushing against me, staring into my eyes. Am I just one of them?

Suddenly it's quiet. The surf ebbs and flows without sound, the dancing spoils of oil, gas, urine and blood pirouette above me on the surface, backlit by the overcast sky like gossamer webs on a dewy morning. A choir begins to sing in haunting but fascinatingly beautiful dissonance. As I submit to the drifting undertow, a tunnel of brightness appears in the distance. The large fishlike shape approaches as anticipated, the brightness encircling it like an aura. It ventures forward without fear, its dorsal fin swaying slowly but determinedly left to right circling my pathetic remains before veering away. Before it disappears, it turns to peer once more in my direction. The beast is transformed into a beautiful sensuous woman — my Aphrodite. She treads water before returning, drawing closer and closer until she becomes accessible to my touch, but my arms don't obey. Her eyes remain fixed on mine; wondrous eyes that beckon me to join her. Her body, naked and desirable, framed by a waist-length coiffure, wavers and dances for me alone in an aquatic ballet. I yearn for her. I reach out to touch her with the last energy remaining but she evades me. I feel abandoned with my excitement unrequited, the only form of life remaining in this pathetic human structure.

She turns once again, my Aphrodite, swimming and dancing her way back toward me until I feel her lips touching mine and her breasts pressing against my chest. I open my eyes to the young beautiful face of Lavinia. I have become my father; I am George Farrell, dying in the arms of his beloved Lavinia, left only with excitement enough to make love to her one last time. But I'm unable. My hardness quickly dissipates at the vision of my mother. She ages decades before my eyes. No longer beckoning me with her sensuous dancing, she swims away. The aura fades from view. I am left with only the darkness and the memories.

I prepare to cede to the elements, any final hope of resurfacing. My body falls limp and settles on the weedy carpet deep below the surface. I stare up toward a dim light. Amid the corpses and debris, a silhouetted figure approaches against the light. Her sensuous body dances above mine: her breasts and her dark hair brush against me as she leans to kiss my lips. Like my Aphrodite and my father's Lavinia before, Naomi's embrace consumes me with desire.

* * *

Naomi hoists Damon to the surface where he gasps and kicks for survival. The sandbar where they'll be able to stand above the waterline is only meters away. The last hint of light in the sky relinquishes to night and the first stars appear. They return to the dock where they stand together shivering in the evening's coolness on the timeworn boards, naked and wet, where Lavinia and her lover, Betsy, must have stood so many times before. Their eyes scan each other's nakedness, bewildered at what has just occurred. They don't dare touch but they both understand that they've experienced something together for the first time. They place their hands into each other's and hold them tight. Finally, without thought, they embrace, savouring each other for minutes without moving.

"We should put some clothes on before we freeze to death," Naomi suggests, wrapping her arm around Damon's bare waist and placing her head against his shoulder while they return to their towels on the dock.

17

The creaking of the wooden porch swing joins a chorus of crickets from the grass as darkness descends on the cottage. Damon and Naomi watch as the emergence of the Milky Way spreads millions of galaxies across the clear black sky, crisp and sharp. They attempt to balance their hot chocolates while the swing arcs to and fro, their eyes fixed at infinity in awe of the cosmic order displayed above them.

"Is there any hope for us?" Naomi asks.

"What do you mean, for us?"

"For all of us, but more specifically, you and I, and our quest for freedom. Look at all those suns, planets, moons and meteors, all organized up there, planned and executed in some monumental way to serve a purpose that we can't even comprehend. Is there any room for freedom at all? Can we, in our infinitesimal positions here on earth, break from that order and create our own unique path, or are we predestined to continue as part of some master plan?"

"We really are so insignificant aren't we?" Damon observes. "It's hard to tell whether we have any independence at all, but, just as some of those solar systems out there are nearing their demise, in fact some are already long dead, I feel compelled to do whatever I can in the short time I have left. Maybe it's good that we're so small and insignificant. That way, when we make some major change in our miniscule lives, it won't matter to the big picture. Regardless of what we do down here, that sky will be the same a hundred, a thousand, a million years from now."

Naomi nestles closer, wrapping her arm through Damon's. "I don't want to change the subject, Damon, but can I talk to you about some of my deepest personal secrets?" Naomi asks.

"I'm always open to secrets."

"But I have to ask you not to get angry or sad. These are just thoughts that I'm having and I need to talk to someone about them."

"Go for it. I promise not to be angry."

She hesitates, unsure of how to begin, until her secrets speak out for themselves.

"I believe that I'm two women within the same body. One draws me toward a man who wants and loves me, who creates an empty sensation in the pit of my stomach every time I'm with him, a hunger that craves love and that tingles whenever I feel his desire against me. I truly understand his needs and wants, and I know that I could give him the kind of love and satisfaction he deserves."

She hesitates again, offering Damon some space to inject an opinion, but he says nothing, allowing her to continue verbalizing her thoughts.

"The other woman within me has desires that no man can ever comprehend, in ways that cause me to tremble with anticipation and that elevate me above and beyond the threshold of ecstasy. I just want, and need, to be loved. I'm tired of being so bloody alone. The trouble is that I think I want both. I want to love this man as much as he wants me. I have the same desires as he does, the same needs. But how can I exist wanting both? How is that possible?"

Again Damon remains silent, sensing that the answer to Naomi's question is meant only for her to discover. They are left with the steady creaking of the swing.

"Damon, do you mind if I spend some time under the pines by myself?"

"Go for it. I understand your need to have some personal time. I do as well. I'm wiped; this day has been overwhelming for both of us. Maybe I'll doodle away on the piano for a while and then head to bed. Do you mind?"

"Not at all. We both need some personal time to absorb everything that's happened here today. Don't wait up for me, I'll come in when I'm ready."

She kisses him on the cheek before stepping off the porch, leaving her sandals behind. The soles of her bare feet leave impressions in the texture of the grass as she treads lightly, in contact with the terrain for as brief a time as possible, as if attempting to defy

168

gravity. Her steps return her to the ancient pine trees where she danced alone so softly earlier following the celebration of Lavinia's life, and where she danced a month ago for Lavinia and Betsy. From her approach Damon can appreciate that she senses an affinity with the grass, the bench, and the brown dried needles underfoot.

Damon returns inside to the piano and flutters his fingers randomly over the keyboard, touching notes and chords here and there without any specific plan or direction. The casual listener might discount Damon's pianistic ramblings as the naive product of an untrained child exploring the keyboard for the first time. To Damon, it represents an empty corridor to wander aimlessly through until some melodic motif or emotional charge redirects him through a newly opened door; it's a form of musical foreplay that may or may not lead somewhere more interesting.

To Naomi, Damon's musical doodling represents the promise of music in the process of becoming, a fresh possibility for connecting the two of them, the raw product that will stimulate her own muse to create alongside him.

Damon's foreplay evolves slowly, at first stilted but gradually easing forward, both technically and emotionally into a cohesive tonal pattern that seeks its own groove; a pulse and a skeletal mannequin upon which Damon drapes the threads of his own creation, weaving strands of melody through ever-changing warps of chordal architecture to produce a tapestry of sound that follows Naomi into the mist and mysticism of Lavinia's ancient wooded domain. Damon watches Naomi respond to the evolution in her own physical way. From the piano bench he observes her lithe body preparing to dance through a series of warm-ups and stretching exercises; her left foot resting waist high on the back of Lavinia's teak bench.

Naomi and Damon mutually accept that their muses form a common bond that transcends any need for intellectual analysis. Damon understands Naomi's inner conflict and that she is dancing to discover her truth within. His only wish is that their collaborative efforts can allow her to travel beyond the need to make choices, and instead, to lavish in the diversity, for once she attains fulfillment, there is no woman, there is no man; the muses alone will provide the satisfaction and serve to break down the barriers that challenge her. She will no longer be bound by conflict, but by a bringing together, a blending of the finest of everything; needs and desires met.

Naomi embraces all of the forces that surround her. Damon's music filters through the pines and the mist, penetrating her body and soul through the pores of her skin; the touch of the earth beneath her feet, from the dampness of the grass to the softness of the decaying pine needles layered from centuries of composting and regeneration offer hope of reclaiming her missing past; the dark stillness of the night illuminated solely by billions of pinpricks from solar systems now deceased that to this night, still spread their points of light like sowing seeds on fresh fertile soil.

* * *

Staring at the earth, the source of life, I follow its vibrating undercurrents as they pass through my soles and toes and ankles and calves and thighs and buttocks, until my entire body trembles with the fullness of its energy. Music in its most original, adventurous and emotionally-charged form strikes me from all directions, echoing from one tree trunk to another and mellowing in the low-lying mist that hangs silent and brooding in the cooling night air. My eyes rise to the firmament to observe the infinite field of stars, within each a distinct solar system, a virtual guarantee that life exists elsewhere in all its forms and stages: birth, procreation, death, decay, rebirth.

"If you're out there, speak to me. Show me a sign."

Across the sky a meteor streaks its response and my fingers stretch to catch its tail. Music, light, vibrations, an endless bounty of possibilities, together they fill my being with a desire to dance and to be free. I circle into a dizzying vortex, my arms still outstretched to the sky and my eyes focused beyond infinity.

* * *

Damon's groove settles into a steady vamp with his left hand spanning arpeggios over two octaves while his right hand hovers above the keyboard anxious to speak. When it does, it strikes down hard in a brief series of tight four and five-tone clusters before relaxing into sequences of pleasing triads and dominant sevenths that resolve logically into their tonics. His vision catches Naomi's movements across the dimly lit lawn.

Naomi's response to Damon's jagged clusters is to soften and temper their edges with subtler, more graceful adjustments to the contours of her body, gradually increasing the tension in anticipation of more harmonically pleasing changes, at which time she explodes into a kinetic swirl of erratic energy that offers counterpoint and balance to their symbiotic performance.

* * *

From the billions of stars surrounding me, two begin to move, adopting human form and flitting about as a dancing couple like a pair of Tinker Bells, ascending to astonishing heights and plunging toward earth without effort or fear; they pirouette in unison and glide into each other's arms. One of them approaches and, through the language of his body, invites me to join him. As he comes within range I accept his hand reaching out; our fingers touch and I'm drawn to him. We soar outward as far as the mind can conceive, just the two of us, alone in the night, passing through galaxies, his former partner receding from my field of vision. There is infinite space for us to dance and we soar through the night like wayward eagle feathers floating freely on a summer breeze.

* * *

Damon's fingers spatter combinations of tonal and atonal colours across the keyboard in open arpeggios and scalar segments that suggest sensations of soaring flight while they respond directly to Naomi's movements as if they are her own hands, sensitive to her muscles and tendons while she bends and contracts and pushes and pulls. They experience her pain and exuberance simultaneously; her perspiration exudes from Damon's skin and his heart pounds as she stretches beyond her limits. Damon's fingers respond directly to every nuance of her movement as they shatter into the keys; tonalities foreign to his own ears surge from the soundboard and splash across the lawn, through the mist and into the pines. With each wave of sound her body vibrates an acknowledgement and proposes alternatives with promises of escalated enthusiasm.

In a frenzy of physical activity, Naomi's fingertips scan and probe the contours of her own torso driven by the intensity of Damon's music and a sense that his very being lives within her own fingers as each chord and arpeggio is stroked. Through her own touch, Damon senses the curves and motion, which he replays to her from the cottage.

* * *

Damon's hands and fingers explore the breadth and depth of me, and I offer no resistance, moving instead, in ways that invite his tactile exploration and encourage his unrestricted access to my vulnerability. He accepts my assistance, embracing my body in synch with my desires as they wander together, his fingers and my mind, from one sensitive region to another. He draws me nearer and wraps his arms around my waist, his hands pulling my torso ever closer as we circle at a dizzying pace through the universe. Our lips touch and my body begins to melt; he wants me and I desire him. In a shower of fragmented particles we explode like a spent meteor, returning to our earthly reality. We blend together as one; the damp grass saturates the back of my cotton dress as we undulate, caressing and exploring, the dissonant jabs of Damon's music thrusting against and through me. As we unite, the sky opens into an electric display of magnificent colour; stabs of green and red and yellow strafe the northern sky, flashing and blazing from one hue to another.

From beyond the fire of the Aurora Borealis a star surges forth, the same star as danced before as Damon's partner. Lavinia emerges from the palette of brilliance and smothers me with her energy. We roll together, Lavinia and I, on the wet ground, enfolded in her spirit as we share each other in unrestricted ecstasy, exploring the curves and folds and wishes of two women as one.

My body heaves with desire, rolling from Damon to Lavinia and back again. There is no question of which one I want; I need them both.

* * *

In the northern sky, the forces of light continue to dance, at intervals slow and subtle, prolonged, sensuous and soft, all the subtleties of the spectrum casting their magic across Naomi's writhing figure. Her movements lead her through a series of gymnastics and, as the undulating hues slowly increase in intensity and tempo, the spirit of the muses grow within her, occupying every possible recess and cavity with unrelenting energy.

Without warning, bursts of light excite the sky in crackling stroboscopic shards of brilliance. Naomi's body reverberates in orgasmic response. As abruptly as it began, the light disappears, withdrawing into darkness. She is left alone, abandoned on the grass, staring upward. Exhausted and spent, her body, gleaming of perspiration, vibrates with sporadic involuntary spasms of satisfaction, and then succumbs. Between the pines, far beyond, there remain the galaxies of the Milky Way, infinite; containing all possibilities.

Still at the piano, Damon wants to go to her, to lie next to her, and to feel the vibrations of her excitement, but he accepts that it's critical for her to pursue her own path. Exhausted from a horrendously emotional day, he quietly closes the piano and retires to his room for the night. In a half-sleep he senses Naomi's footsteps climbing the stairs as she retires to her own room. Satisfied that she's safely inside, he passes into a deep sleep.

* * *

An aura of soft misty warm-toned light passes over me. I sit before a grand piano on a vast outdoor stage, playing background music suitable for the mood.

In puffs of smoke from three decorative urns placed on the ledge of the piano, they appear like genies, one following the other: Aphrodite, Lavinia, Naomi, dancing together in a ritualistic cavorting manner, giggling and touching provocatively. Their frivolity and interplay incite me to respond musically, entering into a fugal dialogue, in which they eagerly participate.

Aphrodite comes forth to perform a solo, apparently intended for me alone. Lavinia and Naomi remain back, gyrating their hips like backup singers in a Motown band. Aphrodite's performance is alluring and overtly erotic as befitting the Goddess of Love, but it lasts only a minute before she recedes into the dark unknown.

Lavinia and Naomi assume centre stage together in a suggestive tango before Lavinia leads Naomi by the hand and presents her to me as she would present a gift. They kiss in a gesture of sisterhood, then Lavinia kisses me on the cheek, curtsies, and bids me farewell, retiring into her urn.

Naomi seizes my attention, holding it for several minutes as we gaze quietly at each other. My eyes wander across her wondrous form, so perfect and finely tuned. Her hands perform a graceful maneuver reminiscent of butterflies before she departs to perform her solo. Only the two of us remain on the stage, as it is when we rehearse in the theatre. She adopts a lotus position and focuses intently before moving; I continue to admire her from a distance as her abdominal muscles inhale and exhale with absolute control and consistency.

* * *

Damon is awakened suddenly by a trio of stray dogs snarling and barking from beyond the gravel road alongside the cottage. He twists and reorganizes the pillow, smacking it several times; his clock indicates 3:06 a.m. Reality has returned. He relaxes and falls easily back into a sound sleep.

* * *

Out on the lawn, the Aurora Borealis flashes and crackles around Naomi. She dances frenetically as if purging herself of demons. I go to her. The grass is damp under my feet. She rises to embrace me but remains in her altered state. Her dress is saturated from the grass and from her perspiration; it clings to her body as a second skin, exposing details that arouse me. She eases me down to the grass and I lay flat on my back as she dances over and around me. Her lips and tongue touch my cheek, my ear, my neck but she remains aloft in constant motion; her breathing is heavy and erratic. She draws the translucent dress over her head and her hair spews water

174

droplets across my face. In only moments we are joined as one, connected in a frenzied state of ecstasy. Suddenly everything becomes passive.

* * *

Damon awakes in his bed, alone, roughing up his already battered pillow. The clock reads 3:24. For some time he lies facing the ceiling, perspiring, pondering what is real and what isn't. There are no answers. He turns on his side with hopes of returning to sleep. It arrives slowly.

* * *

Naomi and I lay together on the grass; her fingers lightly explore my body, walking as if through the Yellow Pages, touching me in spots where I have felt nothing for years.

We return to the cottage, our bodies damp and cold from the grass and the night air. Only the sounds of waves and the wind can be heard from far off in the distance. She shuts the front door behind us and there's a sudden silence. One of the steps creaks as we ascend the stairs and pass together under the sign, 'Damon's Private Room.' She allows her dress to fall freely from her body onto the wide-planked pine floor, and slips between the sheets of my bed. Her body presses against mine and suddenly we are warm.

A deep moan emanates from my throat; my body turns toward her. Her hand follows the contours of my stomach causing involuntary twitches before settling on its destination. My body responds. Unlike the urgency of our earlier outdoor intercourse, we move calmly, trading gestures and whispering soft words. Our carnal magic is performed on each other utilizing every attempt to avoid the inevitable until, once reached, we share our gratification before relinquishing to exhaustion.

* * *

The first hint of morning light diffuses through the sheer curtains on the bedroom window. The luring essence of coffee brewing downstairs draws Damon from the warmth of his sheets to the kitchen. He walks up behind Naomi and wraps his arms around her; she turns and presses against him. They kiss.

"Did you sleep well, Damon?" she probes.

"Like a log," Damon answers.

Naomi chokes on her piece of toast.

"How about you? Did you finally get some sleep?" Damon asks.

"It was wonderful," she beams, pouring his first cup of java, equal in strength and taste to the dark roast he prefers at their favourite café.

"You seem very happy and glowing this morning." Damon flatters.

Naomi approaches him and wraps her arms tightly around him. "I've had a wonderful and insightful night and you played a very big part in it. I've been able to come to several conclusions but I'll need to consult with you about them."

"Very well. Let's have our breakfast on the porch and we can talk."

The night's events play heavily on Damon's consciousness. What was real? Did they make love last night? Was Naomi in his bed or did he merely dream all of it?

Naomi starts, "I want to play a bigger part in your life, Damon, that is, if you want the same thing. You're fully aware of my confusing situation. I'm still not certain where I stand with everything, but I do know that I feel strongly about you; nobody else has ever made me feel this way. The real problem is this; I don't think that I'll be able to totally satisfy your needs and desires and…"

"Stop right there." Damon raises the palms of his hands toward her. "As you already know, you've been on my mind considerably these last few months. We've been lucky to spend so many wonderful hours together, doing things that we both love and care about. You have your dance and I have my music. I also have *your* dance and you, *my* music. We're able to blend these passions into one when we create together. To put it bluntly, we are one hell of a team."

Naomi nods in agreement. "When I walked out under the pines last night I was searching for the real me, the person I've been seeking since I was a teenager in high school. I started to dance in the same area that Lavinia treasured and loved so much. There was a magic that overtook me; a desire to have love, in whatever fashion it came to me. The more I danced, the closer I came to a physical completion of that love; it filled my body, like when your music fills me with energy and desire. I felt the wonder of Lavinia's spirit fill me with her love, a love that I have desired since first meeting her last month, but it still wasn't enough. I felt your music against my skin and I wanted you inside me as well. I wanted it all: you, Lavinia, your music, everything at once. I danced like your Aphrodite, erotically appealing to your baser instincts and beckoning you to join me. Although I was deep in a trance, I felt your presence with me under the pines. I absorbed both you and Lavinia; we all had such urgent lust for each other's bodies and I was so proud that I could be the receptacle for all of that intensity; it was magnificent, but I needed more from you. I needed love, something that was much calmer and peaceful than the lust we first experienced."

"When I finally went to my room, it took me more than an hour to get to sleep. At one point I considered visiting you in your private domain, but decided against it, considering what a harrowing day it has been for you and how you must be exhausted. Once finally asleep however, I entered a dream. The floor outside my bedroom door creaked and the door started to open allowing a band of light to pass across the floor. The silhouette of a man stood between the door and my bed, at first remaining still and staring toward me, waiting for some sign. I assumed it was you so I pulled the sheets away from me to let you know that you were welcome. You approached and lay beside me, pulling the sheets back over us. You responded so sensuously to my touch I knew you wanted me for my love. Together, warm and moist, we made love. We were wonderful together. I have no doubts about how much you love and need me."

Damon has difficulty comprehending what she's saying to him. 'Could it really have happened? Could we really have made such wonderful love together? I thought I had just been dreaming all of it, but she experienced the same emotions, the same responses. Could it be that she was also having the same dream as I was? Is that even possible? Did she visit me, or did I visit her? Or, are our muses so powerful, that we experienced the same love through them?'

There's a long delay while they gaze in amazement at each other, their eyes focusing into the other's, before Damon offers, "Naomi... my sweet Naomi... if you're willing to take a chance on an old geezer like me, I want you to be the one I share the remainder of my life with, however short or long that may be. We have our muses to love and we have each other. Most people don't have anyone or anything. I know there'll be times when we'll question our own sanity but those times will be miniscule to the wonderful experiences we can have. Besides, we can't let our muses down can we?"

Damon and Naomi meander about the grounds with their morning coffees, stopping often to kiss and embrace. They return to the precise spot where they each believe they laid together in a state of ecstasy during the night.

He proposes, "As soon as the paperwork is completed, this cottage will be mine. I want us to know this place as where we came together in this wonderful spirit that we share, and I want us both to consider it our special place."

Naomi hugs Damon tightly in agreement.

Lavinia's remains occupy a moderately decorated urn that sits on the ledge of the grand piano in the parlour. Her wishes asked that they be scattered under the pines, but because of the many years that Damon believed her to be his aunt, he wants her ashes to stay with him for a while.

"Do you think she'll mind staying inside the cottage for a while longer, Naomi? I went for 60 years not knowing my true mother, believing that Helen and Charles were my parents. I just want to extend our time together, mother and me, just a bit longer. I'll keep her urn on the piano ledge, so she can hear me play. One day, when I'm ready, I'll spread them where she wanted."

"I want to be there when you spread them, Damon. I have developed a real affinity for your mother. She and I saw things the same way and besides, she is very much a part of us."

18

Damon finds it difficult to settle into his normal cycle following Lavinia's death. He returns to the college, still at odds over what to do about his early retirement offer. With his inheritance of Lavinia's estate looming in the near future, any financial concerns are taken care of. Besides, once he retires, he'll have access to a full pension from the college, and the Canada Pension that will arrive at the end of each month. He acknowledges that the remainder of his life will be spent without financial hardship, not that he has any intentions of becoming a big spender or world traveller. Aside from replacing his tired old Toyota, he has no immediate plans for large ticket items.

Since the celebration of Lavinia's life, when the explanation of his horrific nightmares came to light, Damon no longer seeks advice from Doctor Kinderman. Naomi, who has managed to dance her way through most of her demons, and has learned to accept her gender orientation status, still searches for her adoptive father and for the answers about her birth family.

Damon's many attempts to locate Naomi's birth parents were temporarily interrupted by Lavinia's death and the ensuing paperwork and legal matters relating to her estate, but no responses have yet to emerge. He still plans to continue the search without revealing anything about it to Naomi for fear of inciting any undue anxieties, considering that a resolution seems next to impossible.

As of September, restructuring in the music program's scheduling has eliminated the theatre from Damon's availability during the afternoons, causing him some difficulties in locating another rehearsal room, especially one that allows enough space for Naomi to dance in. Because he doesn't see Doctor Kinderman on Thursday mornings, he and Naomi no longer meet at the café where they first met.

The Concept remains the only reliable place left for Naomi and Damon to meet and talk, although, for much of the evening, Damon is working. Naomi still loves the music and attends regularly accompanied by her single glass of Chardonnay. Often they go to Damon's apartment after the gig and talk the night away.

On a Friday evening in early November, Damon arrives at the club an hour earlier at Lydia's request. She signals for him to join her at a table near the back wall, under the posters of Trane and Miles.

"Would you like something to drink, Damon?"

"Nothing too strong. I don't like to drink before a gig, you know that, Lydia."

She calls the waiter over. "Bring me a Scotch; Damon will have a CC; make them doubles."

Damon's face pinches up at Lydia's order.

"I think you'll appreciate the drink, Damon."

"I figured there was something up; you never call any meetings."

"How's everything going, Damon? Are you getting things back on track since your mother's death?"

"Yeah, I suppose, although it doesn't seem the same somehow."

"I have some news that might not go down well with you, but I want to tell you personally before you hear it from Tiny, or worse, from somebody else."

"You guys aren't splitting up again are you? I don't think I can handle that again."

"Ah, come on, Damon. You loved every minute of it."

"I didn't hear you complaining either."

"No, it has nothing to do with personal stuff; besides, things are great with Tiny and me." Lydia pauses, looking away to the side before finally turning her eyes back at Damon's and blurting it out.

"Oh shit, there's no easy way out of this. I'm selling the club, Damon. I just can't keep it going anymore. Life's too damned short; I have to do something else for a change, so Tiny and I are going to travel a bit, you know, see the country and all that."

"Are you putting it up for sale?" Damon's thoughts jump into overdrive. "If you do, let me know. I might be interested in keeping it going. I have some money coming to me from my mother's estate, and…"

"Sorry Damon. It's already sold. A guy in a suit came in here last month with an offer; it was too good to turn down. I talked to Tiny and we agreed to the sale within a few days."

"Is it somebody I know? Maybe I can go in with him. That way we can keep it going. There are no other places like this, you know that."

"It's not even somebody I know. It's some numbered corporation. They take over on New Year's Day. It won't be a jazz club anymore, Damon. I'm really sorry." Lydia tries to console Damon, but he stares into the darkness, oblivious to her attempts.

A few minutes later, Naomi enters The Concept and assumes her regular table behind the stage. The waiter brings her a Chardonnay. It's only 8:30 and Damon has already started playing. His double Canadian Club sits on the piano ledge. From his musical output, Naomi senses that something is bothering him. Somber chords emanate from Damon's left hand with the pulse of a mournful dirge, while his right hand, stretched into tenths, peppers the keyboard with churchy motifs reminiscent of Oscar Peterson's 'Hymn to Freedom.'

Damon's mind overloads with the events of the past few months; he tries to make sense of everything with Lydia's news stacked on top.

'I know that Naomi is watching me from behind the stand, and that the other guys are starting to arrive on the scene, probably wondering what's going on, except for Tiny that is; he knows.'

'Maybe I should just call it quits, right now. What's the point in going on with this? It's time to move on, to try something new. I shouldn't drag Naomi through this. She's far too young and has many great years ahead. Besides, she shouldn't be hanging around an old bastard like me; she'll waste her life. Me? I'm washed up. It won't be long before they book me into the home.'

The dirge continues as Damon's mind throbs in double time.

'The new place will probably become some goddam strip club, or some innocuous dance bar, or even a tattoo parlour; worse still, a decorous upscale latte shop with 10 dollar cups of coffee, retro chrome and vinyl tables and black and white linoleum squares on the floor.' He shudders at the thought.

Damon's hands struggle against the dirge, probing further into a minor vamp with Afro overtones like McCoy feeding fire into one of Trane's sermons, when Tiny and the drummer join him on the stand. The vamp surges on, repetitive but increasing in dynamic strength as if the search is infinite until Jesse's tenor enters with quotes from Love Supreme blending with strains of Seraphic Light. The band passes through memory lane on a quest for new directions.

There are no restrictions tonight: no nice, pleasant five-minute tunes for the audience, no birthday or anniversary requests, and no relaxation; it's straight ahead through the detours void of any destination. By the time the band wails the final turnaround and cadence, they've burned through three uninterrupted hours of sweat and relentless energy with a sense of freedom that rarely rises to the surface. No words pass between the musicians as they mop the perspiration from their faces and hands, only nods, smiles, and the collective acknowledgement that they're here. Whether during the next month and half, before Lydia closes the doors for the final time, they will re-experience the high of this night, is anyone's guess. The only important detail is that they are here tonight; this is when and where it happened. There are only memories for the few patrons and fans, for the players, and for Naomi who is weeping with empathy, her body trembling with emotion, still unaware of the circumstances that lie beneath the surface.

Naomi joins Damon in his apartment where they attempt to unravel the news. She embraces him and lets him know she cares.

"That was phenomenal tonight, Damon. I wanted to get up and dance, but I didn't think Lydia would have appreciated that, do you?"

Damon remains quiet, internalizing, trying to deal with whatever comes next. He wraps his arms around Naomi.

Naomi whispers into Damon's ear, "Would you move in with me?"

"Say what?" Damon answers with a start.

Naomi re-utters the words verbatim.

"That's what I thought you said. Why would you want to do that? I'm 32 years older than you and half bald; I have chronic pains in my lower back and my knees ache all the time. I crawl to get out of bed in the morning only to realize that I'm one day closer to turning into some incontinent, withered up old prune. Every possible disease known to man is lurking around the corner to wrap its talons into me and haul me away to the grave: heart problems, prostate cancer, and dementia, to name only the more popular choices. By the time one or more of those diseases get me, you'll only be 40 years old. Think of that for a minute. You would have wasted 12 of the most productive years of your life looking after an old prick like me."

Not the reaction that Naomi expects, she pulls back. "I thought you cared for me."

"I do care for you. I do like to be with you all the time. I'm just trying to spell out the reality for you. You don't want to be the widow of a defunct jazz musician, do you? That has to be a living Hell."

Preferring not to enter into a philosophical discussion with Damon at this time, Naomi accepts that he really does care for her and wants to be with her, so she chooses to discuss the logistics behind her proposal instead.

"By the end of this year The Concept will be history. I know that you will have no ambition to start looking for another jazz venue, and the younger guys will each go their own way. The college's retirement offer is still available. You have just played the best gig of your life and you're worried that they can only get worse from here on. Musically, this is your golden opportunity to explore the freedom you're always dreaming of. These are all signs for you to change your life, Damon, and I want to change my life as well. I've been able to expunge my guilt for what happened to my mother, and I'm learning to live with the person I turned out to be. I'm gay, and I have to live with that, but I'm in need of a partner, someone I can share my life with, and that someone is you. Let's change together. I say to hell with the differences. What does age mean anyway but just a series of man-made numbers? You don't know that you'll die within 12, or even 20, years. Hell, you may only live another five or survive until you're 100. Why be miserable? For Christ's sake, Damon, let's put our lives together. I care deeply for you, and I'm probably the only person who understands you and feels that way about you. Besides, you're the only person in the world who understands me, accepts my strangeness, and can live with my dilemma."

She realizes what she has just said to him, pauses, and then asks for clarification. "You do understand me, don't you, Damon? Please say yes."

Damon stares into Naomi's eyes for the longest time, until his own start to water. "Are you really serious, despite all the odds against this working? If you are, you had better be prepared to relocate because I've already decided that I'm moving to the cottage as soon as the probate is completed. I'm accepting the retirement offer, collecting my incentive, and buying a new car. Are you sure you'd be willing to live in Muskoka year around? It can be pretty bloody isolated and cold in the winter."

"Didn't I already say that I want to share my life with you? Hell, I may even share the sheets with you on those blustery winter nights. This is not about wanting to have wild lust-driven sex of course, but to share the happiness that has evolved between us since we met. I want to feel your warmth next to me, the coziness of the best friend I have, and have ever had. I may, however, want to wear my wool flannel pajamas, and you'll have to remove that bloody sign of exclusivity that hangs above your bedroom door if you want my warm body next to yours."

Damon, obviously acceptant of Naomi's proposal, finally asks, "When and where?"

"Are you asking me when and where I want my body next to yours? How about right now?" Naomi jests and cuddles up to him.

"Just as long as there's no talk about getting married. I've been down that road and I'm not going there again." Damon laughs.

"Can I assume that's a yes then? And, can you live with my idiosyncrasies?" Naomi waits for a response.

Damon slowly nods affirmatively. "It'll be tough sometimes, especially when Mr. Happy wants a warm friend."

"You leave Mr. Happy to me. I'll find a way to look after him."

"Then it's a yes."

Naomi jumps up and wraps her legs around Damon's waist and her arms around his neck.

"Then I suggest we have the party right downstairs on New Years Eve, which is the last night of The Concept. Let's close this joint with a hell of a party."

"What party? I thought we were just moving in together."

"What about all your friends? You can't abandon them without a party."

"I don't have any friends."

Naomi starts counting on her fingers. "Lydia, Tiny, Jesse, the waiters, the bartenders, the guys in the band, other musicians, your students, the patrons downstairs who come out every bloody night to hear the band as regular as Big Ben. We need a party, for all of us, and for The Concept."

"I'll have to clear this all with Lydia, it's her place and she's already planning a final night party."

"I've already cleared that with her, and she's all for it."

Several weeks later, Damon and the band are cooking through Wayne Shorter's 'E.S.P.' Since Lydia dropped the bomb about selling the club, the musicians have been stretching out further than before. It isn't that Lydia ever placed any restrictions on them, but there is a renewed sense of freedom among the players that encourages more adventurous or *outside* playing.

At the end of the set, Lydia approaches Damon. "There's a man sitting over there who wants to talk to you. He said it's a personal matter. Do you want to use my office?"

"Sure, thanks Lydia. I'll go over and talk to him."

The man introduces himself as Doctor Pablo Sandoval, and clarifies that he is not a medical doctor but a professor of Political Science at the University of Mexico.

"What brings you to The Concept tonight Dr. Sandoval?"

"You have brought me here, Dr. Farrell. I am following up on a search you have been making into the whereabouts of a certain Doctor Parsons."

Damon suggests, "Can we drop the formalities? There are too many doctors in the room; it's becoming confusing. Please call me Damon, and may I please call you Pablo?"

"Certainly. And may I start off by stating that there is no Dr. Parsons. I, Pablo Sandoval, am the man you are looking for."

Damon guides Pablo into Lydia's office. "Please sit down, Pablo. The Dr. Parsons I am searching for is the adopted father of a good friend of mine, Naomi Parsons, a father she believes abandoned her and her mother while she was a very young child. She would very much like to know her father, and perhaps he would also have information that can lead her to her birth mother and father."

"I am the adopted father of Naomi, but I did not abandon her as you suggest. Parsons is the maiden name of my former wife, Rebecca, who changed back to it following our separation. But, to explain what happened will result in a very long story, my friend."

"I'm due to be back on the bandstand in 20 minutes. Give me a quick abridged version for now, and maybe the epic version at a later date?"

"I will try, my friend. In the spring of 1973, my wife and I went to Santiago, Chile, where I was working on my doctorate in political science, a study into socialist movements in Latin America. Salvador Allende's Chile was of course, an ideal case to study. While we were there, I befriended a young journalist, Joachim Batista, who was of immense assistance to me in my research. He was also an active member of the Socialist Party of Chile and a personal friend of the President. On many occasions we were invited to his humble home where he and his beautiful young wife, Juanita, served up traditional meals that were delicious and memorable. The four of us became very close friends."

"Suddenly, on September 11, 1973, everything came to an abrupt, crashing end. Allende died, suicide it is claimed, and many people were arrested and killed. The National Guard smashed down Joachim's front door and trashed their home before hauling him away. Juanita was left alone with her worries and they were well founded because Joachim never returned home. Several days afterward, Juanita received a small package left anonymously at her front door. It contained Joachim's eyeball, all bloodied, with a note warning her to leave the country or suffer the same fate. It was later discovered that her young husband was among the thousands held captive at the soccer stadium and one of hundreds murdered there under the orders of the now-infamous, General Augusto Pinochet."

Some of the images suggested by Pablo ring familiar to Damon as flashes from Naomi's nightmares. Damon looks at his watch. "What does this all have to do with Naomi?"

"Following the coup, and especially after Juanita received the warning, my wife and I made plans to return to Canada, and we assisted Juanita with a refugee application. As her sponsors, she was permitted to join us on the trip, and she stayed in our home until she finalized her immigration status. She was just getting settled in Canada when she discovered that she was expecting a child, Joachim's child. She confided in my wife that the child must have been conceived on the same night, the night of the coup. That child would be Naomi."

"Pablo, I thank you for coming and sharing this with me. Naomi will be ecstatic to hear this news. She experiences severe nightmares about many of the details you mention, which swirl in and around her mind without resolution. She also has many questions about you and your wife, events that also have plagued her. It is crucially important that we talk some more? I would like for you to meet Naomi, but it would be better if I had more information before I try to arrange that."

"I can stay here at the club for a while, if you'd like. We can talk some more during your next break. Incidentally, I'm enjoying your music; I'm a huge jazz fan."

"So is Naomi… your daughter. She's become a big jazz fan. She should be arriving here soon, if you'd like to talk to her. I'll bring you together during the next set break."

"No. Not yet. I think you should hear the complete story before you make that decision, my friend. On second thought, maybe I should just finish my drink and come back another time."

"Nonsense, Pablo." Damon's curiosity is piqued and he doesn't want Pablo to escape from the room before he knows the rest of the story. "I'd prefer if you could stay around until we can talk some more. During the next break, I'll just explain to Naomi that I have some business to take care of; she won't mind. She'll stay until the music stops anyway. If you do choose to leave however, is there some place I can reach you?"

"Here, Damon. Take my business card." Pablo writes the number of his hotel on the back. "But I think I will stay for a while longer. At least long enough to see my daughter. Don't worry, I won't approach her until I have talked to you again."

"Thank you Pablo. I look forward to the next break." Damon shakes Pablo's hand and turns toward the bandstand, but stops. "Oh, and just so you don't wonder which of the dozens of beautiful women coming and going in the club is Naomi, she is the most beautiful one; tall, with dark eyes, and her black hair is cut into a bob that frames her gorgeous face. She always sits over there." Damon points to Naomi's table.

Damon returns to the stand and discusses the next set with the musicians. Naomi arrives moments later and is noticed by Pablo, who keeps his promise to maintain a distance. During the next break, Damon goes to Naomi and excuses himself. He returns to Lydia's office where he meets Pablo Sandoval once more.

"Now where were we, Pablo?"

"You are absolutely right about Naomi's beauty. She's the image of her mother, Juanita. Did I tell you that Juanita was one of the finest dancers in Chile at the time?"

"How coincidental can that be, eh?"

"Now, for more of the story. I should tell you that my wife, Rebecca, became extremely religious while we were in Chile. There are many movements there, and throughout Latin America, with missions that originate in the United States; they are quite fundamental in that they focus more of their fanatical attention on the 'eye-for-an-eye' values of the Old Testament than the 'turn-the-other-cheek' message of the New. They are also quite steeped in the so-called Moral Majority when it comes to politics. Rebecca embraced that movement with open arms, which caused some obvious differences between us, especially with my Socialist leanings. I tend to follow more atheistic beliefs, or should I say lack of beliefs."

"How does this affect Naomi's birth mother, Juanita?"

"I'm coming to that. I just thought that the religion information would help you understand the way things eventually turned out. During the last month of Juanita's pregnancy, she started having health difficulties. While doctors were more interested in the health of the unborn baby, Juanita's situation was deteriorating rapidly. It became necessary to attempt an early birth. The birth went like clockwork, but shortly after Naomi was born, Juanita hemorrhaged and died. She never saw her baby. Poor Naomi was born an orphan."

"Rebecca and I wanted so much to give the child a chance so we applied for adoption, and were approved. I should also mention that Rebecca and I were unable to have our own children, so Rebecca treated this as a blessing from God. Once the adoption was completed, Naomi came home with us and Rebecca turned into a zealous monster. Every step of childrearing had to be in line with the mandate of the church she attended and the Pastor became like a surrogate parent, approving or disapproving of every step taken. Finally, I spoke up as Naomi's father. Rebecca ran to the Pastor for advice. He told her that I, as an atheist, was worse than Satan himself, and that she needed to take steps to protect her new daughter from the likes of me.

190

With the Pastor's assistance, she fabricated lies about me that ended up costing me my relatively new position at the university here in Toronto. I eventually found another position at a university in Uruguay."

"What could she possibly fabricate that the university would believe?"

"Rebecca had the good fortune to be born into a wealthy family. Her grandfather was very successful in the early years of the 20th century in an import-export business, which was passed down to her father. Rebecca was an only child and subsequently the sole heir to the family fortune. When she embraced evangelism, she agreed to tithe a minimum of 10 per cent of her earnings to the church, a handsome sum considering her many investments. The Pastor was more than willing to accommodate her idiosyncrasies and to assure the happiness of his most benevolent parishioner, and she wanted his assistance. With the help of the Pastor, and a healthy payoff, Rebecca was able to muster support against me by arranging for several students to come forth with accusations that I had forced them to have sex with me. I can assure you that none of it was true, but to have a religious clergy and some healthy funds against you, the odds against revealing the truth became overwhelming. So, I lost my position here and sought one elsewhere. Fortunately, there are still those among my comrades who know my innocence and keep me informed. They are the ones who passed on your name to me, and so here I am."

"May I suggest that you return here, to The Concept, next week? I will introduce you to Naomi at her table, and the two of you can talk privately. I know that she is very interested in discovering who her birth parents were. To start, I recommend that you focus on that rather than the differences between you and Rebecca."

"Thank you so very much, Damon. I am grateful for your patience and cooperation."

19

When Lydia closes the club for the night, Damon and Naomi retreat upstairs to the apartment. Much of Naomi's conversation revolves around their plans to move to the cottage and the upcoming party.

"Nobody has ever thrown me a party, except for my birthdays when I was a child. At that time, there was only my mother and I, and a small cake. Each year I wished that my father would show up unannounced, but he never did. All the other kids my age had a mother *and* a father. I wanted a father so bad that I started to resent my mother. I think that's why I finally rebelled against everything she believed in."

Damon is tempted to tell her about Pablo, but bites his tongue.

"My birthdays were much the same, as I've already told you. Lavinia and I used to celebrate together; I now know why, but it always confused me that Helen and Charles, and of course, Phil, were never there. It was always just the two of us, except for this year. It was great having a birthday with you and Betsy to share it with. In a way, I'm glad that we didn't know about Lavinia's illness at the time. It would have put a serious damper on things, and I'm certain that's why she hid it from us, and put on such a brave show."

"She was a real trooper. I wish I'd had more time to get to know her. We had so much in common and she was so good to me when I was visiting. You were so-o-o lucky Damon. I've never known any of my relatives; no aunts nor uncles, not even a father, even though I've had two of them; and two mothers as well, although I only knew one." Naomi wipes a tear from her eye with the back of her hand. "And she doesn't know who I am anymore."

Damon can hold off no longer. "Naomi, there's something I want to tell you, and I hope you'll take the news with happiness."

"Somehow this feels like bad news is coming."

"No, on the contrary. I think you'll like the news I have." He pulls her close to him. "For the past few months, I've been searching for your adopted father through my connections at the college and the university."

"What do you mean, you've been *searching*?"

"I put the word out among some people I know at the medical school as well as my colleagues in the arts faculty, that I'm trying to locate a Doctor Parsons. I didn't name you, or reveal why I wanted to find him. I just asked them if they could check around."

"Why didn't you ask me if I minded before you started the search? Did it ever occur to you that I might not want to find my father?" Naomi pulls away from Damon. "He was not a nice man. He abandoned my mother and me when we really needed him, when I was so little that, to this day, I don't have any memory of him."

Damon blurts, "I found someone who has information about your birth mother and father." He stops short of further reference to her adopted father.

Naomi warms up when the subject of her birth parents arises. "What do you mean? What kind of information?"

"A man has come forward with, what appears to me, to be reliable information about your birth parents. You have a very interesting history in your family."

"Are you going to tell me that I'm famous, that I'm royalty, or from some upper crust family? I won't believe that."

"No, Naomi. You're not famous, but, according to the information I received, your parents played a small role in an historic event. Also, the images you're seeing in your nightmares seem to be connected to that event."

"What event? Tell me more, Damon. Who are my real parents? I have to know."

"I only know what this man has told me. He came to The Concept tonight and we had an opportunity to speak."

"That's the guy I saw you with." Naomi points her finger toward Damon. "The guy in Lydia's office. You said you were talking business with him. Why didn't you tell me right away, so I could talk to him as well?"

"Settle down Naomi. I wanted to make sure he wasn't a fraud or a con artist, and that he meant well. I'm also trying to protect you. My gut tells me he's on the level. He seems to know enough about your family to have the right information."

"I have to meet him. I want to talk to him. What's his name? Do you have a phone number?"

"Calm down. I told him that I would talk to you first. He wants to meet with you as well. I'll call him and set something up. How about here at the club? It's a neutral spot, and I'm sure that Lydia will let you use her office."

"Tomorrow would be perfect. Make an appointment."

The following evening, Naomi dresses a notch up from her usual casual attire and arrives at The Concept early, assuming her table. She positions her chair for a more direct line of sight to the front door. It opens several times allowing entrance to regulars and musicians. She watches for the man she saw the previous night. Damon sits at the piano, wiping the keys down with a cloth, also focusing his eyes on the door so he can introduce Pablo to Naomi as soon as he arrives.

Damon called Pablo immediately after Naomi left his apartment early this morning to arrange the meeting. Pablo's voice sounded as eager as Naomi's. It was arranged on the phone that Pablo should deal first with the details of Naomi's birth parents before entering into any discussion about her adopted parents' situation. Pablo was warned about Naomi's ill feelings toward him, and he assured Damon that his version of the story was factual, and that he would tread carefully.

Damon and Naomi both notice Pablo at the same moment. Naomi fusses with her hair and the neatness of her blouse; Damon approaches the door and shakes Pablo's hand.

Pablo admits, "I'm a bit nervous Damon. I have no idea how this will all go down."

"Just stay the course, Pablo. Let me introduce you." They walk toward Naomi's table, and Pablo offers his hand.

"Hello Naomi. My name is Pablo Sandoval. I have looked forward to meeting you for some time. Now, thanks to Damon, I have that opportunity."

Damon suggests they use Lydia's office for privacy. "I'll leave you two alone. I'm going up to play some jazz."

Naomi is the first to speak. Attempting to conceal her anxiety, she addresses Pablo. "So, Damon tells me that you know something about my birth parents."

Pablo starts to explain how he and his wife met a young couple in Santiago, Chile, in 1973. As when he related the story to Damon earlier, he turns a short story into an epic, until Naomi finally interrupts.

"How does all of this relate to me? You and your wife know a young couple in, where was that, oh yeah, in Chile, and they were involved somehow in the Socialist movement? Why is this all important to me?"

"That young man and woman, Joachim and Juanita Batista, were your father and mother."

"You referred to them in the past tense. What happened to them? I always believed that I was born in Canada. I have never been to Chile."

"Your father died in Chile, during the coup. Like so many others, he was murdered by the army, which was backed by the CIA."

Naomi has many questions and Pablo is able to answer every one of them except when Naomi asks who adopted her after her mother died in the hospital.

Damon and the quintet are locked into a steaming blues. Jesse and Zach trade fours with the drummer as Damon jabs open voiced chords into the mix. Until Damon senses Lydia's hand on his shoulder, his concentration has prohibited him from hearing Lydia's office door slam shut and from seeing Naomi stomp out of The Concept into Queen Street. Once aware, Damon leaves the stand; he sees Pablo seated in the office with his face buried in his hands.

'Christ, he must have told her,' Damon concludes, running out into Queen Street in pursuit. After running a block in each direction, he finally notices Naomi's shadow on the sidewalk. She's leaning against a brick wall in the alleyway next to the club.

"Jesus Christ, Naomi. Come inside. Someone will take you for a hooker out here. Besides, it's colder than a penguin's pecker." He wraps his arms around her and guides her to the door.

"Is that man still here?" she asks. "I can't face him right now. Do you know who he really is?"

Damon nods that he does.

"So you're in on this too, are you?" She backs away.

Finally, Damon shakes her shoulders. "Naomi. Listen to me." He stares directly into her eyes. "Pablo is your adopted father. He also told you everything there is to know about your birth parents. I believe his story because everything he told me the other day coincided with the nightmares you have: the army, the foreign language, and the eyeball. Everything falls into place, don't you understand?"

Naomi's head falls on Damon's shoulder. Her voice stumbles through her emotions. "I know, I know," she sobs. "Deep inside, I know that he's telling me the truth, and I don't blame you for seeking him out; I'm glad you did. I just don't know if I'm ready to handle that much truth at one sitting."

"Come back in with me, Naomi. I'm certain that Pablo is still in the club. Maybe if the three of us can sit down, we'll be able to get you through the hard parts. We can go upstairs to my place. It'll be quieter there. What do you say?"

Naomi blows heartily into a tissue. "OK," she inhales and holds her breath for a prolonged moment before exhaling. "Let's do it."

Damon opens the front door for her. Pablo, who has been watching through the window in the front door, is waiting inside. He opens his arms to her and she falls between them against his chest. Damon guides them upstairs to the apartment. A few moments later, Lydia appears with a tray of drinks.

"Call me if there's anything else you need," she offers.

Once settled, Pablo and Naomi open up, allowing their emotional baggage to unload. There is much weeping from both. She tells him about her nightmares and the hatred she developed toward him. He apologizes for not resisting the banning order against him and for leaving the country instead of fighting for her. Naomi told him about Rebecca living in the institution and not recognizing her anymore. She also told him about the events in her younger years that led to the breakup between her and Rebecca.

Finally, when both are emotionally drained, Pablo slowly withdraws two photographs from his jacket pocket, a black and white print of the four parents, birth and adopted, taken in the foothills of the Andes during a picnic, and a faded colour photograph of Naomi as a baby with Rebecca and Pablo while on a summer vacation in Muskoka.

"I want you to have these," Pablo offers. "I have carried these pictures with me for many years. They are the only copies left, as Rebecca destroyed all evidence of me, and of your birth parents. She was very possessive, but you already know that."

Damon, satisfied at the outcome, leaves to return to the bandstand, just in time to play out the last set of the night. Pablo and Naomi return as well, their hands together as father and daughter.

20

New Year's Eve arrives as scheduled and The Concept is decorated for the party. Like everyone connected to the club, Lydia is charged with mixed emotions. When The Concept began, it was her baby, a jazz club that would provide her husband, Tiny, and his close friends, a place to play the real thing, jazz that continued the tradition and the mainstream, and that wasn't immune to stretching out. It was a place for younger musicians to learn their craft on the scene from the older, more experienced players, and for the older ones to adopt some newer ideas in the process. That was Damon's idea, shortly after he started teaching jazz at the college. There was no venue for his students to share the stand with seasoned players. Other clubs in Toronto at the time brought big New York front men into town, backed by local trios. It was a great scene for the working trios, usually drawn from a nucleus of less than 10 musicians, but access to the visiting celebrities was limited. Despite his position at the college, Damon always maintained that the classroom was no place to learn jazz, or any other music for that matter.

The name chosen for the club was also Damon's suggestion. He had studied many treatises on the development of jazz and improvisation; one of those was George Russell's, 'Lydian Chromatic Concept of Tonal Organization,' a work focusing on modal and scalar melodic development, which for many years served as Damon's bible. When Lydia received a handsome sum of money from her late father's estate, she purchased the building on Queen Street West and opened the club, initially called Lydia's. One night, when Damon was introducing the band, he mistakenly called the club, Lydia's Concept, and the name stuck, until the shortened version, The Concept, took hold.

News about the special New Year's Eve bash was delivered mainly by word of mouth, from musician to musician, from jazz fan to jazz fan. After a few announcements from the bandstand several weeks before, and a hand-printed sign stapled on the front entrance, it became evident there would be a packed house. By nine o'clock, every chair and table was occupied and people were standing in the spaces between the tables. The band wasn't scheduled to begin until 10:00, but the crowd seized the opportunity to share memories with each other, and regulars met others they hadn't seen for a while.

Naomi, of course, commandeered her usual table for two and leaned the other chair against the table to indicate that it was spoken for. Pablo, her adoptive father, had promised to attend the party and to sit with her.

The hour before the band is to start playing is reserved for speeches.

"Hi everybody," Lydia shouts over the din of conversation and waves her arms in the air to attract attention. "Tonight is a night that I had hoped would never come. My emotions are running high, so I apologize in advance if I start to cry. You all know that this is the final night of jazz at The Concept. I have no idea what is going to replace the club, but that is no longer my concern. I do know that the musicians have been able to find other venues and bands, thanks to the help of Damon and Tiny who served as headhunters for them since the news was made public. I wish them all very well in their new environments."

Lydia calls the musicians up to the microphone by name and presents each with a gift from she and Tiny, a poster from the walls of The Concept, and a CD, produced secretly, without Damon's knowledge, of the quintet's fabulous performance the night they all heard the news.

Lydia turns her eyes toward Damon, "I am so sorry, Damon. I know how you feel about recordings of your work, but there has to be some permanent record of what happened here, and that night was the best of what happened. If you feel like you have to blame someone, blame me, it was my idea. The rest of the crew just helped me with the technology, that's all. Why don't you step up here and say a few words, Damon? You've been here since the beginning and you know every dusty little secret about this place; don't you dare reveal one speck of that dirt."

Damon strides slowly to the stand amid the applause for Lydia and an advance acknowledgement for him. Lydia hands Damon a personalized copy of the CD and apologizes for the photo she used, an image of Damon in meditation at the piano that looks ominously like he's asleep.

Damon embraces Lydia, accepts the recording with thanks, and begins his address.

"If this was one of my classes, I would have no hesitation to talk at length. Tonight, however, I am lost for words. Not that I don't have the words on the tip of my tongue, but that I will have great difficulty delivering them. This night is a turning point for me in so many ways. Of course, I'll cease performing here, in this building, where I've been a fixture for more than two decades. I have already moved my belongings from the humble apartment upstairs, where I have lived for the same length of time, and where many memories will be buried forever."

He glances around the room, stopping for a fleeting moment at Lydia, whose eyes glisten and turn away. He notices that Pablo is sitting next to Naomi, their chairs together, both facing the bandstand.

"This night also marks a change in my personal life, a change that began in this very room back in the spring, when that beautiful young woman entered this club and into my life." He points toward Naomi, and she blushes at the attention. "We, Naomi and I, are moving on with our lives, and relocating to an idyllic place north of here, in Muskoka, where we hope to live until we die."

After choking back some emotions, he restarts. "There are so many memories here that I could never even begin to catalogue them. Every night on the stand was a new experience, not only for the young cats, and there have been many young guys over the years, but also for us older ones, mainly Tiny and me. Every night, every tune we played, gave us something else to strive for, to stretch out, to live for. That's what jazz is all about: striving for something new, seeing how far you can stretch out and still hold on to the *thing*, and of course, living for it. If any young musicians out there think that jazz is just something to dick away at for a while, stop now and get yourself a paper route, or commit yourself to a lifetime journey of wonderful, exciting, frustrating, depressing, and absolutely phenomenal ups and downs; it's a roller coaster ride, I can tell you."

Again, he takes a pause to clear his throat. "Finally, although nothing is final, is it Naomi? I want to thank a whole shitload of people out there. Some of you I don't even know by name, but you regularly come out here and listen to us week after week, and give us your ears and your hearty applause. It's a real ego booster. I've been guilty of uttering to my fellow musicians that the audience isn't the important factor in this music we play, that we must, first and foremost, satisfy our own desires as the creators of the music. I still believe that. In fact, you the listeners have proven my theory time and again. Every night we strive for the best we can be and we stretch ourselves into zones that many listeners would otherwise tune out, maybe even feel like we're abandoning you at times, but you continue to hang in. There is still an audience for honest, hard-working, talented musicians who want this music, this art form, this jazz, to evolve. That's what happened here, in this place, in The Concept, in Lydia's Concept."

There is abundant applause and a few hearty whistles.

Damon continues. "In just about every other venue in this country, jazz has been eroded so drastically that even a semblance of honesty has been wiped out, or at the very least, reduced to a pile of drivel posing as jazz in the guise of whining, sniveling, self-proclaimed divas who don't know a flatted fifth from a high five, or in the bastardized versions of jazz festivals that place real jazz musicians on satellite stages and in back alleys while half-baked celebrities and their agents usurp the main stages in the name of commercialization and profit. I must also place considerable blame on the media who don't give jazz a column inch of play in the newspapers and magazines, and what passes for jazz radio has become appalling, nothing but wallpaper for offices and commercial establishments who play their drivel 24/7. It's no wonder that young people have no idea what this music is all about."

A deafening applause emanates from every corner of the room.

"Finally… I told you nothing is final… I want to thank all the musicians I've worked with here over the years and especially Lydia. Without them and her, it wouldn't have worked. Thanks again. Have a great party."

Again, the room fills with applause. When it dies down, Lydia returns to the microphone, embracing Damon in passing.

"There's one more thing we must do tonight before the music starts, and it isn't on the official program. I would like Damon to return to the bandstand please. Stand right over here, Damon," she orders, and physically places him in the correct spot. "Now," she looks behind her at Jesse and the rest of the band.

"Jesse, let's get this show on the road."

With Jesse Townsend on tenor, Zach Harris on trumpet, a fill-in pianist from the audience, and the regular young drummer, the band starts playing the head to Horace Silver's, 'The Preacher,' while Tiny Prescott emerges from the back room and steps to the front of the bandstand wearing a robe and a starched white clergy's collar.

Damon stares directly at Tiny. "What the hell's going on, man?"

Tiny shouts to the crowd, "Who stands up with this man?"

From the darkness, Betsy McGinnis struts forward dressed in a formal tuxedo with tails. "I'm the Best Man," she shouts, and stands to the right of Damon, at which point, the musicians start playing a loose interpretation of The Wedding March.

The front door from Queen Street opens wide, allowing Naomi and Pablo to step inside. Naomi is gorgeous in her white silk and taffeta gown with a long train following. Pablo sports a grey tuxedo with black satin lapels. Damon can't remove his eyes from Naomi as she and Pablo slowly pass through the crowd of revelers until they reach the bandstand to face Tiny.

"Who gives this woman away?" Tiny asks.

"I, Pablo Sandoval, father of the bride, do hereby give this woman to thee."

Before Damon can utter a word, Tiny starts the proceedings. "Dearly Beloved. We are gathered here to witness the betrothal of this man, Damon Farrell, and this woman, Naomi Parsons."

Damon interrupts, "Wait! Wait! Hold it, just a minute. I trust that this is all in jest, my dear friends." He looks at Tiny directly. "Please assure me that you have no official credentials to conduct such a ceremony, Tiny."

"Jesus Christ, Damon. Just go along with this will you?" Tiny responds, laughing. He asks the audience, "Is there anyone present this evening who has reasonable cause that this betrothal should not proceed?"

Lydia stands up and steps forward waving a sheet of paper with the headline, 'Reasonable Causes.' Damon stares back at Lydia in a panic, moving his head from side to side and mouthing the words, 'Don't do it, Lydia, don't do it,' but Lydia speaks out.

"I happen to know that the groom, a certain Damon Farrell, is far too old to be married again; and the bride, a certain Naomi Parsons, is far too young and beautiful to be married to such an ugly old fart as this. That should be as reasonable a cause as any."

Jesse speaks out from the bandstand. "I too can produce reasonable cause. The groom, Damon Farrell, will be out of work and homeless after midnight, and therefore has no means of respectable support for this beautiful young woman, Naomi Parsons."

Tiny concludes, "The people have spoken and have produced what I, Pastor Prescott, can accept as reasonable cause. I cannot continue further with this betrothal. But, I will offer this advice to the wonderful couple before me. Why don't you folks just go and move in together; you'll be a lot happier?"

Before the applause and laughter subsides, Tiny continues, "Do you, Damon Farrell, take this woman, Naomi Parsons, to have and to hold from this day forward, for better or for worse, 'til death do you part?"

Damon ponders the legality of the question carefully before answering.

"Damon?" Tiny prods. "Are you there?" He turns to the audience. "I do believe that our groom has fallen asleep."

There's more laughter throughout the club.

"Yes, your most reverent Pastor Tiny. I am here, and in sound mind and body."

Jesse counters, "Are you sure about the body part, Damon?"

The laughter continues.

Finally Damon responds to Tiny's original question. "I do."

Applause.

"Excellent." Tiny turns to Naomi. "Do you, Naomi Parsons, take this decrepit old man, Damon Farrell, to have and to hold from this day forward, for better or for worse, 'til death do you part? Before you answer, Naomi, I must warn you to be very cautious, and to consider the last part of your vow. You do know, don't you, that you're entering into a contract with a man who has, at best, 10 to 20 years left on his ticker, probably less on other parts of his body?"

The audience loses control, causing Naomi to delay her response.

"I know everything about this man, and he is likely to outlive me by 20 years. I do."

Tiny completes the ceremony. "I now pronounce you Soul Mates, 'til death do you part. Good luck to both of you. Damon, you may now kiss the bride, but hurry, because if you wait too long, I'm going to kiss her myself."

Lydia speaks out over the din of the audience. "There's one last item on the agenda before we turn the rest of the night over to the band. There must be a Soul Mates' dance, so clear an area out in front of the bandstand to give them some room."

Naomi, enclosed within her white bridal gown, whispers into Damon's ear. "Go to the piano, Damon. I'll look after the dancing part. Just play to me, like always."

The floor is cleared for Naomi, who stands alone in her dress, the train circling around her. She focuses on a spot on the floor, slowly pulling into her lungs, the energy of the room. Damon chooses some obscure chords at random to set the mood while Naomi remains still. The music intensifies through a series of arpeggios based on some

204

ancient Persian scales before resting into a hymn-like cadence that causes everyone to turn their attention once again, to Naomi.

From her stillness, she turns slowly clockwise, her upper torso seeming to advance faster than her lower in a corkscrew manner. As she rotates, the bodice of her dress slowly begins to peel away and Naomi emerges from the white cocoon wearing a tight-fitting flesh-toned body suit that, in the dim lighting of The Concept, has all the appearance of absolute nakedness. She continues rotating at an increasing rate until she suddenly, but gracefully, folds into a concise bundle on the floor.

Her new stillness offers Damon an opportunity to produce some free-form meanderings in D-Flat that gradually merge together into Body and Soul, one of his all-time favourite ballads, while Naomi waits unflinching for the arrival of the bridge. At the change of key into D-Major, Damon adopts the tempo of the tune and Naomi starts waving her arms like wings on a butterfly that appear to draw her upwards from the floor. Once upright, she circles about the club freely, waving her arms and taking long strides without any apparent regard for the music, as Damon surges into an explosion of dissonant jabs and abstract arpeggios. Without warning, Naomi vaults into a series of high-flying maneuvers, finally collapsing into a writhing mass on the floor in front of the piano, as Damon catches her rhythmic pulses in synch, alternating between his left and right hands in one last orgasmic surge. Naomi rolls from side to side in one final statement, as Damon settles into a fading turnaround before returning to the hymn-like cadence that matches Naomi's final stillness.

The audience, most of whom have never experienced an artistic expression quite like this, is wild with applause and cheering. Lydia takes the microphone.

"There you have it folks; another first for The Concept. What a night. Now let's turn the party over to Damon and the Quintet. Drinks are on the house."

Before the band starts to play, Damon makes one last announcement.

"Let's hear it for my beautiful, talented Soul Mate, Naomi Parsons."

There is another round of applause.

"Naomi and I have been working on this free improvisational merging of our muses for several months now. Although we can never predict what the outcome will be, because it's whatever emerges from inside, we have concluded that it should have a title. We call it, 'Muses and Consummations.' This has been the first public performance. We're so glad you enjoyed it."

The Damon Farrell Quintet plays some of its more popular tunes for the crowd of regulars, a set list that includes Bolivia, Beatrice, Freedom Jazz Dance, Little Sunflower, and a burning rendition of I Love You.

Many patrons remain at their tables while others mingle; some, like Naomi choose to dance. She dances with Pablo, her newly discovered father, and with Betsy, still wearing the tuxedo. She also drags Damon from the bandstand for a slow dance during Sophisticated Lady, clinging to him so tightly that she feels his excitement against her.

At the stroke of midnight, the band, sans Damon, starts into Auld Lang Syne. Everywhere in the club people welcome the arrival of 2003 by dancing, embracing, kissing and drinking to excess. Pablo kisses and embraces Betsy while Lydia and Tiny feign making love on the floor. Damon pulls Naomi tighter to him; they place their lips together in a mutually sensuous exploration of desire, their tongues probing around each other's. Damon wants Naomi and she wants so much to be loved. The year that changed both Damon and Naomi's lives has come to a close.

21

Early in the spring of 2003, Damon and Naomi relocate Naomi's furniture from her cozy apartment in the Annex, to the Muskoka cottage. Over the winter, Damon, who has been running back and forth between Naomi's apartment and the cottage, has fully renovated the coach house into an upscale apartment and studio for Naomi. The main floor, where the carriages were stored during the horse and buggy days, was transformed into a hardwood-floored studio with a small three-piece bath and change room, an ideal location for Naomi to teach dance to local students and to people from the city when they arrive during the summer for the workshops both she and Damon are organizing. The roomy three-room apartment upstairs provides Naomi with a private domicile, a place of her own to retreat to and to conduct her life without interference, as agreed between she and Damon.

The Ikea furnishings from her Toronto apartment arrive in a rented cube van driven by Pablo Sandoval, who has taken a fatherly interest in the life of his adopted daughter. Naomi's upstairs apartment has been totally renovated with new flooring, windows, a large bright bedroom with a queen-sized bed and ensuite five-piece bath, a complete kitchen, Ikea of course, with stainless steel appliances and the latest quartz countertops. Naomi can watch over the property, all the way to the pines, from her balcony that extends out over the entranceway from her bedroom. There is a front entrance with a sign advertising Naomi's Dance Workshop, and a closed in walkway connecting the coach house to the cottage, a blessing on cold winter nights.

Beside the new entrance to the former coach house, Lavinia's vintage two-tone Studebaker rests, awaiting its own restoration. On warm days, Damon can still detect the essence of Lavinia's lavender perfume exuding from the upholstery in the old classic.

Damon's private room upstairs in the cottage remains much the same as it has been for most of his 61 years, including the privacy sign over his door, which Naomi has finally agreed should be kept for 'old time's sake,' and out of respect for both Lavinia and Damon. He continues to sleep in his large brass bed with its vintage steel coil mattress that gratingly announces his movements while he sleeps.

Betsy McGinnis, who was shuffled out of her matrimonial home by her husband, Daniel, only days following her eulogy at the celebration of Lavinia's life, the moment when she removed both she and her lover from the proverbial closet, moved into Lavinia's room at the cottage after being welcomed by both Naomi and Damon. It was believed that, as she had spent much of her life between that room and the area beneath the pines, she deserved to continue living there. Her remuneration to the new householders is amply served through her superb kitchen and cleaning skills, talents which she readily volunteers, and which are more than welcomed.

Damon and Naomi quickly settle comfortably into small-town life and, with ample encouragement and assistance from Betsy, they become active in the local arts scene, Damon with his musical abilities and Naomi with her dance. Both assume part time teaching roles through the summer community arts programs and organize stage concerts in the park intended to highlight young talent as well as present their own collaborations of improvisational works. Both Damon and Naomi attract students from the local area. Through a website, set up by Naomi, they also draw students from as far away as Toronto.

During their first summer in Muskoka, they organize a concert of their own creations on the lawn at the cottage, a fund-raiser that attracts a large audience of curiosity seekers and raises several thousand dollars in support of the library acquisition fund, in the name of Lavinia Hope.

"Lavinia would have been so proud of you two," Betsy tells them, with tears in her eyes, upon receipt of the cheque.

Often, Naomi joins Betsy for a swim and sometimes goes with her to town for lunch and shopping. They maintain a friendship that encompasses discussions about books they've read, the news of the day, and womanly topics that all but exclude Damon.

Damon continues practicing piano and composing original musical sketches that he shares with Naomi and Betsy after dinners, when they're sitting on the teak bench under the ancient pines where Lavinia used to communicate with the spirits.

Lavinia's ashes remain on the piano ledge and her memory continues to inhabit their lives. In quieter moments, usually when Naomi is in town shopping with Betsy, Damon remembers his mother by playing music she would have liked: softer ballads and more lyrical melodies than his usual dissonance.

Damon also keeps in touch with his former band-mates. He emails copies of his original music to Jesse Townsend, his former tenor saxophonist from The Concept, who debuts Damon's tunes with his new band at the Toronto Jazz Festival, and later records them for posterity. While Damon was never keen to perform at festivals nor was he eager to record his own music, he receives some additional income from the performances and radio play in the form of royalties, after agreeing, at Jesse's prodding, to register his tunes with Socan. The following year, Damon and Naomi are invited to perform their extemporaneous collaboration, 'Muses and Consummations,' at the same festival to an enthusiastic packed house, in spite of the rap 'artist' headlining the festival.

Life is good for them during their first couple of years at the cottage. Their spirits are up, they remain in good health, and they create as freely as their muses allow. The demons and nightmares that plagued them both when they first met and which were indirectly the reason they met at the café between their appointments with Doctor Kinderman, have all been expunged from memory and relegated to the past; they are now able to live and create freely in the present.

Pablo visits each June for Naomi's birthday and she looks forward to his visits, even though they communicate regularly in the interim. He usually stays for a few days, taking advantage of the lake for swimming and kayaking and welcoming the company of friends and good food.

The platonic nature of Damon and Naomi's life together dictates that they maintain their own private quarters, Damon in his long-standing private domain, and Naomi in her new apartment. Their agreement is to respect each other's sexual orientation without pressure from either party.

While Damon's long-term abstinence from sexual activity has well prepared him mentally from pursuing intimate relations outside the home, it doesn't preclude his ever-hopeful imaginations that his beautiful Naomi will, on occasion, express a desire for his manly charms.

During the frigid nights of a Muskoka winter, Naomi thinks often about quietly sliding under Damon's sheets and cozying up against his warm body while he's sleeping, but she's unsure of how he might respond.

'What if he rejects me? I'd probably be devastated. On the other hand, what if he tries to seduce me? How would I respond? Would I accept him, or would I try to resist? H-m-m-m. That's a tough one. What would I do if he came to *my* bed in the middle of the night wanting to sleep next to me? He would like that, but I'm uncertain whether I could give him what he wants?'

In the darkness and silence of those same cold sleepless nights, Damon ponders similar questions.

'If Naomi were to join me under my covers some cold night and cuddle up against me, what would I do? It's a no brainer; I'll be hornier than a Billy goat. Could she be so naïve to think that I could ignore her? Christ, here I am getting a hard-on just thinking about it. I wonder what she'd do if I shuffled off into *her* apartment? She most definitely would invite me into her bed, I'm pretty sure about that, but what would happen next?'

His excitement keeps the topic alive.

'Maybe I should just visit her sometime to see what happens?'

One night during their first February, when the wind is shaking the entire framework of the cottage and rattling the cedar shakes, Damon's sleepless mind refuses to eliminate the thought of he and Naomi sharing a bed. After more than an hour of bouncing the questions back and forth, and his libido responding to the idea, he finally rises from his bed and shuffles his bare feet across his floor with full intentions of visiting Naomi in her apartment. Before he reaches the hallway a sudden cracking sound, followed by a crash, shakes the entire cottage. Minutes later, after he's had a chance to take stock of what happened, his bedroom door swings open revealing Naomi's figure silhouetted against the hall nightlight.

"Damon, can I come in? Something happened. Did you hear it? I think the coach house is falling down."

Damon reaches for Naomi.

"Calm down. I think the wind knocked over one of the small trees in the backyard. Let's take a look."

Naomi wraps her arm around Damon's waist and they walk down to the porch door. Damon switches on the porch light. The wind had drifted snow against the door, but the light exposes the broken limb from an old apple tree spreading across the driveway.

"Fortunately it didn't hit the cars or the buildings," Damon observes. "It'll be OK until morning. There's no point in going out there tonight in this blizzard."

They stop in the kitchen to pour a couple of drinks before heading back to their rooms. Once on the landing, Naomi embraces Damon.

"Would you mind if I sleep in your room for the rest of the night, Damon? I won't bother you, I promise. I'm just afraid of staying alone in my room. Do you mind?"

Once settled into Damon's bed, Naomi snuggles against him. He accepts her by enveloping her in his arms. The warmth of her body and Damon's imaginations contribute to the return of his excitement. In consideration and respect for Naomi's preferences, Damon takes special care to avoid pursuing his desires with her but, as she becomes fully aware of the effect she has on him, she quietly, without fanfare, employs a tactile kindness in reducing his anxiety.

Following that night, a milestone for each of them, Naomi and Damon occasionally repeat the precedent set then. There are also times when Naomi invites Betsy to join her in her apartment late at night, events that cause Damon to suffer some minor discomfort, but he suppresses his jealousies by focusing more attentively on musical thoughts using his meditative powers as diversion.

During their second year in Muskoka, Naomi's summer workshop in improvisational dance attracts only three students, two from the local area who are sent by their dance teachers, and one from Toronto who, while already familiar with the basic concepts of improvisation, became aware of Naomi's special talent incorporating meditation through a contact in her former dance company. The local girls arrive each day from their homes in town; Anna, the woman from the city opts to stay at a nearby hotel for the duration.

Anna is an already well-trained dancer of 22, who, like Naomi, has been dancing since she was a very young age. She is tall, slim but muscular, and very much in tune with her body. Upon her arrival, she is immediately attracted to Naomi, and displays her feelings through her dance. Naomi is receptive and reciprocates her feelings. Often, after the two local students have returned home for the evening, Anna remains behind, allegedly to pick Naomi's brain, but her prowess and assertiveness evolve into more sensual activities.

One warm and inviting evening, Damon decides to take a walk through the pines, and down to the lake where he can stroll freely along the shore. Before leaving, he slides open the studio door to invite Naomi on the walk. In the middle of the studio, Anna and Naomi are embracing intensely, their lips pressed together and their bodies gyrating in synch with each other. At first, Damon naively interprets their actions as part of an interpretive dance routine but, oblivious to Damon's presence, they continue to explore each other in the most seductive manner while he remains frozen at the entrance. The sight of the two women both excites and disturbs him but he can't remove his eyes from them. Rather than announce his presence, an act that would inevitably lead to a confrontation, Damon quietly removes himself from the studio and returns to the cottage, abandoning his walk.

'Should I say anything to Naomi about what I saw? I know we agreed to stay out of each other's personal lives, but doesn't this step over the line? On the other hand, I invaded her private space. Why am I so upset? I'm jealous, that's why. For Christ's sake, I'm nothing but a whining-ass jealous lover. I'm just as bad as Virginia used to be. I have no right to expect Naomi to live her life according to my idiosyncrasies.'

Whether he should say anything to Naomi about what he witnessed remains a conflict in Damon's mind for weeks afterward, while Anna continues her workshops with Naomi. He finally resolves to remain tight-lipped about it until after Anna's workshop has finished, as if her departure can relieve the pressure that boils inside him, or that Naomi will return to her normal loving self, but his jealousies cut deeper than he can admit.

During a particularly hot and humid spell, the phone rings.

Naomi, who is in the kitchen with Anna and Betsy, shouts, "Could you please answer, Damon? I'm in the middle of preparing dinner."

Following the phone conversation, Damon calls to Naomi in the kitchen. "We have company arriving, Naomi."

"When? This weekend?"

"No. In about ten minutes. Lydia just called from town. She intended to surprise us but lost the directions to the cottage."

"I'd better prepare another plate. Damon, could you find a nice wine for dinner? Pick something she'll like; you probably know her preferences."

Two years have passed since they last saw Lydia, although she and Damon exchange emails from time to time. Upon her arrival she's welcomed with hugs and kisses from both.

Lydia apologizes, "I know I should have notified you folks that I was planning to come, but the truth is, I didn't do much planning. Everything happened so suddenly."

"Is something the matter, Lydia?" Naomi probes.

"Where's Tiny? Didn't he come with you?" Damon adds.

Lydia attempts to answer their questions, but tears interrupt her response.

"What's the matter, Lydia?" Naomi starts. "Has something happened to Tiny?"

"He's gone. Tiny's gone."

Anna and Betsy retreat into the kitchen to continue preparing dinner.

"What do you mean, gone?" Damon asks. "Has he died?"

"No. Heavens no. He left, that's all. He just got all fired up one day and left me."

"But why?" Damon asks. "Did he give you a reason? And, where is he now?"

"Let me try to explain. After the Concept closed, he looked for other gigs, but he's not as young as he used to be. Who is, right Damon? Not only that, but the younger players have an entirely different approach to playing that's pretty foreign to Tiny. He doesn't like change too much; he never did."

Damon quips, "I can vouch for that."

"Well you know Tiny. As soon as things aren't working out, he heads straight for the bottle. I tried to interest him in doing some travelling, you know, to get away from the city for a while, but he wanted no part of it, so he stayed at home with a jar of whisky and stared at the TV. That's all he did. He didn't even listen to music anymore. He hasn't had his bass out of the bag for almost a year. Whenever I tried to talk to him he just clammed up. Finally, a week ago, I told him that he needed professional help and suggested AA to him. I also told him to look up that therapist that you and Naomi went to, but he just stood up, put on his coat and left. He didn't even take his bass, his wallet or his driver's license. I have no idea where he went, but I just couldn't take it any longer. I had to get away. So here I am. I gave your phone number to everyone I know with instructions to call here if they see him; I hope you don't mind."

Naomi offers, "We were just preparing dinner when you called so we've set another place for you. Why don't we eat, then we'll talk later. You're staying the night I hope."

"If I may. That would be great, as long as I'm not in your way."

Damon adds, "You're always welcome here, Lydia, just as we told you when we left the city. There's a spare guest room upstairs; you can stay as long as you like."

Following dinner, Anna leaves for the coach house studio and Betsy returns to her upstairs room. Lydia pitches in with the dishes and afterward, while the sun is setting over the water, Damon and Naomi take her on a stroll around the property, showing her the lake and the ancient pines.

"I often come here to meditate," Naomi tells Lydia, as they approach the teak bench. "You would just love this northern air. It's so fresh and invigorating. I've never felt as healthy as I do here."

"Oh, I'm pretty much a city girl." Lydia states. "I'm afraid that I'd go stir crazy after a while if I stayed here too long. Are there any bears or snakes up here? They just freak me out."

Damon brings Lydia's belongings in from her car and shows her to the guest bedroom at the end of the upstairs hall.

"You should sleep well tonight, Lydia, especially after the drive and this fresh northern air. If there's anything else you need, just call me; I'm just down the hall, in the room with the sign over the door. We'll see you in the morning for breakfast."

Lydia embraces Damon. "Thanks for everything. I really appreciate this."

Lydia's visit extends for several days. She has some minor success in relaxing but looks forward to returning to the city. During her final evening at the cottage, Betsy and Anna join them for a feast of barbequed shrimp and corn on the cob, which they devour with substantial quantities of wine and laughter. Damon shares some of his musician jokes from the Concept days and Betsy tells anecdotes about Lavinia. At the completion of dinner, Betsy returns to her room; Naomi and Anna stroll to the lake for an evening swim, leaving Lydia and Damon sitting on the porch swing.

Damon tips his wine glass to Lydia's. "Here's to friendship and to your safe journey home."

Lydia counters, "Here's to old friends and old times."

She stares into Damon's eyes. "I really miss those old times, Damon. Once in a while, and especially more recently, I've thought about you and me, and how it might have worked. Do you ever think about those nights up in your apartment after the gigs? Of course you do. We were pretty good together, you and I."

"Yeah, I have thought about those nights from time to time, but that's all history. It's in the past; we made other choices. I'm happy now with Naomi. We've got a good thing happening here together."

Lydia slides her legs up onto the swing and brushes one foot against Damon's thigh. "How much do you think about me and what do you think about when you do?"

"Oh come on Lydia. You don't really want to go down memory lane, do you?"

"Would you like to hear what I think about?"

"I'm not sure I like where this is going, Lydia."

Lydia's foot slides under his shorts and her wiggling toe explores his personal region. His response is immediate and substantial."

"Do you like where it's going now?" Lydia teases.

She watches his expansion as her foot massages him, noting with pleasure that he does nothing to stop her.

"You always liked it when I used to do this to you, Damon."

The warmth of her breath wisps across his lips as she moves closer.

"And you always liked what happened next." She places her lips on his and her hand rides softly up his thigh. "It feels like you still want me."

Damon weakly states his objection. "I can't do this Lydia. It's not fair to Naomi. We love each other so much, and we're happy."

"She can't treat you the way I can. You know that. Right now, she's probably having a lovey-dovey time skinny-dipping with her bosom bimbo, Anna, down at the lake. She's a piece of work, that Anna, isn't she? If I wasn't so straight, I could go for a bit of her myself. Surely you're not so naïve that you don't know what's going on there."

Damon avoids answering by trying to change the subject but Lydia charges on.

"Don't you ever crave for it, Damon? You can't just live like a monk; guys like you need it and you're too good at it to dismiss the need completely. Look at me, Damon. I'm here, ready, willing, and definitely able, and there'll be no hassle, no questions asked, and no complications down the road. Come up to my room with me right now, while they're diddling down at the lake. No one will know. I'll give you some great new memories for the future."

Lydia takes Damon's hand and leads him into the cottage; he offers no resistance.

Once upstairs, they stretch out on top of her bed. Damon remains motionless while Lydia unbuttons his shirt and pulls it over his back before removing her own blouse and nestling her naked breasts against his chest. As her hand slowly and methodically unclasps his shorts and lowers his zipper, she quickly resolves his long dry spell.

After some silent moments, Lydia speaks in a whisper.

"How was that for an appetizer? Why don't we just relax and think about the entrée? Who knows? If you're lucky, I might even think of something sweet for dessert. Just remember, we've done this many times before, so I know every vulnerable spot on your body."

Against the grating of well-worn metal springs and the repetitive creaking of the pine floorboards beneath the antique bed, Lydia and Damon manage a marathon of calisthenics while creating their latest memories before joining each other in a symphony of moans, desperate calls, and demands for more, resisting the inevitable for as long as physically possible until they finally cede to each other at the pinnacle of their synchronized pleasures. They remain clinging together in an effort to remain as tightly connected as possible and fall into a much-needed slumber without loosening their grips.

Outside, in the darkness, while Damon and Lydia are busy creating new memories in Lydia's bed, the giddiness of Anna and Naomi continues to echo from the lake joined on occasion by the calls of loons. By the time Anna joins Naomi in her coach house bedroom,

Damon and Lydia have already succumbed to a deep sleep, oblivious to the pas de deux being performed across the driveway.

Before first light casts subtle shadows across the grass from the pines and penetrates the slotted spaces between the venetian blinds in the cottage windows, Anna has already returned to her hotel room in town and Damon has shuffled back to his own bedroom where he manages an additional hour of sleep.

When the sweet essence of coffee rising up the staircase awakens Lydia, she joins Damon in the kitchen. Her robe untied and open, she embraces Damon from behind, pressing her exposed nakedness against his shirtless back while he pours the coffees.

She whispers into his ear, "Just like old times, eh? Why don't you come back to the city with me Damon? I really need you there. I'll even open another jazz club for you. We could make a real go of it, you and I. And, I promise you many more marvelous memories. How about it, Damon? Please say yes."

"I can't do that, Lydia. My God, Naomi and I, we're a couple. We're as good as being married, and we're in love; really in love."

"But don't you get it, Damon. We make magic together. Besides, I need you to remind me that I'm still a woman, vital and sexy. You do that for me, unlike any other man."

"Last night was a mistake, Lydia. It shouldn't have happened. It must have been the wine."

"But it did happen, and the wine had nothing to do with it. You loved every minute of it, from the toe-in-the-crotch foreplay to that fabulous prolonged orgasm. We were magnificent."

"I can't do it Lydia. As much as we enjoyed last night, screwing each other's brains out, it can't continue. I owe it to Naomi, don't you understand that?"

Lydia, without further recourse, goes for his jugular. "For Christ's sake, Damon. Are you blind or what? Don't you see what's going on here? Do you think Naomi is sitting around wasting herself on some platonic fantasy? No, of course she isn't. She's getting it on with that dancing whore, Anna, and probably with Betsy as well. What in hell do you think they do down at the lake, or when they go shopping together? Naomi's getting hers, you can count on that; you need to get yours."

Lydia spreads the front of her robe open. "And this is the store where you can get it. It's open 24/7."

Damon backs away. "Forget it Lydia. Go back to the city and find Tiny. He needs you more than I do."

"Good morning all," Naomi calls through the screen door in a musical tone. "The coffee smells wonderful; I could smell it all the way out in the coach house."

Lydia quickly turns away and ties the sash around her robe while Damon fills Naomi's cup.

Naomi wraps her arms around Damon. "Thanks for letting me sleep in. I really needed that."

Damon returns Naomi's embrace before handing her the cup. "You sound so cheerful this morning. You must have slept well."

"Oh believe me, I did."

Naomi turns to Lydia. "Will you have some breakfast before you leave for the city?" she asks in the same cheerful voice. "You *were* heading home today, weren't you?"

22

"Do you ever miss the excitement of the city?" Naomi asks, once both Anna and Lydia have finally returned to Toronto.

"What excitement would that be? Would it be the whining of the police sirens or the constant grating of streetcar wheels against the rails? Or maybe it's the drunken reprobates cursing and spitting outside my bedroom window or the college administration imposing more paperwork and guidelines to allow the lowest common denominator to set the bar for academic achievement and graduating without ever waking up, or for that matter, without ever attending classes at all. Is that the kind of excitement you mean?"

"You're making fun of me, Damon. I meant it as a serious question. We've lived here in this relative seclusion called cottage country for two years now. I'm just wondering if the novelty is wearing off, that's all. Are you becoming bored, in other words?"

"Why? Is it catching up with you? Are you not enjoying this anymore?"

Naomi detects a tone of cynicism in Damon's voice that she hasn't heard before. "Why are you answering my question with more questions?"

"I'm sorry, Naomi. I guess I'm just on edge. Maybe it's seeing Lydia and hearing about Tiny. He and I go back a long way."

"So do you and Lydia."

"What's that supposed to mean?"

Before adding more rhetoric, Naomi allows a moment of silence to moderate the discussion.

"Please don't be defensive, Damon. I couldn't avoid seeing you and Lydia from the porch the morning she left, and I overheard some of what she asked you to do; about returning to the city with her, that is."

Damon is speechless, unaware of other details Naomi might have overheard, or worse still, seen.

"I also heard what you told her, and I'm proud of you for sticking up for us; it was a brave and wonderful thing to do. I know that she wanted you to leave with her, and I assume that you and she shared intimacies the previous night. It was only fair, I guess, considering the way Anna and I were acting. After all, why should I expect you to be different than me? Why should my biological needs be satisfied and yours ignored?"

"Look Naomi. I'm not proud of what happened that night, and I don't think that Lydia intended for it to happen when she first arrived here. God knows that I haven't been out looking for sex. She is really worried about Tiny and so am I. What happened that night was more the result of the wine loosening our inhibitions and allowing things to be said that otherwise would be kept under wraps."

"So, you are admitting that you slept with her, are you?"

"Wait a minute. You said that you knew about it. What kind of game are you playing?"

"I only said that I assumed you were intimate, not that I knew. But of course, now I do know, don't I?"

Before Damon can gather his thoughts, Naomi peppers him with more interrogations exposing her innermost jealousies that, until today, she had yet to reveal.

"Was it fantastic sex? Was she great in bed? Does she do things to you that I could never do? How did she screw you, Damon? Did she get on top and ride you like Calamity Jane would ride a stallion?"

Damon is stunned at her outburst. As an act of defense, he counters, "I think Calamity Jane might have been more your style."

Naomi, upset at her own loss of control as well as Damon's response, marches out the front door and proceeds toward the pines. The screen door slams behind her.

"Wait a minute, Naomi. Let me explain." he calls to no avail.

Damon slams a foot against the floor. "What a stupid thing to say. I must be mad."

He remains in the cottage to allow Naomi her space and to gather his own thoughts, and recalls his experiences with Virginia many years ago when she regularly ranted in jealous rages.

'I never once cheated on Virginia and she accused me daily of having affairs with other women, even when she was screwing my brother behind my back. Now, with Naomi, I actually did betray her trust by having sex with Lydia; I wouldn't call it making love, it was just sex, pure and simple. Naomi has a good reason to blow up... or does she? What about when she gets together with Anna, or Betsy, for that matter? How often does she have sex? Is what they do a form of making love, or is just plain screwing? Do they actually love each other, or is it purely a lustful titillation intended for satisfaction?'

He pours a double Canadian Club straight up and sits at the piano, gazing into the strings without focusing. The glass of whisky is placed next to Lavinia's ashes while his fingers probe the keyboard in search of tonalities appropriate to the situation. He is simultaneously angry, embarrassed, and ridden with guilt.

The torrent of chaotic sounds emanating from the piano express his anxiety and confusion through jagged and dissonant clashes that are more traffic noise than music. Upon his realization that he's punishing the piano with his emotional baggage rather than channeling it into something productive, the tones evolve into more tempered and mellow statements. Damon allows the music to carry him toward his personal Zone of Tranquility, becoming lost within his own creation.

Is Damon being held captive by the structures of his life and his art or is he discovering a new freedom by allowing himself to be led solely by his emotions? Whose approach to freedom is valid? Is Naomi's anarchic theory of allowing freedom to occur by chance more valid than Damon's reliance on earning the freedom through a series of structural frameworks?

Among the pines, Naomi struggles with her own demons, not the ugly nightmarish images of her past, but the emotional realities of her present conflict. Her love for Damon can't be equated to the kind of lustful need that she has for Anna and Betsy. They are separate entities, bodily lust and a commitment to love, just like Damon expressed to her when they first had dinner together.

'I don't really love Anna or Betsy, but I crave their intimacy. They make me feel like a complete woman through the variety and depth of how they touch me. In the case of Betsy, she possesses a knowledge that comes from age, and that must result from the explorations she had with Lavinia, right here among these pines. I know deep inside, that Damon can't give me those feelings. I also know that Betsy can't provide me with the warmth and tenderness that Damon always extends to me as a person, especially his sensitivity to my art and his complete understanding of my orientation issues. What other man could do that? However, could his understanding extend to the intimacies I share with Betsy?'

'With Anna, she provides me with her entire body, like a blank canvas, to do with it whatever I wish, and there are so many things that I'd never imagined before that she encourages me to explore. She takes me on such incredible journeys that my body explodes with satisfaction but, in the end, it's just lust; there's nothing more to it.'

'What if I can make allowances for Damon to pursue his natural desires with other women? Could I, for instance, allow Lydia to spend more time with us here at the cottage so she can share Damon's bed the same as I share mine with Betsy and Anna? What if I could encourage Damon to visit Lydia in the city from time to time? I could spend some time there with Anna and we could schedule our personal time together for when Damon is visiting Lydia. That way it wouldn't be in our faces all the time. My God! What am I thinking? This would finish Damon and me; there has to be some other way.'

Without thought, Naomi has already started stretching as she always does before dancing. Damon's music filters through the pines with freshness in the tonalities and rhythms that appeal to her in her current state of mind: tender melodies and pleasing harmonies that incite her to freely express her emotions.

Aside from the unplanned dialogue between their muses during the afternoon, verbal communication between Naomi and Damon in the evening remains minimal. With twilight descending following a quiet reheated dinner, Naomi retires to her coach house to read. Damon stays in the parlour, listening to a recently released Charles Lloyd CD. Upon its completion he retires to his own bed, but sleep evades him, replaced instead by the disturbing events of the day, and the recurring memories from the night with Lydia. The cottage is silent but for the usual night noises until broken by footsteps creaking outside his bedroom door.

"Damon?" Naomi whispers through his door in a barely audible tone. "Are you awake?"

Damon takes a moment before answering in the affirmative. "Is there something wrong?"

"May I come in? There's something I want to talk to you about."

"As long as we don't start fighting again."

Naomi pries the door open slowly in an attempt to avoid the scraping of its hinges, and steps gingerly forward, stopping at the side of Damon's bed.

Damon switches on his reading light, dimly illuminating Naomi in a shiny satin teddy that clings to her bodice and exposes her well-muscled legs.

"May I join you?" she asks in a whisper.

Damon welcomes her by spreading open the sheets.

Naomi snuggles tightly against his warm body. He wraps his arms around her, pulling her closer.

Naomi whispers, "Can we talk about something that's been on my mind for some time?"

Damon expresses his agreement. "Sure, go for it."

"I want to have a family, Damon. A real family: a baby with a real mother and father." Her words crunch together in an excited manner.

Before realizing the seriousness of Naomi's request, Damon quips, "You, and me, and baby makes three. Is that it?"

"Please Damon, I'm dead serious." Naomi places her hand softly against his chest hair, plying her fingers through it while observing how the hair curls around her forefinger.

"I want to be a mother and have a baby; and I want you to be its father."

"A baby? That's what you said isn't it? A baby?"

"Yes Damon, a baby. You know, one of those pudgy little things that cries and laughs and wants to be fed and to whom we tell bedtime stories and provide the wisdom of our experience."

"And who also pukes and farts and doesn't do his homework and gets to be 13 and rebellious and listens to punk music and smokes dope."

"Not if we're really good parents she won't."

"I see, you want a daughter, do you? Why don't you adopt one? That way you'll get just what you want."

"I want a baby, our own baby; I don't care if it's a boy or a girl. I just want a baby that we can call ours. But I can't make a baby all by myself. I want you to be the father, and you know what that means don't you?"

"Well, considering that I'm already 62 years old, that means that I'll be about 77 when he or she starts high school. The parent-teacher meetings will be a blast, won't they? I can't wait for those. They'll think I'm the kid's great-grandfather. Who knows what music they'll be listening to in another 15 years? It won't be jazz, you can be sure of that."

"You'll love being a father, Damon. I know you will. But, even more than that, you'll love creating our baby with me, I'll make sure you will."

"Oh, I have no doubts at all that I'll enjoy that part immensely, but let's try to be practical for just a minute, Naomi. I could very well be dead before the child becomes a teenager, or most certainly by the time he or she starts university. I don't really want to be the father of an orphan."

"Hold on a minute, Damon. I don't have any desire to be dead in 20 years. If you want to die before your time, that's one thing, but I'll still be around to raise our child, so we won't be raising any orphans."

"You'll be a single mom, then. Is that really what you want?"

Naomi delays any verbal response, opting for another tact. While leaning her head against Damon's neck she meticulously slides her hand down from his chest, allowing it to linger on his stomach, her fingers gently exploring the region surrounding his navel.

She proposes, "Would you be interested in having a test run? You know, just to see how you'll like it."

Curious about the extent of her probing, Damon remains silent and still. The anticipation of her actions in Damon's subconscious encourages a sudden interest that invites Naomi's hand to examine further.

With an eager curiosity, Naomi plays with Damon's anatomy as a child in a sandbox exploring routes for her fingers and lips to follow. Applying her own personal sensitivities as a template, based upon knowledge she gained from her own imagination and from Anna's vast experience, Naomi assumes that Damon will share similar sensitivities. Her assumption is proven correct after lightly stroking his lower abdomen with the tips of her fingernails and flutter-tonguing his left nipple.

His anticipatory reaction provides her with the permission she desires to play with his maleness in a much deeper and intense manner while his body jerks and rolls beneath her. Damon's excitement is accompanied by a series of deep throaty moans, while his hand pursues it's own path under her teddy.

He becomes aware that, through Naomi's naiveté with men, she is offering him something totally different from what he had ever experienced, and Damon responds in like manner with her. Without any verbal communication, the two agree to lie absolutely still, resisting any movement, allowing their senses to adjust to, and accommodate, the new revelations.

Thoughts abound in both minds of wants and desires yet untried. A small flicker from Naomi's fingers incites a reaction in Damon's hand, which encourages Naomi's fingers into more adventurous exploration, and subsequently Damon's to probe further. Aside from their digital explorations, and the escalation of their curiosity, their bodies remain dead still. The longer they resist movement, the more

226

intense their breathing and audible expressions become, until neither can contain their stillness any longer. In a sudden and uncontrollable surge, Naomi draws her teddy above her head exposing her excited breasts and absorbs Damon in one continuous movement. His penetration is with a strong virile confidence.

During the final moments, with Damon secure between the tightened, throbbing muscles of her thighs, Naomi cries, "Oh, my God, Damon, don't stop. Please don't stop. Love me! Love me!" while her hips rise and fall in synch to the rhythm of Damon's uncontrollable pelvis.

During the release and silence of their post-climactic reflections they cling together, still maintaining pelvic contact.

Naomi whispers into Damon's ear. "Is this where the lust ends and the love begins?"

He answers, "I've never thought about it quite that way before. Personally, I try to avoid analysis at times like this."

Naomi appreciates that Damon doesn't just roll over and fall asleep, but instead continues to embrace her. She appreciates that his fingers scout the contours of her face, lips, and neck, and proceed across her breasts while his lips follow with sensuous kisses. A fresh surge of desire flames in the pit of Naomi's stomach.

As a tactic of delay, she offers, "Can I pour you a drink, Damon, a whisky, or a glass of Merlot perhaps?"

"Canadian Club, straight up as usual. That'd be perfect right now."

While Naomi leaves for the kitchen, Damon lies in bed reflecting on what has just occurred, not fully comprehending how Naomi, a lesbian by her own declaration, could enjoy him so much, and how she so erotically satisfied his physical needs and sensitivities.

'Where did she learn all of that? She sure as hell looked and felt like she was enjoying me. She couldn't have faked it; she was so into it. I couldn't give her enough of myself, she wanted more and more. How can that happen?'

Naomi, in the kitchen, pours Damon a double Canadian Club and a single for herself, adding some ice to hers.

'My God! Never, in my wildest dreams, could I have imagined such pleasure and intensity. Are all men like Damon? He was a tiger. I'm not supposed to enjoy this; I'm gay, for Christ's sake. Anna and I had some great moments, but there's been nothing like this. Is it possible that this was just a one off, maybe because I was jealous and trying to make up for it, or that my body craves for a child and I need him that much? Maybe, because I have this internal need to have a baby, my hormones have shifted into high gear, or some weird thing like that.'

Naomi arrives with the drinks and slides back under the sheets with Damon.

"Is that what it takes to make a baby, Damon?" She kisses him on the lips.

"Yup. That's what it takes, but we must repeat it over and over again until those little swimmers connect in the right spots."

"What if they already have?"

"For me, that would be a crying shame, because you wouldn't need me anymore. I'll miss out on many wonderful nights, won't I?"

"You don't think that I just made love to you like that for the sole purpose of making a baby, do you? I hope not."

"That's what you want isn't it, Naomi? I'm having some difficulty understanding why you would want me, a man, in the first place, especially loving me with that level of intensity. You did tell me you were gay, right? Are you sure?"

"Damon, I'm as surprised as you are. Believe me, there was absolutely no faking on my part; I want you to believe that wholeheartedly. Every emotion, movement and sound was as pure and real, from the curiosity of my initial explorations of your body to the incredible ecstasy I experienced. Let me ask you again, was that pure lust at work, or did love enter into it?"

"Does it really matter what we call it, Naomi? It was great. Let's just remember it for what it was."

"Do you want a baby, Damon? Don't worry, I won't ask you to marry me; it won't be necessary. This is the 21st century, we can do what we want, can't we? The main thing is that I love you, and I want to have your child."

Damon avoids a direct answer by joking. "But will you still respect me in the morning, after what we've just done?"

She follows his humour with a feigned slap across the face. "Much, much more. This was only the beginning. I enjoyed this far more than I should have; far more than I ever imagined."

When Naomi leans over to kiss Damon she accidentally spills her glass of whisky over his bare chest, the ice cube falling into the hair.

Damon initially screams from the shock but then starts to laugh. "Isn't this how we met in the first place?"

Naomi laughs, plying her fingers through the whisky-drenched hairs on his chest to retrieve the ice. As a joke, she places the cube against his nipple and it hardens. She follows her fingers with her lips allowing her tongue to lap up the whisky and encircle his areola.

"Before tonight, I didn't know that men had sensitive nipples; I thought that was just a woman thing. Does that mean if I play with them for a bit, you'll get excited again?"

"There's a lot you don't know about men, but I get the feeling you're a quick learner. I'm giving you an 85 for your first exam."

"Is that all? What do I have to do to get 100?"

"Practice, practice, practice, that's all it takes."

Naomi draws back the sheets to watch his excitement return. In a moment of levity, she quickly applies the ice cube to his genitals. Damon jumps and yelps from the initial shock. He grabs the ice and replicates Naomi's adventurous foray, by slowly drawing the cube from Naomi's firm breasts downward.

Naomi determinedly resists moving, her stomach muscles tightening. From this moment, nothing imaginable is ignored. She suddenly jumps from the bed, teasing Damon to follow her. During a cat and mouse chase through the cottage with a momentary stop for intimate contact against the kitchen counter, Naomi escapes outside to the pines, with Damon in anticipatory pursuit, where she performs an erotically charged dance for him before the lovers finally conjoin on the grass for unlimited and unbridled fantasies.

23

Neither Damon nor Naomi is quite sure about how to communicate following the events of the previous night. There is a quiet closeness that accompanies their breakfast on the porch. They touch in ways more appropriate to friends than to lovers: a slight stroke of a hand on one's arm, a soft cuddle of understanding, or a kiss pecked on the cheek, all contrasting the enthusiasm they exhibited in Damon's bed and under the pines. There is no immediacy in their actions, an apparent complacency that displays new confidence in a relationship that has suddenly matured. Their conversation focuses on housekeeping subjects: whether more groceries are needed before the weekend, or whether the phone bill has been paid.

"Would you like me to warm up your coffee, Damon?" Naomi asks.

"Please." He hands her his mug with musical motifs etched into the side.

"I might go into town today to pick up a few things. Would you like to join me? We could drop into the restaurant for afternoon tea and scones, if you like."

"Sure. Sounds like a plan."

Damon sits on the porch swing with his fresh coffee; Naomi remains standing beside the swing holding her coffee mug with both hands. The loons announce themselves from the lake.

Damon finally breaks the silence.

"What happened last night, Naomi? How did that all come together? It was like all the dreams and wishes I've experienced since I first met you suddenly coming together in a tsunami of intense desire and satisfaction. And where does the baby thing come from? Don't get me wrong. I'm not against us having a baby, although I still have some real concerns about my age and my mortality. I'm just curious that's all. I've never heard you mention anything about it before."

"H-m-m-m," Naomi sighs while wondering how to start. If I tell you, there's a real risk that you'll think of me as weird, eccentric, or severely demented."

"Which one would you prefer," Damon jokes, and pats his hand on the seat of the swing. "Come and sit closer to me. I won't bite your head off."

Naomi joins him, balancing her coffee as she maneuvers herself onto the rocking swing.

"Most of it has to do with Lavinia, your mother. She talks to me."

"Come again?"

"I knew you'd think I was crazy. Lavinia and I communicate with each other, usually when I'm out under the pines, but sometimes when I'm alone in bed at night, or even while I'm sleeping; I have dreams where we talk about all sorts of things."

"You never mentioned anything about this before. I thought your nightmares were a thing of the past."

"Oh, these aren't nightmares; quite the opposite. They're real conversations, pleasant ones, not scary like my previous nightmares. Your mother is a storehouse of information, you know."

"You mean she *was* a storehouse of information. Besides, you only met her once, a month before she died; hardly enough time to get to know her very well."

"Oh I disagree, Damon. We got to know each other very well. Even during that one overnight visit, she and I talked about many topics, from my relationship with you and what it's like being a lesbian with a close male friend and confidante, to my dancing and your music and our collaborations. Mind you, she never revealed to me that she was gay herself; I didn't discover that until the funeral, the same time as you found out. She and Betsy were very good at hiding all of that from me. The same goes for her being your mother. I didn't know that either until you showed me the letter. She did however, tell me stories of when she was in the theatre and she offered some amusing nuggets about the local area's characters, of which she was definitely one. She was very talkative."

"I have to agree with you there, Naomi. She could talk the night away."

"She still does."

Damon's face scrunches up and his brow tightens in a gesture of skepticism.

Naomi continues, "I mean, her spirit still does. Do you remember when I went dancing out under the pines after the funeral was over? Maybe you didn't notice; you were quite upset about the news you received that day."

"I do remember. I still have an image of you that day, wandering alone, passing small groups of others as if they weren't there at all. You were walking ever so lightly on the grass, like you wanted to defy gravity and lift yourself above the trees. It actually appeared quite magical; you were almost ghostlike, as if you were about to disappear in a puff of smoke."

"I danced out under the pines, where Betsy said they used to make love. It was very trancelike being there, as if I'd meditated deeply to find my zone, but I didn't have to. It was very mystical and quiet. The sounds of all the other people's voices disappeared, leaving a complete absence of sound. When I neared the bench I thought I heard a voice calling my name but I was alone. The voice repeated my name and I recognized it as Lavinia's voice. Very quietly she addressed me and said that we shared an affinity with each other; a common bond that brought us together. Part of that common bond was our mutual love of you, Damon. The other bond was as women who live our lives with the anxieties of needing attention from other women, but each of us caring deeply for a man. She mentioned your name and confirmed that she was ecstatic that you and I had found each other and that we were destined to remain together forever as a couple."

"That's weird, because she wrote in her last letter to me, before she died, that she wanted me to always love you, and that you were a keeper."

"Do you remember when you called me on the phone to tell me that your Aunt Lavinia had died? Do you also remember me telling you that I had a dream in which she visited me in my sleep and told me that everything would be OK?"

"Yeah. I remember we both thought that was weird."

"Well I did think it was weird at the time, but I now know that it was just the first of many visits I would have with her spirit since."

"This is getting pretty odd, Naomi. Are you sure you're actually hearing my mother's voice, or is it something from deep inside your imagination?"

"Oh, it's her voice alright; I'm sure of that. Yesterday afternoon, after we had our spat, I went to the pines for some solitude. I started to cry over what was happening to us until I heard you playing the piano. It was like a gift to me, like nothing I'd heard you play before, far more sensitive. I started to dance freely with the music inside me, a freedom without any structure, the kind I've always yearned for."

"That's odd. I was playing without any concern for structure as well, a complete abandonment of everything I have always believed in. I suddenly felt a freedom to embark on a new journey, with no destination in particular, just to follow wherever the music pulled me."

"During my dancing, I heard Lavinia's voice blending with the music in me. She told me how much she liked my dancing and that she loved me very much. She expressed how much she appreciated that you and I were committed to each other, but was sad that we were having difficulties. She encouraged me to work things out with you and that we, you and I, should express our love for each other more intimately."

"And I suppose that's how the baby thing started, because my mother's spirit told you to be more intimate?"

"Heaven's no! Please don't make fun of me, Damon. I'm being dead serious. And stop calling it *the baby thing*."

"I'm sorry, Naomi. But can you please tell me where you got the idea to want a baby?"

"After I finished dancing and communing with Lavinia, I sat alone on the bench. I was afraid to come back to the cottage in fear that you might still be angry with me. Thoughts started to saturate my mind about how much Lavinia loved you, and how, despite the trials she was faced with most of her life, she managed to give you her love and her guidance throughout your childhood and as an adult."

"I wish she'd been more forthcoming about the details, at least while she was still alive."

"I know Damon, but who are we to question her motives?"

"I'm her son; if I can't question her motives, who can?"

"Please Damon. I'm trying to explain the baby."

"Go for it."

"Another thought that entered my mind was how sad it was that my birth mother, Juanita, never even knew me. I was born, and she died, in with one new life and out with an old one. The problem is that she was still young, younger than I am right now. Think of it."

"My father never knew me either. He died at the same time I was born; half a world away, and he was only 18. I still can't fathom that."

"Then there was my adopted mother; as domineering as she was, she sincerely wanted the best for me. She tried to be a good mother; maybe she tried too hard. Nevertheless, I let her down, and I still suffer from guilt about what happened, especially about aborting the baby I was carrying. That's what sent Rebecca over the edge. I killed her grandchild."

Naomi slumps over weeping.

"You weren't responsible for what your mother did. You did the right thing. Just remember where that fetus came from; it was from that disgusting bastard that raped you. If you had raised his child you'd be spending your entire life looking into that bastard's eyes. Think about that."

Damon caresses Naomi while, with a few sniffles, her weeping slowly draws to a close.

"There's one more thought that entered my mind. I kept thinking of your son, at least the son you thought you had. You've lived your entire adult life lamenting the first nine years of it, wishing you'd never met Virginia and that you'd never raised Graham."

Tears emerge from Damon's eyes. "That's all history now, Naomi. I've forgotten all of that."

"Balderdash! Those tears tell me that you'll never forget."

Together they weep openly, the tears flowing over each other's shoulders.

"Finally," Naomi offers, "Lavinia wants us to have a child. She didn't say it outright, but during her visit to me the night she died, she saved the baby from the fire and brought it to me. Don't you see? That was a sign. We must create a new child to replace the unborn one."

Naomi's voice struggles to speak between the sobs. "That's why I want us to have a baby, Damon, for all of those reasons. I want *us* to have our own child, one who'll be loved and for whom there'll be no regrets."

Damon reiterates his concerns about his age and warns Naomi that he could become ill, or drop dead, while their child is still young, leaving Naomi to care for the child alone.

"I'll make sure you aren't financially strapped at least," he assures.

Naomi slaps him playfully. "Don't say things like that, Damon. You scare me sometimes. Think about what you always tell me. We live in the present. That's all that matters."

"On another, albeit related, topic. How did you ever learn to make love like that, Naomi? For a lesbian, you sure know how to make a man happy, but how and where did you learn that?"

"From your mother."

"Lavinia? My mother, the lesbian, told you how to make me happy during sex?"

"It's a bit more complicated than that, Damon. First of all, let me explain. In a strange sort of way that you'll probably have difficulty understanding, I believe that Lavinia lives inside of me. She visits me

236

in my meditations and during my dancing, or sometimes while I'm sleeping, and she's the catalyst for my freedom to lust for Betsy and to love you. Lavinia has offered me some guidance in ways to accept a man, and a few techniques intended to please him in the process."

Damon asks, "Just for the record, Naomi, was I making love with you last night, or was it, in some weird distorted transference, with my mother?"

"Oh come on, Damon. It's not like that at all. It wasn't so much that she told me how, but after we communed, I started to sort out how we could go about having our own family. It occurred to me that women and men aren't really that different."

"Betsy showed me a lot too, probably things that she learned from Lavinia over the years, and I just put two and two together. I discovered very quickly last night, that if I touch you in certain ways, you reciprocate and touch me in similar ways. Logic says that your organ and mine have to eventually get together to make this work so-o-o, I started to work on yours, and you worked on mine. It's a no-brainer, Damon."

"Not that I really care, Naomi, but only because I want to get something off my chest, what did you learn from Anna?"

"Don't go there, Damon! You don't really want to know any of those details; well, maybe you do. No! Forget it. There is nothing that would interest you; certainly nothing that I can apply when you and I make love. Like you always tell me, teaching and learning happen at the same time. Oh, did I tell you? I must have forgotten. Anna knows your piano student really well. Do you remember, Sandi... with an 'i' who plays at the Italian restaurant? They used to be roomies; well, partners, like... you know... a couple... like us."

Damon chuckles. "With my wildest imagination, I can't visualize how Anna and Sandi can be partners like us, Naomi."

"That's true. Suffice to say that you don't really want to know what I learned from Anna."

"Fair enough. OK! I agree. We should have a child. Should we plan our strategy or do we just keep doing it until something happens?

I must admit. I'm not terribly clued in on making babies, except for the lust of it all, the part which, incidentally, I will enjoy immensely."

"Well, we could just get together when the cycle is ready, which gives us a small window of opportunity. I'll let you know when that time arrives, and we'll get together. The other possibility is, that I move into your room and we sleep together. When the mood arises, we do whatever seems right at the time, and we hope for the best. I think that's how most babies are created."

"I opt for the second scenario. You can move in tonight."

"I thought you might prefer that option."

Damon adds, "While we're going through this, this creative collaboration of making a baby, is it possible that Betsy could limit her personal visits with you for awhile? I've accepted your relationship with her since we moved to the cottage, but I do have some minor jealous tendencies that I didn't think I possessed until recently. It would be better for me if I didn't have to compete for you."

"You're so old-fashioned, Damon." Naomi kisses him. "Believe me, I already talked to Betsy this morning while you were still sleeping. I told her that we were working our way through some things and suggested that she and I keep our distance for the meantime. She was cool with that, and wished us well."

24

Juanita Lavinia Parsons-Farrell arrives at three o'clock on a frosty April morning in 2006, bringing with her fresh adventures for Naomi and Damon. The birth occurs at the cottage with a midwife present and Doctor Flanagan assisting.

Naomi insists that Damon play the piano during the event so the child's first conscious sense will be one of their muses. Damon jokes that, if it were humanly possible to do so, Naomi would prefer to dance among the pines while giving birth. Among the selections Damon performs is the Thad Jones classic, A Child is Born, which Pablo records on his new video camera, accompanying graphic images of Naomi screaming and moaning and the emergence of, and first cries from, Juanita, producing a home movie of epic importance in Pablo's mind. Betsy remains close at hand during the final moments, fidgeting and repeatedly offering her assistance.

Pablo arrived several days before the event to assist around the cottage and to secure his position as a grandfather. It doesn't escape Damon's attention that Pablo, the grandfather, is six years younger than the new child's father.

Betsy has been buzzing around the cottage for several weeks helping Naomi prepare for the birth by washing clothes and bedding, cooking and freezing meals, and baking cakes and cookies, mainly to keep busy.

Both Pablo and Betsy appear more excited than the new parents, although Damon is beginning to display some anxieties about assuming care of normal parental duties like diaper changing and burping.

With the arrival of Juanita, their lives change instantly and radically. Damon's occasions at the piano are limited to times when the baby is awake, and Naomi's dancing is dictated by Juanita's appetite, although she is anxious to return to a physically active schedule, as much to curb any permanent weight gain as for any creative purposes.

Pablo returns to the city but arranges more frequent visits to coincide with everyone's birthdays, Christmas and Easter, and holidays for all nationalities, ethnicities and religions. During his visits he arrives burdened down with gifts for his granddaughter, the first of which is a DVD recording of her first cries. He threatens to release the recording of his epic video on the new phenomenon called YouTube for the entire world to see and hear, but Naomi's violent opposition to allowing a public performance of her birthing screams and views of her personal regions overrules his perceived Oscar nominee.

As soon as Juanita is able to sit up on her own, Damon settles her next to him at the piano to play duets, and as time progresses, her talent for picking out melodies for children's songs and copies of some of Damon's original tunes emerges.

Juanita regularly accompanies Naomi to the pines where they dance together and, when Damon is playing, Juanita is encouraged to dance freely with the music, imitating her mother's movements. By the time she's three, Juanita adopts the lotus position and meditates quietly with Naomi before dancing.

For Damon the time passes quickly. He has little opportunity to worry about his age or his life expectancy; Juanita continues to challenge him with her curiosity and questions him on every subject, from why bumblebees are yellow to what causes the Northern Lights to flash in the sky. Whenever possible, Damon responds to her as he would an adult, with emphasis on the truth. However, Juanita's incessant curiosity sometimes demands answers that delve into regions of fantasy.

Naomi's approach to parenthood is an evolutionary process in which Juanita is encouraged and allowed to pursue anything and everything that challenges her curious mind. All regulatory duties are administered by Damon: how to hold a fork, when not to cry or scream, where and when to eat, as well as the basic lessons in hygiene like teeth brushing, hair washing and toilet functions.

240

The roles of each parent soon become etched in Juanita's consciousness as she quickly learns to take advantage of the parent most appropriate for the situation. If she's hungry she appeals directly to Damon, who discusses with her, the correct time for meals. If the timing isn't to her liking, she darts immediately to Naomi who always manages to supply a handful of cookies or other treats that require no preparation. Of course, if Auntie Betsy is around, Juanita employs her as the first contact when food is an issue. When Grandpa Pablo visits, Juanita quickly identifies him as an equivalent to Santa Claus who arrives with gift boxes and bags of toys and candies.

At the age of three, Juanita is exposed to pre-kindergarten. Damon drives her to the school each morning and Naomi picks her up at noon, often taking her to the restaurant for ice cream before starting home. Juanita immediately takes to the new school experience and loves playing with the other children. She's an outgoing and imaginative child who shares stories with them about her mother who 'talks to *spiriks* and *medicates* under the pines.'

For her fourth birthday, Damon and Naomi arrange a party where all of Juanita's classmates are invited.

"I want to make sure that she never has birthdays alone," Damon promises. "As much as I thoroughly enjoyed those annual visits with Aunt Lavinia, I always wondered why Helen and Charles, and especially my brother Phil, never celebrated with us. Birthdays are a joyous occasion, not a time for weeping."

"Let me remind you of that come August, Damon, when you'll be celebrating your 68th birthday. No moaning or complaining that the years have slipped away, or that you're going to die before Juanita becomes a teenager."

The day of Juanita's birthday party arrives. In addition to Grandpa Pablo, with his car brimming with wrapped gifts, and Auntie Betsy, with her special birthday cake based upon Lavinia's own recipe, vehicles with pre-kindergarten kids and their parents arrive en masse from town. Although some of the 'townies' are familiar with Naomi and Damon's summer concerts and workshops, many of the parents arrive for the party to satisfy their curiosity about the home lives of the city-bred jazz musician and the dancer who *medicates* and talks to *spiriks*.

Naomi concocts a fruit punch for the children and Damon creates an alternative version incorporating Cuban rum in a separate bowl for the adults. Food is in ample supply that, except for the sweets, is guaranteed by Naomi to be nutritious and healthy. Plates of celery sticks, seedless grapes, carrot slices, mushroom halves, and dips of humus dot the tables outside, contrasting a plethora of tarts, cookies, candies of all colours, and of course, a double chocolate birthday cake from the kitchen of Betsy McGinnis that is topped by a dancing girl in a tutu.

The children were asked to dress in the costumes of their favourite characters. Aside from the usual array of Sesame Street Muppets, Disney princesses, and Bob the Builders, one boy, Jeremy Sampson, dresses as his own father, sporting a plumber's overalls complete with tool belt and a P-trap. For the occasion, Juanita dons a tutu that her mother wore in a production of The Sugar Plum Fairy when she was just a small girl herself.

The games, organized by Betsy and Naomi, are designed to serve as icebreakers for both children and parents, some of whom, neither Naomi nor Damon have met before this day.

In the three-legged race, each child teams up with another child's parent, an event that challenges both adult and child due to the differences in height; like setting a camera atop a tripod with two uneven legs and a broken one.

For another competition, teams of four people each are organized for the utmost in diversity by teaming up short and tall adults with other parent's children and asking each team to balance together with all eight feet on one upturned 45-gallon drum; each person must simultaneously trust the others to maintain their position on the drum longer than the other teams by hanging on for dear life.

Damon, of slightly less than normal height, is teamed up with two hearty children and Mrs. Sampson, the substantial wife of the 275 pound plumber, who teeters awkwardly on the edge of an oil drum with Naomi and a couple of short girls of anemic proportions. Fortunately for Mr. Sampson, Naomi's strength contains all four members of her team long enough to win the prize: Kinder Surprise Eggs for the children and 649 lottery tickets for the adults.

Following the games, Damon accompanies Juanita on the piano while she shows off her dancing prowess. Dressed in her tutu she dances a story of a little princess who becomes lost in the woods until she's discovered and saved by a massive grizzly bear, played by the accommodating Mr. Sampson sporting an odoriferous, mouldy bear skin borrowed from a local taxidermist. Juanita troops on with the dance while other children, frightened by the grizzly Mr. Sampson, escape into the cottage for refuge.

Before the day is over, children and parents alike demonstrate their collective talents in a sing-along accompanied by Damon. One of the children and Mrs. Sampson are taken ill from overindulgence: the child from cake and candies, Mrs. Sampson from the special adult punch. She's last seen being squeezed into the cab of a Ford F-150 pickup belonging to Sampson and Company, Plumbing and Heating. An assortment of metal and plastic pipes and fittings, as well as porcelain American Standard water closet, rattle against the pickup bed as they maneuver the gravel road from the cottage.

In time, the property is once again returned to Damon, Naomi, and Juanita, who, along with Betsy and Pablo, clean the premises of paper cups and plates, wrapping paper and ribbons, the remnants of food and drink containers, and toys.

Juanita hugs her parents before snuggling into bed. "That was the *bestest* birthday ever. We have to do this every year."

The adults finally settle in the living room for an after-party drink. Damon and Pablo help themselves to more chocolate cake. Betsy falls asleep on the sofa. Naomi dances outside under the pines.

25

One morning early in May of 2011, Naomi experiences some shortness of breath after a brisk walk along a trail that follows the shoreline. It's a spring morning full of promise; the sun is shining and the temperature rises above the average.

"I must be out of shape," she complains to Damon, bending forward and placing her hands on her knees, "it's been a long winter."

She blames her own laziness during the winter months for her heavy breathing, but it persists, one morning after another, and lasts longer as the days pass until each episode leaves in its wake, a dull pain and a tightness that makes dancing increasingly difficult.

Believing that she may be experiencing a bout of pleurisy, or even a mild case of pneumonia, Naomi seeks the advice of Doctor Flanagan, who immediately sends her into the city for tests.

Naomi informs Damon that she has some meetings to attend in Toronto with a dance company that is interested in having her conduct some workshops for them, and asks if he would mind caring for Juanita while she's gone. Pablo has driven up to the cottage at Naomi's request, to drive her to Toronto. He asks no questions, but is always at the ready to oblige.

"I should only be gone a week," she promises. "Betsy will help you out with things I'm sure."

Damon calls. "Juanita, come and say goodbye to Mommy. She's leaving now." There are hugs and kisses all around before Naomi and Pablo depart.

After the first series of tests, others follow, until the results prove conclusive: lung cancer. The oncologist suggests treatment, chemo and radiation, but Naomi is insistent that he first reveals the probabilities of survival to her.

The oncologist pauses, feeding Naomi's worst nightmare.

She demands a response. "How much time do I have left, Doctor?"

"Six months, maybe less, and any treatment will only serve to prolong your life a few months. It can't be stopped."

Before revealing the final news to Damon, she already decides on her fate: no treatment. She admired Lavinia for the stand she had taken against the poisoning of her body when the final results were so conclusive. Naomi adopts the same stand.

Damon senses changes in Naomi's demeanor throughout May and June. At times she prefers her solitude and often leaves food on her plate at dinner. She is occasionally abrupt with Juanita, passing her over to Damon and leaving the room. One evening, after ignoring most of her dinner, Naomi sits with Juanita on her knee, but the child wants no part of it, preferring to run around the room instead.

"If that's the way you're going to act, then get down. Run around if you want, but don't come to me for attention anymore." Naomi sets Juanita on the floor and quickly stomps from the room. Juanita begins to cry and seeks consolation from Damon.

Damon, concerned about Naomi's sudden change in behaviour, pursues her, but only to observe her next step.

Naomi walks over to the piano and picks up the urn containing Lavinia's ashes. She pulls the urn over her heart and whispers.

"It won't be long now Lavinia."

Damon is devastated when she tells him everything. "Is there nothing they can do? What about chemotherapy?" he asks her in a pleading voice.

She tells him what her decision is, and why, and he reluctantly accepts it as a wise choice.

"It's your body, and I respect that." Uncertain about what lay ahead, they immediately begin discussing how they can savour their final precious months together and how Juanita will be affected.

Considering that both Damon and Naomi were adopted, and suffered dearly for it, they agree that Juanita must remain with her father.

"What'll happen when I get too old to look after her?" Damon asks.

Naomi chuckles, "By that time, she'll be old enough to look after you."

"Jesus, Naomi. This isn't a time to be flippant, or to joke about things."

"If I can't have a sense of humour right now, when do you think I might acquire one, a year from now, or maybe when I reach your age?"

"Oh Christ, Naomi. I'm sorry."

Short walks around the property are possible for the first while, usually ending at the bench in the pines for some rest and spiritual reinforcement. They take Juanita with them whenever possible, but occasions arise when they just want to be alone together. Betsy volunteers her assistance to look after Juanita whenever necessary.

On a heavily overcast afternoon, several months after receiving what Naomi calls her 'life sentence,' Damon is practicing at the piano after downing a third whisky.

* * *

A fleeting motion in the corner of my eye interrupts my concentration. Upon closer examination, I see Naomi walking toward the lake. Her determined gait raises some concern for me that she might be up to something sinister so I follow her at a distance and watch her from the security of the woods. When Naomi arrives at the dock, she carefully removes her clothing, uncharacteristically folding and placing it neatly on the dock, before adopting her familiar lotus position. Facing across the lake, she meditates for quite a long time until she lays back on the wooden slats and stares upward at the grey, clouded sky; a trancelike expression casts across her face like a veil. I watch intently while remaining hidden from her view.

The wind picks up speed and the clouds move more rapidly overhead. From across the lake the waves increase in size and frequency and batter noisily against the pilings of the dock. As the sky darkens further an aura appears around Naomi's still figure from which a series of transitional figures appear as if representing some historical chronology.

Aphrodite, in all her beauteous splendor, rises from Naomi and dances above her in an appealing call to me before she dives magnificently into the increasingly choppy water of the lake. Naomi remains still in an apparent lack of awareness. The image of Virginia appears next, pregnant, I assume with Graham, and beckons me to join her as she plunges into the lake after Aphrodite. The storm increases rapidly and the waves surge over the top surface of the dock rolling over Naomi's body without causing her any noticeable distress.

The aura brightens against the increasing darkness illuminating the emerging image of a naked Lavinia, just as I remember her from when I witnessed her swimming years ago. She offers me a motherly embrace before sliding off the dock into the water, soon followed by the image of Lydia, who completes the cycle, leaving Naomi alone with her aura.

While trying to comprehend the meaning of these women in my life chronologically disappear into the stormy surges, I watch Naomi rise to her feet and spread her arms out, gradually moving them above her head, the aura following her as she dives headlong into the water.

In a panic, I run to the edge of the dock and launch myself into the air. Before I hit the water, I hear Naomi's voice calling me.

* * *

"Damon, can you hear me? Could you please bring me something cool to drink, a juice or some water? I'm parched."

Damon looks for her in the direction of her voice and sees her out among the pines. He mixes a pitcher of iced tea and takes it to her. When he arrives, Naomi's mind is wandering; speaking in a muttering whisper, words that Damon can only assume are intended not for him, but for Lavinia.

Several days a week, Betsy sits with Naomi and Juanita, while Damon provides background ambiance at the piano. On good days, Naomi attempts some of her warm-ups and several times actually dances to the amazement of both Betsy and Damon.

Nearer the end, Naomi and Damon seek the assistance of Doctor Flanagan, who prescribes appropriate dosages of pain medication, which unfortunately removes Naomi from participating in some of their more involved discussions. She begins sleeping for more hours a day than she's awake.

On one of Doctor Flanagan's home visits, Damon inquires about what Naomi might be aware of.

"When she's sleeping, does she know what's going on? Does she have any ability to think or to comprehend while she's sleeping? Is she sleeping, or is she in some kind of coma? Does she even hear me when I talk to her?"

Doctor Flanagan is extremely accommodating and even consoling, but he can only offer that the medication is quite strong because the pain would otherwise be intolerable. He doubts that there could be much comprehension on Naomi's part.

Prior to Doc Flanagan's departure, he turns to Damon. "Your voice is quite raspy I've noticed. Let me take a quick look at you." The doctor peers into Damon's open mouth and probes around with a cotton swab. "It looks a bit reddish, some minor irritation, probably a bit of a cold; nothing to worry about. Stress can cause all kinds of things. Do try to get a bit more sleep."

Several weeks later, on the afternoon before Naomi dies, her eyes open and she stares into Damon's face for the longest time before uttering in as strong a voice as he's heard her use in weeks. "I'm so-o-o sorry Damon, for destroying our dream."

On what becomes Naomi's final afternoon, Damon rolls her bed out to the porch where she can feel the warm late sun against her face. He improvises at the piano and watches through the screen door for a smile, or some visible sign that she can hear him play. Damon never accepted Doctor Flanagan's theory that she wouldn't be able to comprehend her surroundings. Science has no explanations for the kind of spirituality shared between Damon and Naomi. Even after she fell into her final coma he has continued talking to her about the wonderful events they shared in their short time together, and has offered one-sided discussions on topics that drew them together in the first place.

While Damon's fingers pass lightly over the keys, he carries on both sides of a dialogue about freedom in art and in life that seem an extension of one of their overnight discussions; one that still remains unresolved.

In the midst of his playing, Damon suddenly knows. Some force beyond his control governs the placement of his hands and fingers, not to any recognizable melody or rhythm at first, but to an emotion that he and Naomi sensed together many times. While his playing evolves into the quintessential jazz ballad, Body and Soul, Damon, blinded with tears, senses Naomi dancing before him in such alluring movements that he feels a part of her. As she moves, slowly at first, he moves with her and the music swells in synch until a level of shared excitement carries them both to places only imagined. It's when she suddenly disappears from his vision that he's drawn to her bedside.

With Naomi's hand in his, Damon sees Juanita quietly stepping through the screen door; she joins her father. Although Damon and Naomi had methodically prepared their daughter for the inevitable, Damon still experiences considerable agony trying to decide on the best words that could explain Naomi's passing to Juanita. He opts for the truth, straight and simple.

"Mommy just died, Juanita, just after you stepped through the door."

"Did she say goodbye, Daddy?"

Realizing that the truth is more difficult than he anticipated, Damon explains in terms the five-year-old can fathom. "I felt Mommy saying goodbye to both of us just as you arrived here. I was holding her hand and she squeezed it to let me know she's moving on. She waited for you to come out before she decided to die. Wasn't that nice of her?"

"Uh-huh." Juanita stares at her mother. "When is she moving on? Where's she moving to?"

"She's gone to be with your Grandma Lavinia, in a place far away from here, but not so far away that you can't talk to her from time to time."

Juanita places her hand on Naomi's. "Don't worry, Mommy. I'll talk to you every day. Say hello to Grandma Lavinia for me. I'll send you an email."

Damon and Juanita stay with Naomi awhile before he calls to tell Betsy.

"Betsy," he calls into the cottage, "It's time."

She joins them for a few minutes beside Naomi's bed before Damon asks her to take Juanita inside.

"Auntie Betsy is going to make you a hot chocolate before you go to bed, OK honey? I'll come up and read a story before you go to sleep."

An hour passes before Damon calls Doctor Flanagan. Numbed by the process over the past few months, Damon is unable to weep at first. He just sits, staring at her face, so beautiful, so innocent, and still so young.

After some time, his anger erupts. "Why her?" he shouts into the pines and his voice echoes back from the lake. "Why not me? I'm old enough to go. Take me instead. Where's the fucking justice in this?"

After calling Doctor Flanagan, Damon turns out the lights and positions himself beside Naomi on the porch in total darkness.

"I warned you about moving in with an old fart like me with only a few years left to go. How stupid. And how totally unfair this is. Why did I waste my breath? What's all of this worth anyway? It's worth shit."

Uncontrollable tears and trembling take control over his body. When the doctor arrives he wraps a blanket over Damon's shoulders and escorts him inside. A few minutes later, the hearse arrives. They allow Damon a few more minutes with Naomi before moving her.

Once Naomi's body is removed, Damon spends the remainder of the evening consoling Juanita and telling her stories that stimulate her imagination, like how her mother talked to Lavinia's spirit under the ancient pines.

250

A celebration of Naomi's life occurs at the cottage several days later, attended by a smaller, but dedicated, contingent of friends and relatives than attended Lavinia's celebration nine years before.

Pablo Sandoval, with tears of sorrow mixed with guilt, utters a few words about how, in such a short time, Naomi had filled his heart with love.

The Concept is well represented: Lydia and Tiny, Jesse and Zach, and a number of others known only to Damon by their familiar faces, attend to support him in his bereavement.

Oberon Claxton and Doctor Flanagan appear together as a couple, freed from their life of secrecy by Betsy McGinnis' eulogy to Lavinia.

Betsy, who prepared an abundance of fresh baking and finger foods, delivers a moving tribute to Naomi and to the bond of friendship they had developed since Naomi and Damon moved into the cottage. She refers to Naomi as worthy of the spirit of Lavinia and expresses her confidence that the two will share their space in the beyond.

She also mentions Juanita. "What a treasure that Naomi contributed to our world. Young Juanita will travel in her mother's and her grandmother's footsteps beyond the end of time."

Helen arrives with Graham, his wife, and a young man in his twenties. They had picked Helen up at her retirement residence in Toronto and driven to the cottage; Charles was unable to leave the nursing home, where he has spent the past four years in a state of advanced dementia.

Damon, with Juanita sitting on the teak bench beside where he stands, finds it extremely difficult to deliver his thoughts about Naomi. So much of their life together had been without words, and Damon struggles with trying to verbalize the essence of their relationship. How does one explain a love that exists on another plane, one complicated by ambiguities and special understandings, through meditation and by searching inside of one's own being in order to communicate the full spectrum of feelings for another?

"It is with extreme difficulty and sadness that I find myself, once again and so soon afterwards, talking publicly about someone I love and cherish. I stand before you with no script, no charts, no maps, and no prepared statements. In true fashion, I am creating as I go. That's what Naomi would have wanted. What I will say to you now comes from my current emotional state, full of devotion, fear, and a small dose of guilt."

Damon sips some water. "Fate brought Naomi and I together. Every moment I ask myself, what if... What if we both didn't have some weird nightmares about events that occurred before we were born, and which steered us toward the assistance of Doctor Hilary M. Kinderman?"

He peers out into the gathering and locates their therapist. "Thank you Doctor Kinderman, from both of us."

"What if we hadn't both decided to drink coffee in the café outside the therapist's office between our appointments? What if Naomi had been a financial advisor, or a dentist, without any desires for artistic freedom? What if she had belonged to a fantastic and adventurous dance company instead of the boring and dreary company that it was? What if I had been married to someone I still loved, or conversely, what if she'd been married? What if I hadn't the opportunity to perform in a great jazz club like The Concept, especially on that fateful night when, because she was bored out of her skull, Naomi sought an experience that would blow her mind with creative energy, and found it? What if neither of us had been born amid conflict and what if neither of us sought a life of peace and freedom? There are many more 'what ifs;' I could go on for hours."

"Naomi and I both spent a goodly portion of our lives seeking freedom in our chosen creative fields, she through her expression of dance, and I through my music. Together we explored and discovered new vistas and we eventually found our freedom. She contributed an anarchistic approach and I provided the evolutionary avenue through the foundations of theory and experience. Neither of our individual approaches provided that freedom. Our freedom was discovered through our mutual love and respect for each other. Life proved to be our freedom, and now, half of that freedom has moved on to a greater liberty, a liberty void of any structure whatsoever."

"It is said that differences attract, an old adage that, in our case, has proven to be true. Those differences, with which Naomi and I initially struggled, were resolved and manifested into this beautiful living doll that sits beside me. Every waking day that I have left, I will look at Juanita and see the ones I loved above all else in this world: her mother and mine."

Damon stops to gather his final thoughts. "I will miss the freedom that Naomi provided for a while, but I look forward to the day when…" His voice breaks. He sips some more water.

"I have lived a life as a confirmed atheist, and something about my words seem to be out of character." Damon raises a goblet of Merlot. "Goodbye Naomi. I love you."

Juanita looks up toward the sky and waves. "Bye, bye, Mommy. I love you too."

Following the celebration, Graham and his family approach Damon to offer their condolences. Graham embraces Damon with tears flowing over his cheeks.

"I'm so sorry Dad, for all the pain we put you through. We had no right to treat you that way."

Damon backs away, confused. "Dad?"

Let me explain. "Awhile back, Naomi contacted me and told me not to say anything to you about this until after she was gone. She had arranged for Doctor Flanagan to take a sample of your DNA and send it to the lab. They checked mine against yours and came up with a match. It was all Naomi's idea. Of course, if it proved otherwise, I was not supposed to tell you and leave everything the way it was."

Damon remains confused. "That means that you're still my son."

"And you're my Dad. And Great Aunt Lavinia wasn't my aunt at all, but my Grandmother."

The flowing of the tears grows contagious. Damon peers through saturated eyes at the young man standing next to Graham. "Then this must be…"

The man steps forward, extending his right hand to Damon. "Hello Sir. I'm William Charles Damon Farrell. I guess that makes me your Grandson."

Damon embraces William. "There's one sure thing about our families' funerals. They're guaranteed to contain shock value." He pauses. "Welcome back to the family boys."

Graham introduces his wife, Genevieve, to Damon. At Damon's suggestion they all retire to the porch for some Merlot. "What do you do for fun, William?"

"I'm at university, a second-year music student. I play piano. Sometime later, can I pick your brains, Granddad?"

"Have you ever played a vintage Steinway, William?"

26

After ranting at the ancient pines about old age, and consuming a quantity of Canadian Club in the process, Damon settles into taking care of what has to be done. Betsy joins Damon at the bench as prearranged with Juanita in tow. She picks up the urn containing Lavinia's ashes. The night sky above them is ablaze with the pulsing, alternating hues of the Aurora Borealis.

"It's a perfect night for this, Damon," Betsy reflects.

Damon agrees and explains why it has taken so long.

"As you know, Betsy, I've been keeping my mother's ashes on the piano ledge since she left us. Many times I've asked myself why, and have been unable to answer, except to rationalize that I went for so many years not knowing her as my mother, that I was afraid to let her go. It took more than a year before I could even call her my mother; my voice kept saying Aunt Lavinia. But here we are, under the pines, and I now understand why I kept her ashes for so long. I needed her as a mother for awhile, before she was sent away."

Betsy pulls Damon toward her with her arm and together, they hug Juanita. "I understand completely, Damon. It's been difficult for me as well."

"It's time, Betsy. We must let them go. We've kept them from their odyssey long enough."

Betsy opens the urn containing Lavinia's ashes and pours some of them into the urn containing Naomi's. Damon and Juanita take Naomi's urn and reverse the action.

"They belong together, these two wonderful birds of a feather." Betsy suggests.

Once the ashes are blended, Damon, Juanita and Betsy spread them up into the air beneath the ancient pines with several sweeping motions, remembering to save a small sampling to spread out over the lake as both Lavinia and Naomi requested.

Damon shouts, "You have finally found your freedom, Naomi. Dance! Dance! Dance!"

As Juanita adds, "Goodbye Mommy. Say hello to the *spiriks* for me, and don't forget to *medicate*," two branches from the northern lights stretch out across the midnight Muskoka sky, meeting and blending before dissipating into darkness.

"Mommy will be happy now, won't she?"

"I'm pretty sure she is, honey. She's been waiting for this freedom for many years."

They take the remaining ashes down to the lake where the urns are emptied off the end of the dock. The moon streaks across the water while loons offer their final calls of the season. The three connect their hands in a gesture of friendship and of comradeship with their two lost loves.

Following a prolonged silence, Juanita asks, "Will I ever see Mommy again?"

Damon responds, "Whenever you want to see Mommy, just close your eyes."

ABOUT THE AUTHOR

photo by Scott Wicken

Canadian writer, jazz musician and photojournalist, Douglas Wicken, has remained dedicated to all three of his life's passions for most of his 70-plus years. He currently calls Kitchener-Waterloo, Ontario home, but during his lifetime he has lived in Hamilton, Guelph, Montreal, Toronto, Belleville and Picton.

As a jazz musician for more than 50 years, he continues to perform on double bass and flute, in addition to writing many of his own original compositions.

His documentary photo essays culminated in the publishing of two well-respected books: Nicaragua Portfolio (1991), and Manitou Miniss (1982). Between 1987 and 2015, he taught in the prestigious Photojournalism Program at Loyalist College in Belleville, Ontario. An award for excellence in Documentary Photojournalism bears his name.

Wicken's writing began as a necessity in preparing his first book, Manitou Miniss, documentary photo coverage on the people of Wikwemikong, a First Nation community in Manitoulin Island. After writing the text for his second book, Nicaragua Portfolio, Wicken turned his attention to fiction, initially writing short stories, but always with a desire to complete a novel.

Muses and Consummations, his first novel, draws on his experiences as a jazz musician and educator. It examines the relationship between two unlikely people who become drawn together through their art and discover more than that in the process.

www.dougwicken.net

CPSIA information can be obtained at www.ICGtesting.com
Printed in the USA
LVOW11s0704261015

459735LV00003B/8/P